RAINBOW BLUES

KC Burn

Dreamspinner Press

Published by
Dreamspinner Press
5032 Capital Circle SW
Suite 2, PMB# 279
Tallahassee, FL 32305-7886
USA
http://www.dreamspinnerpress.com/

Rainbow Blues
© 2014 KC Burn.

Cover Art
© 2014 Catt Ford.
Cover content is for illustrative purposes only and any person depicted on the cover is a model.

ISBN: 978-1-63216-009-6
Digital ISBN: 978-1-63216-010-2

Printed in the United States of America
First Edition
June 2014

Readers love *Pen Name - Doctor Chicken* by KC BURN

By KC BURN

Grand Adventures (DSP Anthology)
Pen Name - Doctor Chicken
Rainbow Blues

TORONTO TALES
Cop Out
Cover Up
Cast Off

Published by DREAMSPINNER PRESS
http://www.dreamspinnerpress.com

ACKNOWLEDGMENTS

Thanks as always to my support/editing/brainstorming crew: Alex, Dottie, Chudney, and the book club girls (who put up with my moaning about writer's block). Special thanks go out to Andrea M from my newsletter group, who helped me come up with Luke's name.

CHAPTER 1

LUKE JORDAN opened the door to his apartment and walked in, slinging his keys on the counter. The door slammed shut behind him, echoing in the empty silence. He hung up his heavy winter jacket and ditched his work boots in the rubber tray by the entrance.

As he did every day, he stripped off his dirty, sweaty clothes and popped them in the washing machine. His apartment might be small and shoddy and located in an area of questionable safety, but it had a washer and dryer that he loved. His affection for his washing machine and the way it allowed him to avoid the Laundromat possibly bordered on unnatural, but then again, his social life was sorely lacking, aside from weekly visits from his son. His relationship with his washer and dryer was an unholy trinity that might be the best relationship he'd had since his divorce.

A quick peek into the machine told him he could wait another day or two before it was full enough to run. Naked, he strode into the bathroom and turned on the shower.

With a groan, he stepped under the steaming spray and stood there for a few minutes, letting the heat and the pattering of the water ease the muscles bunched and knotted under his skin. Every day, it seemed, the weight on his shoulders got heavier, and he didn't know if the tension would ever go away.

He slicked soap over his skin by rote. His soapy hands slid down to his groin, but after a few halfhearted tugs, he sighed. He was only forty-three. Life shouldn't make him so weary he couldn't even be bothered to masturbate. Should it?

Without any other detours, he cleaned up quick, got out of the shower, and walked the short distance to his bedroom. The drawer on his dresser stuck, and he rattled the handle to get it to slide free. The thing was a piece of shit, bought on clearance from Walmart… or Target…. Sears? He didn't recall. Furnishing his apartment after the divorce had been a necessity, but not a memorable one. He should have spent more. It wouldn't have put too big a dent in his bank account, but at the time he hadn't seen the point. And now, it seemed a waste to replace his almost serviceable furniture for something better. No amount of fancy furniture would turn his apartment into anything other than a squat concrete bunker. No decor could disguise the bleakness of his life.

He pulled on a pair of flannel pajama bottoms and a T-shirt before slouching back into the kitchen. He opened the freezer door and eyed his selection of cardboard boxes masquerading as meals. Once upon a time he'd cooked regularly for his tiny family of three. But the effort of cooking was too much for just himself.

After selecting Salisbury steak—again—he slung it in the microwave and grabbed a beer from the fridge. One a day was all he allowed himself. At least while he was alone. Bleak was one thing. Drinking himself into a weeknight stupor was a whole different story.

A few minutes later, his "gourmet" dinner was ready, and he placed it on the coffee table in front of the couch. With a practiced hand, he flipped on the television. *NCIS* reruns first, then at eight there were other things on. Nothing new, unfortunately. This close to Christmas, everything was on hiatus.

He didn't even have to check the guide to know when to change to which channel. Was this what he had to look forward to for the next forty years, or however long he had left? Appetite gone, he shoved his half-eaten meal away and laid his head back on the couch. Was this all there was for him? Could he put up with this… monotony for the tiny weekly bright spot of Zach's visits?

The divorce had seemed like such a good idea. He and Kelly had been growing apart for years. Hell, they probably should never have gotten married in the first place, but with Zach on the way, and both he and Kelly still teenagers, it seemed the thing to do. He and Kelly were still friendly, but she'd been the social one of the pair of them. Once they'd split, Luke discovered most of their friends were her friends, but since their separation had been completely amicable, he hadn't noticed the loss. Not until Kelly married and got pregnant in short order. Her new husband had been a widower with two kids under ten, and Kelly's whole life changed. Suddenly, Luke's entire social network, however peripheral he'd been in it, was gone. And he didn't know how to build a new one.

Luke's entire social interaction was watching various crime solving teams on TV do their stuff. Kelly and Zach knew why Luke had divorced Kelly, but he hadn't told anyone at work the real reason. He didn't dare. None of those guys were his friends. They respected him as their boss, but if they knew the truth, he wouldn't even have their respect. So Luke never accepted any invitations to bars or parties or dinners, not even when he'd been married. After all, he'd been grappling with the truth for so long, and he was afraid if he got too close to anyone, they'd figure it out. The truth would likely be career suicide.

And what did he have to show for his carefully kept secret? A miserable lonely apartment and a miserable lonely life. He was too young for this, but he was too set in his ways to change now.

Not even the sexy DiNozzo's antics were engaging enough—*the fourth time I've seen this episode*—to distract him. It wasn't even eight, but maybe he'd go to bed.

His breath gusted out in a heavy sigh. He didn't even the energy to hoist himself to his feet.

The phone rang—the landline. Luke glanced over in surprise. He'd only bothered getting a landline because it was the only way the front door buzzer would work, but once he gave his son a key, he hadn't used it. In fact, the phone had a thin layer of dust on it.

"Hello?"

"Uh, hi, LJ?" Despite the hesitation, Luke had no difficulty placing the voice. Only one person called him LJ. "It's me, Ryan? Zach's friend?"

Panic stole his breath. Why was Ryan here? Had something happened to his son?

"What's wrong, Ryan?"

Luke took the handheld receiver to the closet and had one arm in his jacket before Ryan spoke again.

"Nothing, just Zach wanted me to meet him here, and he's not here yet. Can you buzz me up? It's cold out here."

Luke paused, letting his parental concern ease away while he took a few breaths. "Uh, sure thing." He barely remembered which key to press to activate the front door release, but he waited until he heard the familiar squeak of the hinges before he hung up.

It was Wednesday. Sure, Zach had skipped the past weekend's visit to study for exams—it was his last year, and he was poised to get his bachelor's degree in the spring with a great grade point average— but Luke hadn't expected him to visit midweek.

Nor had he expected Ryan to join him. Ryan and Zach had been inseparable for years, but Luke hadn't seen him much since the house was sold two years ago.

He hung his jacket back up and quickly cleared away the detritus of dinner. Already this was more exciting than any weeknight he'd had… pretty much since he moved into this apartment.

A few minutes later, he poked his head out the door. Ryan hadn't come up yet, nor had he buzzed again. It didn't take that long to get to his apartment, he didn't think. Luke shut the door again and paced. Although he wanted more than anything to give his son the benefit of the doubt, Zach showing up midweek with Ryan as a buffer likely meant bad news. After all, when Luke admitted he was gay and that was the impetus for divorcing Zach's mom, he'd half expected Zach to hate him. When the opposite occurred, he'd been so grateful, even though Kelly had told him it wouldn't be a problem. Despite their youth when they had Zach, they still managed to raise a good kid between them, which was why this midweek visit was so disturbing.

Frowning, he shut the door again. Maybe he'd just fallen asleep on the couch and dreamed the whole thing. Odd for his subconscious to add in Zach's best friend, but there was no accounting for dreams. Hell, if his brain had any sense, he'd have been dreaming about having sex with a hot guy—and not Zach's best friend. He shuddered.

He flopped back down on the couch, wondering if he should flip over to a *Law and Order* rerun, just to mix things up a little.

THE CLICK of the deadbolt turning sent a spike of adrenaline through Luke, and his pulse picked up. The door swung open, and Luke leapt to his feet, fists clenching in the absence of anything that might be considered a weapon.

"Hey, Dad!"

Luke blinked at the talking pine tree in his doorway, which then waddled its way into his apartment. Like an overly cheery Christmas special, a grinning head appeared from either side of the tree. Zach was a taller, lankier version of Luke, right down to the reddish brown hair, ruddy complexion, and hazel eyes. Kelly's contribution to their son was to make Zach's features and build sharper and more refined, so Zach looked a lot more elegant than Luke. Elegance would be wasted at Luke's job on the construction site anyway.

Ryan, on the other hand, had sprouted some blue streaks in his black hair that hadn't been there the last time Luke had seen him. He was shorter than Zach, and he'd been past the age of majority before he stopped looking like an underage kid.

"Hi, LJ! I found Zach before I came up."

"I figured, Ryan. What are you two doing here? Aside from apparently delivering me a Christmas tree."

The two young men propped the tree against the wall, and Zach dragged in a big cardboard box from the hallway.

Zach peered around Luke's apartment with a frown, and Luke had a moment of satisfaction that he'd at least cleared away the remains of a dinner that positively screamed lonely and pathetic. Otherwise his place was clean.

"I knew it." Zach's frown hadn't disappeared.

"Knew what?" Luke still suspected this might be some sort of weird dream.

"You haven't done anything to decorate for Christmas. Just like last year." Zach got up in his face and squinted. "You're not spending Christmas alone are you?"

Luke put on his most innocent face. "Of course not." The first Christmas after the divorce was final, Kelly had graciously invited him over. She knew better than anyone how uncomfortable he'd be with anyone else. Unfortunately, he'd been even more uncomfortable than he'd ever guessed. Interacting with Kelly's new husband and getting to know Zach's new siblings had been awkward and just plain fucked-up. Like he'd been dropped in another dimension and everyone except for him was completely different.

Instead of going through that again, he'd told Zach he was spending last Christmas with friends, when he really spent it with a bottle of Jack Daniels, the twenty-four-hour marathon of *A Christmas Story* interspersed with the *Die Hard* movies, and more than a few tears. Not so much because he thought the divorce had been a mistake, but somehow he thought things would be better. Instead, he'd only been able to mourn the comfort of a cordial, shared parenthood and the presence of his kid, which he hadn't realized how much he relied on.

"Bullshit."

Luke's eyes widened. "Zach!"

"Sorry, Dad, but I didn't believe it then, and I don't believe it now."

Probably he shouldn't be surprised. After all, aside from the big secret of his sexual orientation, he'd made it a practice not to lie to his son or wife. Granted, keeping the gay thing under wraps for so many years was a pretty big secret, but the weight of it made any other lies completely untenable. And since he never had sex with men while he was married to Kelly, it made his conscience mostly clear. Last Christmas was the first time he actively lied to his son, but it had been so very necessary to his sanity.

"You should. I'm perfectly capable of keeping myself occupied."

Ryan squished himself into a corner as far away from them as he could, in an attempt to give them some privacy, but Luke didn't really want to discuss this now or ever, whether Ryan was there or not. Ryan's home life made him extra sensitive to tension, and Luke had spent many of Ryan's younger years trying to make sure Ryan was comfortable.

"Oh, really? And how do you keep yourself occupied in this place? Gonna cook a turkey dinner with all the fixings?" There was a hint of something pained in Zach's tone that Luke didn't quite recognize. Luke was the better cook between him and Kelly, and holiday cooking duties had fallen to him as well. Since he'd waited until Zach had moved into an apartment near the university campus before he and Kelly had moved forward to dissolve their marriage, he hadn't realized that maybe the new family dynamic wasn't any easier on his son than it was on him. But he wasn't given a chance to respond before Zach stalked over to his refrigerator and flung open both fridge and freezer doors.

Boxes of no-name frozen dinners glared reproachfully from the freezer while the entire contents of his fridge consisted of beer, milk, cold cuts, mustard, and some limp lettuce. No hint of any of the groceries that should be in there, although at two weeks before Christmas, the only thing he'd have bought if he was making dinner was a turkey. At least Zach hadn't looked in the cupboards as well. He had cereal, bread, and maybe a couple old cans of soup.

Zach's shoulders slumped, and he turned back, his eyes glittering. Even at the grand old age of twenty-four, Luke couldn't bear it when his son hurt. And for whatever reason, Luke's new life hurt Zach in some indefinable way. His burgeoning irritation with Zach's intrusion disappeared in a flash, and he wrapped a hand around his son's neck and pulled him into a hug.

Scrunching down a few inches, Zach laid his head on his shoulder and squeezed Luke with unexpected strength.

"It's okay, it's okay. I love you." It had been a long time since he'd comforted Zach like this, but over the years there had been many, many occasions thanks to skinned knees, split lips, broken bones, and broken hearts. And despite the fact that it was all his fault, Luke couldn't suppress the frisson of pride that Zach still needed his dad.

After a few minutes, Zach rubbed his eyes against Luke's T-shirt and pulled away. Just like his dad, Zach couldn't cry without the whole world knowing, not with those red-rimmed eyes and glowing red nose. Luke was glad that Zach's friendship with Ryan was such that he didn't mind showing emotion with him around.

"Dad, you can't do this. The whole point of the divorce was so you could be happy."

"I was happy with your mother. You have to believe that."

Zach snorted and wiped a sleeve across his still-wet eyes. "You know, I used to believe that. You might even still believe that, but I've seen Mom with Mark. Neither of you were truly happy when you were together. Not the happy that comes with being in love."

Luke tilted his head. "Are you seeing someone?" Zach hadn't mentioned dating anyone seriously during his entire post-secondary schooling, but despite several crushes that had come to nothing in high school, he didn't think his son had been in love for real. He almost hoped he hadn't, because it would kill him to realize he'd missed such a milestone in Zach's life.

Zach slammed the fridge and freezer doors shut.

"No. Jeez, Dad, this isn't about *me*. But I'm an adult, and I'm not stupid. Mom is almost a completely different person. The way she looks at Mark and the way he looks at her...." Zach couldn't hide embarrassment any better than he could hide crying and a blotchy red flush colored his cheeks. "Well, I've never seen you and Mom look at each other like that. Not ever. You always looked at each other the way... the way... Ryan and I look at each other."

Lifelong friends. Yes, Kelly was definitely that, even if she'd moved on to a new life filled with babies, while Luke was slowly turning to middle-aged dust in a barren apartment. Luke darted a glance at Ryan curled up on the couch with his legs tucked under him. Luke had almost forgotten he was there, observing. Ryan gave Luke an abashed little grin. Since Luke didn't exactly know how to respond, he turned back to Zach.

"It's going to take time to get used to living on my own." Luke didn't know what to say to make this better.

Zach rolled his eyes. "But that's the whole point. You're not supposed to be living on your own like a damned secluded, celibate monk. It's not like you have to mourn your relationship. You were both more than ready to move on, and although it came as a shock to me at the time, I should have seen the signs a long time ago. You and Mom were... are... friends, but the divorce was right for both of you. But you *haven't* moved on, and there's no good reason for it." Zach's voice climbed louder at the end, his frustration growing and amplifying Luke's own frustration with his pathetic new life.

"I… I…." Luke didn't want to admit to his son that he just didn't know how to move on to a new life. Right after the divorce, he'd hit a few gay clubs. But they made him every bit as uncomfortable as Christmas at his ex-wife's. The flash and sparkle of the clubs didn't suit him, and he had no idea how to go about finding dates.

"Zach, I'm a construction manager, for God's sake. No one is particularly gay friendly at work, and even if they were… they're not my peers. How am I supposed to find a date? I tried clubs, but I hated the music, I had nothing in common with anyone, and most of them were *your* age."

Luke supposed he wasn't like most men, who'd feel pride getting sexual attention from younger people, but it had only made him vaguely ill. Not to say he hadn't managed a few encounters with a few guys closer to his age. They weren't entirely satisfactory, but he still hadn't had anything in common with them aside from a love of dick and the need for a shared orgasm; he wasn't about to share that information with his son.

With a sad smile, Zach gripped his shoulder and a sudden burning in his own eyes caught Luke by surprise.

"I want you to be happy, like Mom is. So, we're here to decorate for Christmas, get you into the spirit. And I want to know you won't be alone on Christmas."

Luke didn't choose to be alone. Never had, never would, but the alternative was worse. Spending time with Zach's newly reconstituted family only made him feel more alone than his solitude.

"Zach, I appreciate the tree and all. It's a great idea, and it will definitely cheer the place up. But I will be fine on my own." No point in claiming to be visiting friends again. Zach wouldn't believe the lie.

Clearing his throat, Ryan stood. "I'm just going to pop out for a smoke. I'll be back in a few." He grabbed his coat, gave Luke a comforting pat on the arm, and left before Luke could say anything.

Luke turned a frown on Zach. "Since when did he start smoking?"

Since Zach grew up without siblings, Ryan, who was also an only child, had become as close as a brother. Or as close as Luke assumed brothers being. Ryan didn't have a very good home life, and he'd almost been like a second son for him and Kelly. They might have made a lot of mistakes, becoming parents so young, but Zach had always come first. Unfortunately, Ryan's parents never had that same attitude.

Zach waved a hand in the air. "You worry too much, Dad. He's just giving us some privacy. If he was going to take up smoking, he'd have started earlier than twenty-four."

If Ryan had been hoping to spare any of them embarrassment, he was about ten minutes too late for that "smoke."

"Look, I'll be fine on my own. Really." He might feel like an old man some days, but he certainly wasn't at the point where his son needed to look out for him. His social issues weren't Zach's problem.

"I worry about you, Dad, and I don't want you to be alone. You and me, we're going to spend Christmas together."

"No! Your mom will miss you, and you'll have a traditional Christmas with them." Luke couldn't take that away from his son. Kelly would be pissed if Zach wasn't there.

"Dad, this is what kids from broken homes *do*." Zach put a little whine in his words, like a petulant teenager, to let Luke know he was joking, but Luke didn't quite understand the joke.

"Your mother would kill me."

"My mother would kill me if I let you drink yourself stupid again this year."

Shock made Luke's eyes widen. "How did you know?"

"Dad." This time, there was no joke in Zach's exasperated my-parents-are-stupid tone. "Adult, remember? I came over the next day, and it wasn't hard to see the signs. I understand why you don't want to go to Mom's. I do. But kids alternate homes for the holidays with divorced parents all the time, and I don't care if it's not totally traditional. I don't need that. I'm not a kid. We can have a great time, you and me."

"What about Ryan?" As soon as Ryan had been old enough to leave his own home, he hadn't ever returned, to Luke's knowledge, and started joining their small family celebrations. Then Luke realized how the question sounded. "I mean, obviously he'd be welcome to come, too."

Zach smiled that genuinely happy smile that he and Kelly had strove to keep on his face without spoiling him with material goods they couldn't always afford.

"Good. So, it's settled. The three of us bachelors will hang out and have a man Christmas."

Luke rolled his eyes. He'd have to have a personality transplant before he'd call it a "man Christmas."

"Guess I'd better start making a grocery list." Luke wanted to laugh. Spending Christmas with his son and his almost-son would be fantastic. But he couldn't rely on Zach forever; he needed to find a life of his own that didn't involve conversing with television detectives or waiting for whatever scraps of time Zach could afford to throw him. "Aren't you going to text Ryan, tell him to come back in? I think it's a little cold out there for him."

Zach's gaze slid away like Luke was covered in Teflon.

"What? What have you done that I'm not going to like?"

His son bit his lip and pulled a folded sheet of purple paper out of his pocket and handed it over.

Luke opened it, the sight of a rainbow flag making him cringe ever so slightly. Advertising his orientation didn't seem like something he'd ever want to do.

> *Are you working in a blue collar profession? Do you find it hard to meet people? Do you feel uncomfortable being honest with your coworkers about your orientation?*
>
> *If so, Rainbow Blues might be for you. Rainbow Blues offers a safe environment where you can be yourself and meet other men like you.*
>
> *Yearly membership $100.*

"Merry Christmas," Zach said.

Luke sucked in a lungful of pine-scented air. The traditional scent evened out his fury a bit, but not entirely.

"You signed me up for a dating service? Zach, that is not your place. Cancel it. Immediately."

Zach finally looked at him, chin thrust out and spots of color appearing high on his cheeks. Luke groaned. Zach was his son, through and through, and he could be stubborn as hell when he set his mind on something, and Zach was wearing his stubborn face. Which meant Luke needed to give in to whatever this was, or he and Zach were going to have a huge argument.

"No. I won't. First off, it's not a dating service, it's a social group. They specify quite clearly on the website that their purpose is for blue collar workers to find other gay friends. Because, Dad, you need some fucking friends. You probably also need to get laid, but getting laid is a hell of lot easier than making friends."

Luke's face heated up. The truth didn't just hurt, but it could humiliate too. He also was a little worried that Zach was too naive to recognize a sleazy hookup site masquerading as something reputable.

"I also paid for you to go to their holiday party, which is their next scheduled get-together. It's Saturday night, so you've got plenty of time to find something nice to wear."

"Zach, what the fuck?"

Luke wanted to bite back the words as soon as they escaped, doubly so when his son paled. Luke didn't swear at his son, not ever. But right before his eyes, his son proved he was a man. Instead of caving or running away, Zach merely narrowed his eyes and pulled his shoulders back, staring Luke right in the eyes.

"I would never presume to know what you'd look for in a potential boyfriend. Maybe if I'd ever seen you date, I'd know what you liked or what you didn't. I checked out the website. I checked out reviews. I checked to see if they'd had complaints with the Better Business Bureau. This isn't some skanky meat market because, ew, I wouldn't send you to one of those, even though it might get you to loosen up a bit."

The silence lengthened as a calculating look appeared on Zach's face and a thread of panic wove its way into Luke's belly.

"No. I don't know what you're thinking, but no. I'll go to the holiday party, just forget whatever you're thinking right now." Luke wouldn't put it past him to figure out a way to send Luke to an orgy or hire him a rent boy or something. The last time Luke had seen that particular look, Zach had ended up overdosed on caffeine. That particular brainwave had been a combination of a late term paper and a sleep-deprivation study with himself as the only subject, which he'd managed to get an A on. The time before that, he and Kelly had ended up with a tub full of lime Jell-O and had to explain to Ryan's parents how both their kids ended up with matching black eyes and split lips because they'd thought the idea of a pool full of Jell-O was cool and a bathtub was the nearest they could manage.

"You promise to go to the holiday party?"

"I promise. I swear." Besides, if it was a skanky hookup, well, maybe getting laid wouldn't be so awful. It had been… months since he'd gotten off with a hand that wasn't his own, and pretty much the only time he'd gotten laid since his divorce had been in seedy club hookups. He'd find a way to tell Zach he'd never be going again, without letting him know his Christmas gift was a fairly expensive cock.

Luke got another big, happy smile for his capitulation. "Good, because if you didn't agree, I was going to tell Mom how you spent last Christmas."

Zach pulled a phone out of his pocket and started texting while Luke tried to breathe. His breakup with Kelly might have been mutual and amicable, but he sure as shit didn't want her to know he was a pathetic asshole. No one wanted their ex to know that. Bad enough that his son and probably Ryan were fully aware.

Moments later, Ryan bounded back in the apartment, and the three of them settled into setting up the tree. This close to Christmas, the decorating selections were limited, or so Luke had to assume based on the eclectic mix of colors and styles Zach had purchased for his tree. Or perhaps his son had suddenly become color-blind or just plain blind.

They ordered pizza in, Luke's barely touched frozen dinner nothing more than a bad memory.

The finished product came together beautifully, and he'd have died rather than tell Zach anything different, but the cheery addition only illustrated how dismal his life had become.

LUKE STOOD outside the community center. He might have to rethink his conclusion that this was a skeevy hookup party. Surely that would be held at a club of some sort, wouldn't it? He wedged a finger under the unfamiliar collar and pulled, trying to make the new shirt comfortable. At work and on his personal time, he was much more a T-shirt and jeans sort of person. At least he'd been able to talk Zach out of a tie. He hadn't worn a tie since his wedding… no, wait, there'd been a couple of funerals over the years. Nevertheless, there was no way he could possibly manage socializing with complete strangers while being strangled by a fancy strip of silk.

He'd promised to give it a shot, and Zach had spent good money to give him this opportunity. Even if the purple flyer had caught his eye, it's unlikely he would have bothered looking into it further.

Another deep breath and he walked in, trying to pretend he wasn't completely out of his depth.

The interior was decorated like a high school Christmas dance. But the room was filled with a bunch of men. He'd half expected to be the youngest guy in a room full of dinosaurs, but there was a substantial age range; he was neither oldest nor youngest. Hovering in the doorway, he wasn't sure what to do. Going straight for the food—or the cooler that he prayed contained bottles of beer—seemed a little rude. Surely he wasn't supposed to just walk up to a random person and start talking, was he?

Sweat popped out on his forehead, and his breathing got shallow. The room wasn't huge, but there probably weren't more than thirty guys here. Not an overwhelming number and certainly no reason for his panic, except he hadn't tried to make friends with strangers since he'd been in school. Kelly had been his social committee for so long.

"Hey man, no passing out." A strong hand clamped down on his shoulder, and Luke suppressed a startled yelp.

Luke cleared his throat. "Uh, hey." A slight turn to his left and a dark-haired guy, who was probably about ten years younger and carrying about thirty pounds more muscle than Luke, came into view.

"You're new here, aren't you?" The guy was also wearing a dress shirt, but he seemed far more comfortable in it than Luke was in his.

"Uh, yes."

The dark-haired guy peered around the room. "Usually our fearless leader greets the newbies, but I don't see him anywhere."

Luke took a breath and jumped into the deep end. "I'm Luke Jordan."

"Nice to meet you, Luke. I'm…." He sighed loudly. "I'm Bennett Adrian Walker."

Luke blinked. Was he in the right place? But Bennett just laughed.

"I can see what you're thinking. I'm an electrician, but my parents were hoping for another doctor in the family and named me accordingly."

"Another doctor?" That was a lot of pressure to put on a newborn, but the name certainly did suit a doctor.

"Yeah, Dad was a surgeon, Mom was a registered nurse, and my two brothers are both doctors."

"How come you became an electrician?" Luke coughed. That was kind of a tactless question, since becoming a doctor wasn't always a question of determination. Intelligence, skill, and grades were defining factors. It wasn't like just anybody could wake up and decide to become a doctor.

Bennett laughed again, without a hint of bitterness. "Rebellion? No, the sight of blood just freaks me out. I supposed I could have gone lawyer or something, but I sort of fell into an apprenticeship, and I like what I do. My father sees it as an almost criminal lack of ambition, but hey, isn't that the job of the baby in the family?"

Luke grinned. Maybe this socialization stuff wasn't so bad after all. "I wouldn't know. I'm an only child, and I only have one kid."

"You've got a kid? Wow. How old?"

"Twenty-four."

"Shut up. Testing the heterosexual waters as an infant, were you?"

Luke grinned even wider at the subtle compliment about his appearance. "I was pretty young, yeah."

"So what do you do?"

"Construction manager."

Talking shop all night wasn't really what he wanted to do, although he wasn't about to proposition Bennett either. The guy was good-looking, but there wasn't much of a spark. Luke hadn't gone through all this just to force a sexual attraction that wasn't really there.

Bennett wiggled his beer bottle. "C'mon. You need a beer, and I need a refill. Then we can stand along the walls and wait for the boy of our dreams to ask us to dance."

Luke snorted out a laugh. "That's pretty close to what I was thinking. Are all the meetings like this?"

"Nah. This isn't our usual room. And while it's a social group, there's usually a little more formalized interactions, like icebreakers and shit."

"Have you been a member long?" Luke wasn't sure about the weird note in Bennett's voice.

"Just a couple of months. It's a good idea, but it's also sad that it's necessary. Coming to the meeting makes me feel like a failure. Like I couldn't find the right words to make the guys I work with just… accept who I am. Like being afraid of someone reacting to my 'gayness' makes me inadequate."

They'd reached the cooler while Bennett was talking, and Bennett rummaged around for a couple of bottles for them. After opening them, he handed one off to Luke and the two of them stepped out of the way of the cooler. If the other guys were like Luke, the cooler would be the most popular spot for the evening.

"I know how you feel. My son was actually the one who found the group for me and signed me up as an early Christmas gift." Luke had never really been comfortable with someone so quickly, especially not to talk this openly and easily. If only he was attracted to Bennett, he might propose this second.

Bennett lifted an eyebrow, and Luke snorted. "I know. I mean, he was right. I was in a complete rut, doing the same thing day in and day out. I don't feel comfortable talking about my sexuality with the guys I work with, and that makes going out for drinks or whatever really tense, because I'm afraid I'll say the wrong thing with too many beers in me."

With a nod, Bennett clinked their beer bottles together in wordless accord.

"But it's a bit embarrassing that my son saw enough to figure out I don't really have friends anymore. Not since I divorced my wife."

"Oh, you were married, too? That can be tough."

"I was lucky, I think. My ex is a good person, and we got along really well, but we definitely made better friends than spouses. The split was easier than many I've seen, but...." Luke glanced around the room and swallowed a large mouthful of beer hoping to cool his heated cheeks. "I'm not a very social person. The friends we had were mostly Kelly's. There weren't any sides, exactly, for them to take, but it was her they connected with, not me."

Oh God. Luke bit his lip. Now he'd just told a complete stranger that he was a complete loser. This wasn't how to make friends. Wasn't he supposed to pretend to be fun or interesting?

"I'm so sorry." Luke slid his gaze to the door. "I didn't mean to spill all that."

Bennett laughed and punched him lightly on the bicep. "Don't worry. You were more circumspect than my last date."

Luke let himself relax, and they talked for a bit before Bennett took him around and introduced him to a few other guys. A few guys looked like they were going to hook up, and one of them gave him a look that Luke had no trouble interpreting, but for the most part, they were just a bunch of guys hanging out. Bennett never left his side, but he didn't feel like he was being smothered. He just sensed a guy who he got along with, and whose company he enjoyed.

"You want to hang out again sometime? We could swap phone numbers or e-mail or something." Bennett's expression was a little hesitant, and instead of the confident, outgoing man he'd been hanging out with all evening, Luke saw a crack in the confidence, a guy who also just wanted a friend.

"I'd like that, Bennett." Shit. He didn't think he was misreading Bennett's signals. Luke might not have spent much time trying to find dates or friends, but he didn't think Bennett looked at him as anything but a friend.

It was a fucking shame he wasn't attracted to Bennett, but at least the lack of sexual attraction was mutual or this could get uncomfortable. They'd moved to a spot along the wall, watching the intermingling of guys who were strangers to Luke before this night, but he could have come across any of them during the course of his job. Luke was pleasantly buzzed, so he'd switched to coffee. Last thing he needed was to hit a ride program doing spot-checks.

But he did need to clear up any potential misconceptions. "Uh, as friends, right?" Luke shut his eyes and bit back a groan. If he'd had more finesse, he should have applied some… any… to his words.

Bennett just laughed. "Oh, Luke. Yes, friends. Maybe our first meeting isn't the place to discuss it, but you're not my type, and I'm pretty sure I'm not yours. But I'm glad I met you."

"I'm glad I met you, too." Luke heaved a sigh of relief. So many times tonight, Bennett could have headed for the hills, but he hadn't, and Luke was ready to call the evening a success. One friend, with the potential for a roomful of them, was an excellent start.

"So, this might be a loaded question, considering… well… considering we're all here, but are you doing anything for Christmas? I mean, you've mentioned a son and ex-wife, but do you have any other family?" For all that Bennett had implied it was a loaded question, Luke couldn't tell if Bennett was going to be alone on Christmas and was angling for company or if he assumed Luke would be alone and was prepared to offer a place to go.

"My son and his friend are spending Christmas with me. Did you want to join us?"

A wide, happy smile made the corners of Bennett's eyes crinkle. "Thanks, I appreciate it. I'll let you know, if you don't mind? I have a job that might keep me in the city, instead of heading home for the holiday."

Luke had to call the evening a success.

CHAPTER 2

LUKE WRAPPED his brand new rainbow scarf around his neck to protect himself from the whipping wind. Zach had given him the scarf for Christmas, and while he wasn't particularly intent on proclaiming his sexuality like a flag tied around his neck, there wasn't any reason for anyone to suppose a rainbow automatically spoke to sexual orientation. Or so he kept telling himself.

The colors themselves were much brighter than anything he normally wore, and it was the idea he was drawing attention to himself that made him more uncomfortable than letting people know he was gay. After all, he was really only worried about coworkers, not strangers on the street. By the same token, though, he wasn't quite sure how "out" he was expected to be now that he was out.

Squinting at the front of the playhouse, he wondered if the long-dead designers were rolling in their graves because the beautiful, historical building had been surrounded by tall, square modern buildings that magnified winter breezes into near tornado status.

Shivering, he rubbed his hands together and stomped his feet. January was so fucking cold, and he should have known better than to let Bennett have custody of his ticket. Sure, Bennett was well on his way to becoming a great friend, but Luke had already discovered Bennett wasn't especially punctual.

"Luke!"

He turned and grinned at a red-faced Bennett.

"Sorry, man, had to park really far away. It's fucking freezing out here!"

Luke laughed. "I know. I've been waiting almost twenty minutes. I got a good spot, though, so I can give you a lift to your car after."

"You want to grab a drink or a late dinner after? You're not working weekends in this weather, are you?"

"We'll see. The job site's shut for a couple of weeks, but if the weather gets worse, might be better to just head home." Fucking winter. He should be grateful, though, because he was rarely out of work.

"Sure thing, boss." Bennett handed over Luke's ticket. Bennett had spearheaded a movement to get the Rainbow Blues discounted group rates to see the performance, and Luke had already acknowledged a couple of familiar faces while waiting for Bennett.

Luke had never been to a proper play before, never mind on opening night, and he was unreasonably excited.

They headed into the playhouse, and Luke hesitated for a moment before handing over his ticket, but the stragglers behind him crowded into the warmth at the door and in the interest of not blocking people from getting in, Luke released his grip on the ticket.

Inside, the cozy warmth was almost painful against his wind-seared cheeks.

"You okay, Luke?" He must have spent longer at the door than he'd thought, because Bennett had already shed his coat and leaned against a wall waiting for him.

He nodded, but accompanying a gay man to a play about a gay man coming out, while wearing a rainbow scarf… this was a pretty big step for him. Scary as fuck, but he finally felt like his life had taken a few halting steps forward out of stagnation.

With a grin, he followed Bennett to their seats.

JIMMY ALEXANDER couldn't stop smiling. He loved this play. He loved his role as the romantic lead in a cutting edge story about two men falling in love, *with* a fucking happy ever after. He loved that they'd played to a full house, and best of all, opening night had been an astounding success. Odds were good they wouldn't ever be able to recapture the magic they'd created tonight, but hell, he probably couldn't handle that much perfection anyway. Besides, if they were going to get it right, opening night was the night to do it, since so many reviewers and critics would have been in the audience.

"Jimmy, you were fabulous out there." Damian, the director and his best friend, hugged him breathless. Damian was one of the most supportive directors he'd worked with and never played favorites with him enough that the rest of the actors grumbled. When preparing for plays and rehearsing, Damian was a strict, unsmiling taskmaster, but outside of his directing, he was effusive and fun, and Jimmy knew he wasn't the only one who was going to get lavish praise and hugs.

He and Damian had met during teacher's college, and discovered their mutual love of theater, but Damian didn't like teaching as much as Jimmy did, and was a professional substitute teacher, on top of his directing duties.

"Thanks. Everything just fell right into place. We all fit together like magic."

Performing was a high he rarely got from anything else. Sex, sure, if the guy was any good. Teaching, well, when a student would come along whose desire to learn got fired up in one of Jimmy's classes, that was a pretty good high too. But performing was what he lived for. It was what he got up in the morning for. It was why he slogged through the 90 percent of craptastic bureaucracy, sullen teenagers, and illogical, irate parents, who only seemed to care about their children's education if they could spout abuse at one of the teachers.

He stripped and toweled off before getting dressed in his street clothes. There was supposed to be another snowstorm heading in overnight, but Jimmy didn't care. He wanted to enjoy the high. Nothing like accolades to buoy up his spirits. Most people who didn't know him would say it was rejection by his family that made him seek acceptance and love from the strangers in the audience. Except, they'd be wrong. His family had always been supportive, even to the point of financing a year in Hollywood for him to attempt the whole "trying to be a movie star" thing. But he'd been a good-looking, talented young guy in a fucking sea of good-looking, talented young guys, and he just hadn't stood out.

But acting in plays at the local playhouse? That gave him more satisfaction than scrambling from audition to audition and surviving on ramen three meals a day most weeks because his parents' allowance hadn't left any wiggle room for any extravagances, like alcohol. Probably because he'd been too young to buy it himself, although that hadn't stopped him.

By rights, he should slip out the back and get home ahead of the snow, but there was no way he was giving up his reward. He'd given up the dream of movie stardom on a hot day at the end of summer in a scuzzy shared apartment in California when he was twenty. In the eighteen years since, he'd carved out a comfortable life for himself. There were fans out there, waiting to greet him. He wasn't famous, but he loved it, regardless.

He was ready long before his fellow actors. Rocking back and forth on his feet, he was only able to make himself wait a minute or two before he couldn't stand it any longer. He slipped out to the foyer.

There were a few folks waiting near the door with flowers, sending a twinge of sadness through him. He'd told his friends and family he only wanted to be greeted with flowers from the love of his life. At thirty-eight, with no candidates for a long-term relationship in sight, he was just about ready to let go of that dream as well.

"Jimmy! You were incredible!" Karen Harper swept him up in a hug and kissed him on the cheek. Karen was the chemistry teacher at his school; they had adjoining classrooms and had become great friends from almost the first day. Of course, if Jimmy weren't out and proud, Karen's unabashed affection would have the entire faculty thinking they were more than just friends.

"Thank you." Jimmy smiled and hugged her back.

Karen proffered him a glass filled with bubbles.

"Champagne?"

"Well, if it can't be flowers, it's got to be champagne. We need to celebrate. You had a spectacular performance, your best ever."

His eyes burned a bit from the praise. Would have been nice if his family were here as well, but his parents had left the cold and snow immediately after Christmas, and his brother and sister were scattered far enough around the country to make it difficult to come back, especially in the winter, just to see one of his performances. Wasn't like he was on Broadway or anything. It was basically just a hobby. A time-consuming one, to be sure, but certainly not the focus of his family's life.

Within moments, he was surrounded by a group of friends, who all congratulated him. His friends usually tried to make it to his opening-night performances, and this one had been especially dear to their hearts as it was the first play he'd been in that had been about a gay man and one who got a happy ending. While there had been some heartwrenching moments, the whole play was about hope and love, and no matter how jaded and bitter some of his friends had become, love was what they all wanted for themselves.

"GIVE ME your coat check ticket, and I'll get both of ours." Bennett held out a hand with a smile.

"Sure, thanks." Luke pressed himself against the wall and waited.

Instead of a mad rush for the exits, most of the audience seemed to be mingling around, and a few even seemed to have fresh drinks. If the weather was bad enough that people were reluctant to leave, maybe he and Bennett should just head home, not bother with dinner.

A door opened not too far away, followed by a flurry of activity. Luke stared, then the actor came into view. The one who played Gary, the closeted married guy, who had seemed destined to die alone until he got up the courage to come out. Luke had been entranced, and not just because the story had many parallels to his life, to the point he could relate to the play's title of *Walking Wounded*.

The actor had been stunning. Jimmy Alexander. Tall, blond, slender. Expressive hands with thin fingers that punctuated his words. His face wasn't perfect and plastic, like generic models on magazine covers. His smile was wide, his eyes a little narrow, and his nose a trifle too big for his face. But Luke couldn't keep his eyes off him. Near the end, he'd almost lost track of the story line, so intent was he on memorizing every movement of Jimmy's mouth.

When they'd first entered the theater, he hadn't understood why anyone had bothered wasting money on the program. Sure, maybe a page or two for "credits" but the booklet seemed excessive. During intermission, however, he'd been thankful for that little booklet as he flipped through it to Jimmy Alexander's page. The actor was apparently thirty-eight years old—had to be a typo—and had starred in a number of plays, most of which Luke had never heard of. Luke would have much preferred to know what his turn-ons were and whether he was gay. Maybe the program wasn't all that useful after all.

Within minutes Jimmy was surrounded by people. He shook hands, accepted kisses on the cheek, and drank fizzy champagne. When he threw his head back and laughed, Luke strained to separate the sound of it from the din of the rest of the crowd. It had been a long time since Luke had wanted anything as much as he wanted to lick the long, smooth column of Jimmy's neck.

More of the cast came out of the door, and more people gathered about, a number of them carrying bouquets of flowers. Luke kept moving, but it was getting harder and harder to get a clear view.

When yet another person crowded next to Jimmy, blocking Luke's view, he shifted restlessly trying to find a break in the crowd to keep his eye on Jimmy.

"See something you like?"

Bennett's hand on his shoulder made him jump.

"What? Oh, nothing. Thanks for getting my coat."

Bennett handed the coat over but tilted his head, inspecting Luke. His ears heated, but there was no way Bennett could know Luke had managed to develop a sudden, intense crush on an absolute stranger. Much like the days when he'd pretended to like Duran Duran just for their music, but oh, it was even more for their eyeliner and tight, slender forms. Pathetic for a man, a father, of his age, wasn't it?

"It's more than acceptable to introduce yourself to the cast. That's why they come out like this." Bennett waved a hand toward Jimmy and the rest.

Luke's ears got hotter, and his cheeks joined in.

"Is it? How do you know?" Not that Luke was going to do that. There was no way. The way he felt now, like his skin was too tight and his heart racing, he'd probably spring wood and drool, and there was no way on God's green earth he was setting himself up for that sort of humiliation.

Bennett rolled his eyes. "This isn't my first rodeo, pardner."

A laugh escaped at his polished, urbane friend attempting a Texan drawl. Poorly. But Luke had forgotten Bennett had grown up in privilege, and still had enough money from an inheritance to never work again if he so chose. Bennett had been to tons of plays.

"Let's go introduce ourselves," Bennett urged.

Luke glanced over at Jimmy. He was gorgeous, happy, and animated. There was no way he was going over there. What would he say? "No, no."

"So… you want to leave now? Go get something to eat." Bennett grinned and shoved Luke's coat and scarf at him.

"Now?" He wasn't quite sure he was ready to give up his view of Jimmy. "We could have a drink first."

Luke had seen enough fresh drinks to know there was a bar serving in the foyer somewhere.

Bennett's grin morphed into a knowing smirk, but Luke was okay as long as he didn't actually admit anything.

"You could head closer to the actors while I go grab us a couple of beers."

"That's okay."

Bennett wended through the milling crowd and Luke pressed back against the wall. Holding his coat felt weird, so he slipped it on, bunching his scarf in his hands as he returned his gaze to Jimmy.

A moment later, Jimmy's gaze roved over him. Panicked, Luke looked away. What the fuck was the matter with him? Oh, yeah, he'd never really done much with another guy except anonymous pickups at a few clubs… where he was pretty sure the guys were either desperate or they felt sorry for him. He'd never caught the gaze of a guy he really liked. Not that he knew anything about Jimmy aside from what he saw on the stage, but he was infatuated nonetheless.

After a minute or two, he dared another look. Jimmy was no longer looking at him, and he breathed a sigh of relief—until Jimmy glanced his way again and smiled. Luke averted his eyes and ducked behind another group of theatergoers, his heart pounding.

Then he shook his head. There was nothing to be afraid of, no reason to act like a child. But he couldn't stop that breathless gasp when Jimmy looked at him a third time.

"Come on, we're going over there." Bennett waved an opened beer bottle in front of him.

"Christ, Bennett, don't scare me like that." Luke hadn't noticed Bennett's return, so intent he'd been on Jimmy and his gorgeous smile.

"Let's go."

"No, no, we don't need to."

"Luke, you were interested in coming to this play with me, but the second the character of Gary strode out onto the stage, it was like you'd been electrocuted. We'll go over there. Introduce ourselves. It's only polite to tell him how much you enjoyed his performance. Actors really appreciate that, trust me."

"I don't know."

Bennett gave him a reproachful look. "Surely you don't want him to think he did a bad job, do you?"

Well, no, he didn't want that. But he wasn't sure he was ready for this today.

"I...."

"Nope. We're going. If you don't come with me, I'll make up a totally embarrassing story about you. Got it?"

Luke took a deep breath. He really needed to man up, because this was unacceptable. He'd been the sole support for his family for many years, he and Kelly had raised a self-sufficient college-age son, and he had a good job where he oversaw a number of employees. He could handle a simple introduction to a man and a compliment about his work, even if he was the most compelling man he'd ever seen.

Find your fucking balls, Luke.

JIMMY DARTED another glance at the broad, auburn-haired man. The guy had been sending dark looks his way ever since Jimmy stepped out into the room, and he made Jimmy nervous as hell. Maybe the guy's wife was talking to the actors? If the guy hated the play so much, why was he sticking around? It wasn't fucking fair that straight guys could be so gorgeous even when they hated you.

With effort, he dragged his attention back to another well-wisher. When he let himself glance back, he hated himself for the little niggle of disappointment that the guy had finally taken his leave. Jimmy'd taken leave of his fucking senses if he thought a big, muscled straight guy was going to want Jimmy drooling over him anyway. Then, an older couple shuffled a few steps, and Jimmy sucked in a quick, surprised breath. Hot guy at two o'clock and closing in fast, with a fierce, determined look on his face.

Desperately, Jimmy tried to follow the conversation with... with.... He couldn't even remember who he was talking to, so he just smiled and nodded like an idiot. Surely even a straight guy wasn't going to cause trouble here in the foyer if he'd been comfortable enough to watch a play about a guy coming out and finding love with another man. Unless. Oh. Unless he somehow hadn't realized what he was getting into. Sometimes people didn't bother reading descriptions. This guy was so damn sexy and built, and Jimmy was probably going to cry if he got yelled at. Jimmy didn't spend a lot of time working out or taking self-defense classes. This guy could sweep the floor with him if it weren't for the fact he was surrounded by friends and fans.

Only a few steps away now, and Jimmy would have to face the guy. Who darted out a tongue to lick sharply defined lips. Jimmy's heart hammered, and his palms dampened. He wasn't sure if he was going to run away or drop down on his knees, mouth open, when confronted with one of the sexiest men he'd ever seen. He squared his shoulders and prepared to be harangued.

An urbane dark-haired man stepped in front of him, just as Jimmy had plastered on a wide smile, hoping it would hide his jitters.

"Hello. I'm Bennett. Terrific performance."

Jimmy smiled and nodded, somehow unable to formulate a response since he'd been gearing up to defend himself or maybe faint.

"And this is my friend, Luke."

The dark-haired man shoved a darkly scowling Luke in front of him, and Jimmy couldn't breathe.

"Uh, hi. You were... really great."

Jimmy blinked, trying to process the words while simultaneously wondering if he'd already passed out and conked his head.

"Thanks." Jimmy wrinkled his nose. His voice wasn't normally quite so breathy. Luke wouldn't meet his gaze, but that was okay.

Jimmy glanced down and noticed the rainbow scarf Luke gripped in his hands. A rainbow wasn't definitive proof, but it was a good sign and restored some of his customary confidence. He took two small steps, enough to encroach on the border of Luke's personal space.

"I like your scarf." This time his voice had dropped and was breathy in a good way. Startled, Luke lifted his head and stared at him. Wide hazel eyes framed by short blond lashes ensnared Jimmy in the very best way. Freckles scattered across pale skin, making Luke appear younger than the crinkles at the corners of his eyes attested.

"Thanks." Red stained Luke's cheeks, and he almost defiantly wound the scarf around his neck, while his pupils expanded.

Now that they were looking in each other's eyes, Jimmy didn't want to look at anything or anyone else, and based on Luke's focus, he felt the same electric connection.

Luke swallowed heavily and took a tiny step closer. "I don't suppose you'd want to have dinner with me?"

"Tonight?" Jimmy didn't care who else wanted to meet with him or that he'd been planning to head straight home to avoid the oncoming storm.

"If it's a good time."

"Yes. Come with me backstage? I'll grab my jacket, and we can go somewhere."

Just like that, Luke's frown smoothed out and in the face of Luke's smile, Jimmy's knees wobbled.

"I'll just head on home, then, will I, Luke?"

He and Luke both turned their attention to the dark-haired man who'd introduced Luke. Barry? Ben? Jimmy didn't quite remember. Everything aside from Luke had receded from his awareness into the haziness of a dream.

"Uh. Oh. Bennett. Did you want to…?"

Right. Bennett.

Bennett laughed good-naturedly. "Not a fucking chance. You have fun and give me a call tomorrow." He clapped Luke on the shoulder, shook hands with Jimmy, and left in a swirl of expensive cologne.

"Come on."

Luke glanced around. "Don't you have to stay and mingle?"

Jimmy stepped even closer, enough to tell that Luke didn't wear cologne but smelled clean and male and warm.

"Not necessary."

He grabbed Luke's hand and pulled him through the crowd. Jimmy made sure to keep a smile on his face, but he wasn't about to stop and talk to anyone. If they stopped, this strange magic spell might be broken and Luke would suddenly remember he was a straight man. Or even just change his mind about leaving with him. When he was younger, he could pass for a twink, but at thirty-eight he found it more difficult to attract guys who attracted him.

Backstage in the dressing room, Jimmy's navy peacoat waited for him. Perhaps it wasn't quite as warm as it could be, but he looked hot in it. As long as he didn't get himself trapped in a blizzard, he'd be just fine.

He snagged it off the hanger and turned around, only to find Luke right in his face. The silence in the dressing room made it seem like they were the only two people in the world.

A tiny sound, a cross between a gasp and a squeak, emerged from his lips. The spell, the bond between them, intensified with the speed of a lightning strike. He let his coat fall to the floor and curled his hands around the open sides of Luke's jacket, pulling the man closer.

Meeting with no resistance, Jimmy paused, lips almost touching Luke's.

"I don't normally do this," Jimmy whispered before he gently pressed their lips together. He didn't. He wanted to be a good role model, so his days of anonymous fucks dried up as soon as he'd been hired by Rivercrest High School. But it had been even longer since he'd wanted someone so intensely at first sight.

Luke exhaled, and wrapped his arms around Jimmy's waist.

The kiss stayed soft and gentle for a few moments before Jimmy parted his lips and licked at Luke's lips. With a gratifying moan, Luke opened his mouth and let Jimmy in.

Jimmy's breath came faster, and he used his body to guide Luke back against the door. Didn't matter that their mouths were fused together and their tongues twined. He needed to be closer. Needed it more than the breath he was having trouble drawing.

When Luke couldn't move back any farther, Jimmy let go of the death grip on Luke's lapels and moved them up to his cheeks and wedged himself between Luke's legs. God. He was so fucking hard. Between both sets of jeans, though, he wasn't quite sure if Luke was as into this, although the guy wasn't trying to get away or anything.

Like his thought had spurred Luke into action, he wrenched his head out of the kiss. Jimmy had never been more disappointed by the loss of a kiss.

"I… I'm sorry. I just couldn't help myself. But I wasn't lying. I don't usually just pounce on guys I've known for a minute." Jimmy was embarrassingly close to panting. Guess there was no chance of getting naked right here in the dressing room. He stepped back, just a bit, to give Luke some room.

He hadn't misread the situation too badly, had he? After all, Luke's pupils were blown out, almost obscuring the hazel irises, and he, too, was breathing heavily.

The wide smile made him relax, just a bit. Maybe he hadn't fucked this up too bad.

An adorable flush darkened Luke's cheeks. Jimmy didn't know how old Luke was, but between the blushes and freckles, most people probably pegged him younger than he was—which happened to Jimmy all the time, although in Jimmy's case, it was the combination of his name and his manic energy that made him appear youthful. Was he younger than Jimmy? Younger guys didn't go for him often, at least, not once they realized he wasn't in a position to support a boy toy. Luke, though, looked like a practical soul who maybe worked with his hands. Not a typical mani-pedi-ed, highlighted boy-toy wannabe.

"I don't either. It's just, uh…." Luke's gaze dropped, and Jimmy's automatically followed. Luke adjusted a healthy erection that had obviously been trapped in an uncomfortable position. There was no stopping Jimmy's smug smile, and when Luke lifted his eyes again, he drew in a sharp breath.

This time, it was Luke pulling them together, their clothes the only barrier from hip to chest. Jimmy moaned, and this time the kiss was wild and wet and deep. He'd cracked the seal on some untapped well of Luke's passion, and he was reaping the benefits while Luke fucked his mouth with his tongue.

He didn't want to push Luke into something he didn't want, but Jimmy needed more skin. He scrabbled with Luke's sweater and got his hands underneath to the warm, lightly furred chest. He couldn't suppress a shiver of delight. There wasn't much better than rubbing up against a guy with enough hair that you could tell he was a man. It made Jimmy feel safe and protected in some indefinable way, while making him desperately, desperately horny.

Luke's hands inched down over his ass and gripped, firmly enough that Jimmy had to pull his mouth out of the kiss and bite back a yowl. So fucking perfect.

"Love that," he whispered.

Luke licked his reddened, kiss-swollen lips, a look that suited him. If Jimmy had his way, Luke would sport this look often. He wanted Luke to fuck him, suck him, bring him off right now, again later tonight, and then maybe tomorrow or all fucking weekend if he could get away with it.

"This?" Luke gripped his ass even tighter.

"Oh, yeah." Jimmy moaned again before dropping his head forward, seeking Luke's neck with lips and teeth.

This time, the shiver came from Luke, and he made a humming sound deep in his chest while his hands continued to knead Jimmy's ass. They were both rubbing their groins together so fast and hard Jimmy almost expected their jeans to start smoking.

His balls tightened just as someone thumped on the door. Jimmy sprang out of Luke's arms, definitely panting this time, while Luke spun away from the door and behind a rack of costumes. Jimmy clenched his hands into fists and concentrated on his lines in the play, the tests he still had to grade for his freshman biology class, anything to stave off the orgasm he'd been mere seconds from blowing into his briefs.

Fuck, fuck, fuck. Been a long fucking time since he'd been that worked up.

The thump on the door came again, this time with a voice. "What the fuck are you doing in there, Jimmy? We're locking up for the night. Go the fuck home, already."

"Yeah, yeah, I'm heading out now." Thankfully his voice was steady. More or less.

He didn't dare try looking at Luke, not yet. If Luke was as close to blowing as he was, he wouldn't be able to hold back his orgasm.

Concentrating on his breathing, he pulled his coat on. After a few moments, he was still hard as iron, but he wasn't about to blow in his jeans.

Luke poked his head out, the tips of his ears red. "Uh, yeah, so… that was close."

Jimmy grinned. "Me, too. Want to pick it up again at my place?"

The disappointed look on Luke's face effectively dashed cold water on his dick. "Or not."

Luke shook his head. "No, I mean, I'd like to, sure, but I thought we were going to get dinner. Uh, first."

Dinner? Jimmy was a sure thing, and Luke still wanted to just hang out? That didn't happen very often. Most guys found him too manic to date, although they sure didn't mind his energy in the sack.

"You really want to go for dinner first?"

Luke stepped toward him, his coat and scarf obscuring the belly Jimmy had uncovered and the package that might still be hard for him.

"Yeah, I do. I mean, I can get laid, you know. Dates are a little harder to come by. And I really did think you were great. I've never met an actor before. I'd like to talk some." He licked his lips again. "Although the kissing. Yeah, that was damned good."

Jimmy grinned. A date. He could do a date.

"We'd better get out of here, before they lock us in. Got a preference? There's a decent Chinese place and a Greek place not far from my apartment. They should both be open late."

He led Luke out the back door and rocked to a halt. Luke stepped out beside him. Fat, fluffy snowflakes fell from the sky, a few inches of accumulation covering any recent activity in the tiny parking lot behind the playhouse. Either everyone was home in their beds already or the snow muffled the sounds of the traffic on the other side of the playhouse, the strange serenity snowstorms brought.

"Holy shit." Luke's voice was low, as though unwilling to disturb the silence that enveloped them.

"It's pretty bad out. I don't live far from here, but I'll understand if you want to do this another night." He'd understand, yes, but he'd be disappointed, and his cock would be pissed right the hell off. He hadn't had a date with a sexy man in so long he didn't want to let this one slip through his fingers. It wasn't just that, either, because he truly wasn't that desperate. But they fit together like two halves of a whole, and he wanted to find out if he was under the delusion of some ridiculous romantic notion or if he'd imagined the connection he felt with Luke.

Luke peered at him. Jimmy wanted to project whatever would be most likely to convince Luke to come home with him, but he had no idea what Luke was looking for.

"I like Chinese," Luke said.

Blinking, Jimmy didn't know what to do with that. Was that a statement of future intent or were they going to continue to have their date?

Luke drew in a deep breath, like he was gearing up for some big pronouncement. "Maybe they do takeout. Do you... uh... have breakfast food?"

Oh, by all that's holy and the patron saint of actors. Luke was spending the night.

Grabbing the ends of Luke's rainbow scarf, he pulled Luke close and gave him a kiss. With the snow coming down, and the feeling like they were alone in the world, this was maybe the most romantic kiss he'd ever had. Somehow, Luke understood, and neither of them deepened it beyond the sweet press of lips.

Jimmy pulled back and dusted the snow from Luke's hair. "I'm all for takeout, and I have plenty to feed you for breakfast. I only wish I had a fireplace to warm us up later."

"A fireplace would be good, but I'll warm you up."

With effort, he held in a swoony sigh. How was Luke able to keep saying the right things when he didn't have much experience dating? Someone this sweet and sexy should have been snapped up a long time ago. But if no one else had recognized this gem, Jimmy sure as hell wasn't going to complain.

"Let's get my car unburied, and get going before this gets any worse." That would be just his luck. First promising date material in months and Jimmy wraps his car around a telephone pole on the way home.

CHAPTER 3

"HERE IT is, home sweet home." Jimmy opened his front door with a flourish. Or as much of a flourish as he could, carrying a Chinese takeout bag and stomping snow from his feet. It wasn't the place he wanted to live for the rest of his life, but it would do in the interim.

They'd been lucky to get to China Garden when they did. Even they were closing early because of the storm.

Jimmy set the takeout bag on the hall table and took off his gloves and jacket, hanging them and Luke's over the old-fashioned radiator. Best way to dry out soggy winter clothing. He caught sight of himself in the mirror and groaned. The falling snow had turned his carefully styled hair into a wet, bedraggled mess. Dragging his fingers through it only made it worse.

Luke came up behind him with an evil grin and scrubbed his palms all over Jimmy's head making him look like a blond porcupine. But he couldn't be mad, not when Luke looked so happy. Jimmy didn't want to see that fierce scowl ever again.

"Hey! Messing up my hair is reserved for people whose last name I know." He spun around, and Luke tugged him close, dropping a light kiss on his lips. Jimmy deepened it, just a bit, before hunger had him pulling back. They had all night for kissing. Jimmy stared into Luke's eyes. He didn't know Luke's last name, and all he could think about was how comfortable and perfect his place was in Luke's arms. He'd never really thought he had room in his life for a boyfriend, not anymore, but if no red flags popped up and Luke was interested, Jimmy would make time.

"Jordan."

Oh. Red flag number one. The warm, fuzzy feelings became cold and jagged in his stomach. "Uh…. Jimmy. I'm Jimmy."

Luke started laughing. Laughing hard enough he had to let go of Jimmy and wrap his arms around his stomach. A grin threatened to surface at the infectious nature of Luke's full-on belly laugh, but it was a little weird smiling because Luke couldn't remember his name. God, that was fucking depressing.

Wheezing slightly, Luke straightened. "My name. It's Luke Jordan."

Mortified. He'd never been so mortified that he was rendered speechless. Jimmy could almost always talk—it was a gift, or a curse for his listeners—but now he had no words. Should he apologize? Laugh? Explain himself? If they were at Luke's place, he'd probably just leave.

A tiny frown crossed Luke's face, and he gathered Jimmy in his arms again. "Hey, hey. Don't get upset about it. Probably I shouldn't have laughed, but man, that was funny."

Holding himself stiffly, Jimmy cracked a smile. Maybe it was a little funny. Luke grinned at him and kissed him again, this time with big smacking noises, and Jimmy gradually relaxed.

"It was a reasonable conclusion." Jimmy couldn't let it go without some explanation.

"Yeah, I know." Luke framed his face in strong, callused hands. "But the second I looked up your name in that program, there wasn't any way I was forgetting it, Jimmy Alexander."

Jimmy smiled. "It's nice to meet you, Luke Jordan."

Luke's stomach rumbled, and Jimmy finally relaxed. "Let's get you fed."

"And we can find out more than each other's names, eh?"

A few minutes later, they had the cartons all opened on Jimmy's kitchen table. Much to Jimmy's surprise, Luke chose to sit beside him, instead of across from him.

"All the better to feed you," Luke proclaimed before aiming a small piece of General Tso's chicken toward his mouth.

Jimmy took it, again at a loss for words, momentarily. While he chewed, he couldn't keep his eyes off Luke and picked up a slice of green pepper in his chopsticks, offering it to Luke, who slowly sucked it into his mouth.

The warm feeling in his belly returned tenfold, and his cock took a renewed interest in dinner.

"I thought you said you didn't do this much."

Luke raised an eyebrow. "Eat dinner?"

A laugh spluttered out. He had assumed Luke would be super serious, based on how fierce he'd looked at the theater, but he'd played in the snow, made Jimmy laugh, and managed to be sweet and sexy at the same time. But that was the reason for the question. How could a guy this great be single?

"Date, obviously. You're a natural. Unless you've had more practice than you mentioned." The words didn't sound so awful in his head, but as soon as they escaped, Jimmy realized he'd just accused his sexy date of lying. Lying like a rug wearing pants on fire.

"Um… I mean…." What the fuck was wrong with him tonight? No wonder all his past dates and boyfriends had been nothing better than passable. Apparently he sent the good ones running away with his motormouth.

Luke squeezed his hand. "I'm glad I'm getting it right." He scooped some more food onto his plate. "I really haven't dated much. This is just sort of how I imagined dating should be. And I've spent quite a while imagining it."

The smile that split Luke's face was breathtaking, like he thought Jimmy was doing everything right. Then again, maybe that only supported Luke's statement that he hadn't dated much, because Jimmy was doing a piss-poor job of it.

"I got my high school girlfriend pregnant, and we got married as soon as we graduated. We hadn't done much actual dating like adults, mostly group things. After Zach was born, we were too focused on making ends meet and raising our son to date. Once we were on better financial footing and Zach was more independent… well, it was clear to us that we weren't right for each other and trying to have married-couple dates at that point would have been a waste of time. Since we divorced, I haven't had a lot of opportunity for dating. Mostly because I really don't know what I'm doing." Luke let out a self-deprecating laugh before stuffing a breaded shrimp in his mouth.

"Oh, right. You mentioned your son. The one that gave you your scarf." Was he ready to get involved with a guy who had a kid? Jimmy wasn't sure about that. This was only the first date, though. Maybe he was getting ahead of himself. "I take it he knows you're gay, then? Or was the rainbow a happy accident?"

"A gay old accident, you mean?" Luke grinned, and Jimmy grinned back. "Yes, he knows. And obviously he doesn't care."

"That's awesome." Of course, that might change once Luke's son became a teenager. They were ornery, contrary fucks, as Jimmy had good reason to know.

Luke smiled again, but this one was full of love, and Jimmy melted a little inside. If Luke loved his son that much, Jimmy wasn't giving up a chance to get a little of that for himself. He'd figure out how to get along with a kid, because if Jimmy had anything to say about it, things would be getting serious with Luke.

"How long have you been divorced?" The whole getting married before coming out was more common than Jimmy liked, but he guessed he could understand it. He'd seen firsthand how unforgiving some of his friends' families were.

"Two years."

"Any relationships since?"

Luke rolled his eyes. "No, of course not. I can't figure out dating, how am I going to find a relationship?"

Jimmy smiled at him. At least he hadn't said he wasn't interested in a relationship. But if he'd been divorced two years and had problems finding dates…. "What about sex?"

"As in, have I had sex since I got divorced? Yes, I have."

Jimmy pursed his lips. He wasn't sure, but he might actually be disappointed he hadn't got himself a virgin. Mostly, though, he was glad those other horn dogs hadn't figured out what a great guy Luke was.

"And did you know you were gay when you got married?" Jimmy hadn't ever had a moment's indecision or oblivion about the matter, but he'd been lucky because he'd known his family would be open and accepting. Not everyone was as self-aware, or was willing to be as self-aware as Jimmy.

Luke fed him a pot sticker while answering. "Oh, yeah, I did, but I wasn't ready to come out. My parents were religious and weren't gay-friendly at all." He snorted. "Getting my girlfriend knocked up wasn't much better in their opinion. Even getting married didn't fix my relationship with them. Kelly's family wasn't thrilled either, and they weren't well off. With my in-laws' help, we managed to keep food on the table, and Kelly eventually got her degree, but that was it. My parents died shortly after Zach was born."

Jimmy raised his eyebrows. "I'm sorry, Luke."

Luke shrugged. "Shit happens. I've had a lot of time to get over it. But enough about my boring life. Tell me about acting. I've never met an actor. Do you do movies or television as well as plays?"

Now Jimmy was a bit embarrassed. He sure as shit wasn't going to tell Luke about his pathetic attempt to break into Hollywood when he was… probably the same age as Luke when he was dealing with a newborn baby and new wife.

"Oh, well, I'd certainly like to get into film acting, but I love the plays. It's really only a hobby. Actually…."

"What?"

Jimmy couldn't believe he was going to tell a new guy about this, but something about Luke drew him out. "I spent a whole year in Hollywood. My parents knew I was passionate about acting, and I'd done a number of school productions. They paid for me to live out there, while I did the whole cattle-call auditions and waiting tables thing."

Luke looked so interested, and he'd always been embarrassed to admit this, but he believed Luke wouldn't judge him.

"And?" Luke prompted.

"I got nowhere. Absolutely nowhere. I wasn't pretty enough, muscular enough, definitely not good enough to compete with everyone trying to make it big."

"But you're such a good actor. And you're sexy as anything."

The praise pleased him, but Luke was likely biased. Most of the guys he dated thought his acting was a waste of effort and only took away from time spent with them. Perversely, he wasn't sure how comfortable he was with Luke acting almost starstruck. Most of his roles received critical acclaim, but he was no star.

"Thanks. Anyway, after a year, I came home and went to college. Went with my backup plan. My day job is a high school biology teacher."

"Really?" Luke's eyes darkened, and he leaned forward while pressing his thigh firmly against Jimmy's.

"Yeah. Why? You got some unresolved crush on an old teacher?"

"No. But a teacher seems a little more attainable for a construction manager."

Jimmy's heart leapt. That had to mean Luke was thinking about a relationship, too. God, he would be so fucking disappointed if things with Luke didn't work out.

"For construction managers named Luke, I think either teacher or actor is pretty damn attainable." He lowered his voice to a husky, sensual rumble.

"Oh, yeah?" Luke speared a piece of sweet and sour chicken and used it to stroke sticky orange sauce down Jimmy's face. Before Jimmy could ask him what the fuck was up with that, Luke leaned in and licked it off his cheek.

Jimmy shivered, and his cock pressed insistently against his fly. Luke nibbled his way down Jimmy's cheek, along his jaw, and teased his neck for a moment before latching on to his neck like a lamprey eel, making Jimmy's bones melt. Except for the one tenting his pants.

Luke lifted his head. "Good spot?"

"Uh, yeah," Jimmy managed to get out. "But I've got some other ones that need attention."

"I wouldn't want to miss any of them. Bedroom?"

Jimmy glanced at the remains of dinner. To his surprise, they'd managed to eat almost everything. Faced with the choice of sex right now and putting the few leftovers in the fridge, he chose sex. Of course. He was almost as turned on and horny as he'd been in the dressing room.

"Bedroom." He got up from the chair, Luke following with a clatter.

Luke pressed right up behind him, wrapped his arms around Jimmy's waist and whispered in his ear. "I want you so bad."

Jimmy let out another swoony sigh and sped up. "I want you, too."

THIS WAS already turning out to be a better date than any Luke had ever had or imagined. Talking with Jimmy had been easy and comfortable, aside from a few minor hiccups. Amazingly, Luke had been able to talk and tease. There weren't many people he was able to connect with so quickly. And now, the most talented, beautiful man he'd ever met was ready and eager to get naked with him. Best day ever, aside from Zach's birth, and even that had taken a few days to get over the "he's so fucking tiny, what if I break him" mentality. This… there was no downside.

He pulled Jimmy back against him, arms firmly wrapped around his waist, halting their forward progress to the bedroom. But he couldn't wait any longer to taste Jimmy's skin again. Jimmy giggled as he licked and sucked along the smooth skin of Jimmy's neck. The scent of man and the salty taste of skin was one of the best combinations ever. Sure, he'd had sex before, but rarely was he in a position to explore his partner's body like this. Never lifting his head from Jimmy's neck, he slid his hands under Jimmy's sweater, splaying his palms across Jimmy's soft belly. He toyed with Jimmy's narrow treasure trail and navel, enjoying Jimmy's wiggling and breathless gasps. There was no choice in the matter—he pressed his groin into Jimmy's denim-covered ass, giving his erection some much-needed friction.

The teasing could only last so long before it broke Luke's control, and he dragged a hand down to skim over Jimmy's cock. Jimmy huffed out a breath like someone had punched him in the stomach.

"Bedroom. Now." There was no mistaking the need and desperation in Jimmy's voice; he sounded almost as eager as Luke.

"Go." With reluctance, Luke opened his arms to let Jimmy go, or he was going to strip him down right here in the hall.

Luke took a few minutes to breathe, try to bring himself back from the edge—again. Jimmy made him want, and this was the second time this evening he'd been on the verge of coming in his pants.

When he got himself under control, he walked into the bedroom, and nearly doubled over from the stab of lust knifing through him. Jimmy was already naked, stretched out on the bed, ruddy cock standing at attention for him, a shiny pearl of precum calling to Luke's tongue.

He spared a moment to thank his physically demanding job, because he was damn fit for his age and wouldn't feel like such an old man next to Jimmy's lithe form. Luke stripped as fast as he'd ever done in his life, and sprang on the bed, his own cock leading the way, hungry and eager for Jimmy.

Straddling Jimmy's legs, Luke crawled up the bed, taking a moment to lick the precum off the tip of Jimmy's cock. When Jimmy groaned and jerked his hips, Luke realized neither of them was going to last for any sort of lengthy exploration. At least if they continued to date, he'd have all the time he wanted to learn Jimmy's body.

He finished moving up the bed and lowered himself on Jimmy, cock to cock and chest to chest. Luke promised himself that sometime soon he'd lick Jimmy all over, touch every bit of skin, but for now, he needed to come. Needed to make Jimmy come.

The touch of lips to lips was like a spark that ignited a wildfire. Luke devoured Jimmy's mouth as Jimmy used his tongue to fuck Luke's mouth. Their groans mingled as they rutted against each other, Jimmy's hands clenching on his back. A flash of memory from the dressing room at the theater had Luke flipping them over so Jimmy was on top, but their mouths and hips never stopped moving.

With Jimmy above him, Luke had easy access to his ass, and he dug his fingers into the firm flesh, kneading and massaging the cheeks.

It was exactly what Jimmy needed. Stiffening, Jimmy's cock jerked, spilling hot and wet over Luke's cock and belly. Luke managed a few more thrusts in the slippery warmth before his gut tightened and he added his load to Jimmy's, his vision darkening as the pleasure wracked his body.

Jimmy lifted his mouth off Luke's, probably wise since they both needed to catch their breath, but it left Luke inexplicably bereft. Jimmy sagged, his body relaxing atop Luke's, his forehead resting on Luke's, chasing away that feeling of loss. He rubbed his hands slowly along Jimmy's sweat-slicked back and just breathed, the earthy scent of their cum heavy in the air.

Long before Luke was ready to move, their cum cooled and became sticky. With a laugh, Jimmy peeled himself away and padded to the bathroom, returning all cleaned with a damp washcloth.

"Sorry that was so quick." Jimmy climbed into bed next to him.

Luke grabbed the cloth and wiped himself down, because letting Jimmy do it for him was a little embarrassing.

"It's okay. It was great." The words weren't adequate to explain how perfect the moment had been. "Better than great."

No, that wasn't any better. Thankfully, Jimmy grinned and kissed him, settling in on his side so he could look at Luke.

"It was great. Awesome, stupendous, mind-blowing…. But fast. You just… do it for me, Luke."

Luke took a deep breath and stroked Jimmy's cheek, the blond stubble rasping against his fingertips. "You do it for me, too, Jimmy. A lot. If I were a young guy like you, I'd love to go again tonight, but I'm not sure my recovery time is up to it. There's always tomorrow morning, right?"

He'd been incredibly presumptuous earlier, pretty much telling Jimmy he was planning to stay the night. Jimmy hadn't minded then, but Luke wasn't naive. Guys thought differently when the blood flow wasn't split between brain and cock. It would suck to have to find a cab at this time of night, with weather like this, but he didn't want to wear out his welcome. Judging from the way Jimmy's mouth had dropped open in shock, though, Luke would be on his way sooner rather than later, no matter how complimentary Jimmy had been about the sex.

"Young guy like me?"

Frowning, Luke tried to reconcile the fact that Jimmy wasn't refuting morning sex, but his age.

"What do you mean? I'm thirty-eight. I thought you said you read my bio in the program."

Luke rubbed at his nose. "Well, sure I did. But I thought that thirty-eight was some sort of weird typo. You sure you're not twenty-eight?"

Jimmy laughed and kissed his cheek. "You are just the sweetest man ever. Wait." Jimmy frowned. "You are talking about how I look, right? You're not calling me immature or anything?"

This time it was Luke who laughed, partly at Jimmy's odd self-consciousness and partly relief that they were closer in age. However hot it would be to say he'd hooked up with a much younger man, Luke wasn't looking for a hookup, and he was pretty sure he'd have more in common with someone closer to his age.

"Mostly your looks, yes. But your enthusiasm, too. And not just in bed."

"I was right. You are the sweetest guy." His sweetness got him another kiss, which Luke wasn't going to complain about.

Jimmy stroked over the hair on his chest, a gentle exploration that didn't feel like Jimmy was trying to wind him up. Luke took the opportunity to observe Jimmy with touch as well as sight. Unlike himself, Jimmy didn't have a lot of hair on his chest, just a bit of blond fuzz covering his pecs and then a slightly darker treasure trail leading to dark gold pubes that had clearly been trimmed. Hopefully Jimmy didn't mind that Luke hadn't ever manscaped. Jimmy was slender, without much muscle definition. A soft belly and the merest hint of love handles—which might be more pronounced if he wasn't working two jobs—said that Jimmy loved food. Luke would like to cook for Jimmy. If they kept dating, he'd have to go grocery shopping. Soon.

Despite the fact Luke suspected he'd fall asleep long before he'd be recovered enough to go another round, Jimmy's soft cock and blond fuzzed balls made his mouth water.

Without thinking, he reached out and stroked those balls. "I'm glad you don't wax." It looked hot in porn, but when he was touching a guy's balls, he wanted them to be a man's balls and not like the naked suede of one of those sphinx cats.

"Oh, yeah, well. I used to. When I was hitting the clubs. But it always took three or four days afterward to be comfortable, and let me tell you, the desperation of not being able to scratch or readjust sore, itchy balls because you're stuck for hours teaching a bunch of teenagers just waiting to find any weakness they can exploit or make fun of… well, it just didn't make sense anymore. For a few years, I'd wax again during the summer break, but after I hit thirty, I just couldn't be bothered."

Luke grinned. He could see Jimmy at the front of a classroom, trying not to twitch and telegraph his discomfort to everyone.

"God. I didn't think I'd be up for another round tonight, either, but if you keep doing that, I'm going to want to."

Sure enough, the time Luke had spent stroking Jimmy's balls had had a positive effect on Jimmy's cock, plumping it a bit from its previous sated state. Gorgeous. He licked his lips. It wouldn't be any hardship at all to suck Jimmy off, even if he couldn't get it up again.

"And I think you might be, too."

Luke glanced down his body and grinned. "Apparently you're good for my recovery time."

This time it was Jimmy frowning. "Wait. How old are you?"

Somehow, he'd been hoping to avoid answering that question, but that reluctance had been more intense when he was afraid Jimmy might be fifteen years or more younger than him.

"Forty-three."

"Shut the fuck up. You are not."

All it would take was a good look in bright light, which, to be fair, hadn't been in supply since he'd met Jimmy. Even Jimmy's kitchen light was a subdued, yellowish shade that the contractor in him wanted to fix. In the bedroom, Jimmy was lit by the cold white light of the moon reflected off snow. Moonlight flattened color and smoothed imperfections, which Jimmy didn't have, but Luke did. Having them masked the first time they were together made it easier for Luke to enjoy and let go of his inhibitions, pleased he didn't appear to be the oldster he felt like most days. He just shrugged and nodded.

Jimmy sat up, the gentle touches forgotten as he stared down at Luke.

"How old is your son?" The tone was almost accusing, confusing Luke.

"Twenty-four."

Jimmy flopped back on the bed, laughing. "Oh my God. As soon as you mentioned a son, I've been grappling with the concept of dating a guy with a kid. It's a big responsibility and all, and I was worried about how it would all shake out, assuming we get serious. But I thought he was, like, ten. Maybe fifteen at the most."

Relief flooded Luke. Not only was Jimmy assuming they'd be continuing this relationship, but the odd moments of hesitation he'd sensed in Jimmy could easily be attributed to his concern over Luke's son.

"Nope. Zach is all raised up and on his own. Well, he graduates from college this year, and has a scholarship for grad school next year. Assuming he keeps his grades up, I won't be on the hook for any more tuition, but I'm prepared if he needs it. I try to see him every weekend, if his schedule allows. Dinner or something. Sometimes catching a game. This week, it's brunch on Sunday."

"I guess you won't need any advice from me about dealing with a sullen teenaged boy."

Luke laughed. "Nope, although I could have used some back then. He could be a moody son of a bitch. Thankfully that's long past." Luke bit his lip. Maybe it was too soon to admit this to a man he'd only known a few hours, but those hours had been just about perfect, and the man himself was... right, somehow. Right for him, he was almost certain, and he wanted to find out where they could go, together. "I'd like you to meet him."

"Meet him?" Jimmy gulped. "You don't mean already, do you?"

"Well, no. But if you're serious about seeing where this goes, probably pretty soon."

Jimmy rolled over, draping himself over Luke's chest, his slowly thickening cock nudging Luke's hip. "I'm serious. I don't want one-night stands, and I like what I know about you. I think we could be good together. But I think we need to stop talking about your kid before I feel like a total perv."

"We can do that."

Luke kissed Jimmy and let himself revel in a slightly less frantic encounter with his new lover.

WITH HIS arms wrapped around a nice warm body, Luke drowsed in those comfortable moments prior to falling asleep. The scent of Jimmy's clean sweat and the musky scent of their sex lulled him into a deep contentment. It had been so long since he'd fallen asleep tangled up next to someone. He wanted to say he missed it, but lying next to Jimmy, skin to skin, the hard planes of their bodies merging like they were meant to be, well… he'd never had this. He'd missed the facsimile he had when he and Kelly were still pretending to be a couple. But this… if this was what it would be like having a lover like Jimmy, he wasn't going to want to live without this.

Underneath Luke's arm, Jimmy's breathing became slow and regular, his skin warm, and Luke imagined he could feel the slow, steady thump of his heartbeat.

Slowly, Luke sank closer to sleep. Until a phone blared some music he didn't recognize, and Jimmy sat straight up.

"What?" The word slurred out Luke's mouth. "What's wrong?"

Jimmy glanced at the clock, which displayed the ungodly hour of three in the morning, before leaping to grab his cellphone.

"Damian?" Jimmy didn't sound nearly as awake as he appeared as he stumbled naked out of the bedroom.

Who the fuck was Damian?

Luke debated waiting in the bedroom. After the connection he and Jimmy had made—or he imagined they'd made—was Luke going to find out that Jimmy already had a man in his life? Surely no one in their right mind would be making booty calls in the aftermath of the snowstorm that had paralyzed half the city.

Perhaps it was insufferably rude, but Luke had to know. The evening with Jimmy had been so perfect, he had to know—right now—if he'd been imagining it all.

Jimmy murmured into the phone while making his way to the next room—an office. He sat down at a desk and opened a laptop. Luke stood in the doorway, watching, but he wasn't able to hear enough of Jimmy's side of the conversation to figure out what was going on and why some guy named Damian would be calling Jimmy in the middle of the night. There was nothing in Jimmy's demeanor that would indicate an emergency or a death, which is what Luke always assumed when the phone rang in the middle of the night.

After a few minutes clicking on his computer, Jimmy sucked in a breath, his whole body vibrating as he read something on the screen.

"Thanks, Damian." Jimmy let the phone drop on his desk, and he spun around, catching sight of Luke.

The smile on Jimmy's face was like he'd won the lottery, and Luke couldn't help but smile back. Then Jimmy launched himself out of the chair, right for Luke.

Wrapping his arms around Luke, Jimmy kissed him, a quick smack before he pulled back. "We're a hit!"

"A hit?" What was Jimmy talking about?

"The show! There are about half a dozen reviews posted, and they're all great."

"That's awesome, Jimmy. I'm not surprised, mind you. You were stunning."

Jimmy grinned and kissed him again. This time, when their lips parted, Luke had a question. "Why did that guy call in the middle of the night? Isn't that kinda weird?"

Even if Damian wasn't making a booty call, was there some reason, some history between the two men that made him comfortable enough to call Jimmy at any time?

"No, not really." Jimmy led him back into the bedroom. "I mean, Damian's my best friend, and I've had to bail him out of some sticky situations in the middle of the night. But on opening night, this isn't late. Normally, the cast will hang out together somewhere and wait until the reviews are posted. Back in the day, it was the morning paper, but now there are reviews much earlier online."

Oh God. "Why didn't you say something? We could have… gone out a different day." Luke had been so caught up in the gut-punch of attraction for Jimmy it had never occurred to him that he was being selfish by giving in to his desire for Jimmy.

Jimmy wiggled his eyebrows and pulled Luke down on the bed. "Don't be ridiculous. With the storm coming in, we'd already decided it would be better not to have our customary cast party. Even so, the second I realized you were gay and interested, I wasn't going to let you get away that easy."

Oh? If he hadn't already come twice tonight, those words would have him raring to go again. He kissed Jimmy, long and thorough, and his cock gave a valiant effort to revive, but failed.

"Mmmm. I'm wired from those reviews, and you're sexy as hell, but…." Jimmy glanced down at his groin. "The flesh isn't as willing as I'd like."

Luke chuckled. "Mine neither. Rain check?"

"I'll hold you to it. But I don't think I'll be able to get back to sleep right away. If you're tired, I can just go watch television."

The thought of sleeping by himself in Jimmy's bed… was better than sleeping by himself in his own bed, but he wanted Jimmy with him. "What about a nice long shower? We can get properly cleaned up, and the heat and steam might get you sleepy again."

"You are brilliant." Jimmy bounded out of bed, and Luke followed. Jimmy was getting a kiss for that; it wasn't often people told Luke he was brilliant. Of course, if Jimmy was as sexy in the shower as he was out of it, Luke might be able to accommodate with a little more than a kiss.

CHAPTER 4

LUKE STRETCHED and kept his eyes closed, trying to hold on to sleep just a little longer, despite the light banging on his eyelids. The scent of Jimmy, indelibly imprinted on his brain after only one night, permeated the sheets. Flipping over, he buried his nose in the pillow and inhaled like a lovesick teenager. But he didn't have to moon over Jimmy's scent. Not when he could kiss and touch and taste the man himself. Eyes still closed, he reached out… and reached out. The sheets might still smell like Jimmy, but they were cold from a man who'd long since awoken.

Some of Luke's comfort bled away. Sitting up, he opened his eyes. Jimmy was nowhere to be seen, and Luke had slept in later than he usually did at his apartment. A couple of energetic orgasms with another person were better than any sleeping pill ever invented. Waking up alone, though, was unexpected. The door to the bedroom was shut, and Luke was certain they'd left it open after their midnight shower.

Without Jimmy's facial expressions to guide him, Luke was lost. Was he supposed to wait here? Leave? They hadn't exchanged numbers, but if Luke had imagined the connection between them last night, maybe that's what Jimmy wanted. In the cold light of day, Luke found it easy to understand if he'd misread the situation. After all, having an emotional connection so quickly was impossible, wasn't it? That didn't stop the jagged wrench of grief at the loss of something special, no matter how briefly he'd thought it had been a part of his life. Stupid. He was too old for this nonsense. Falling in love was something for young people. Boyfriends were for other people, not someone who'd been so repressed his whole adult life he was imagining hearts and flowers and forever after one spectacular one-night stand.

As he yanked on his clothes, he took a closer look at the mounds of snow outside the window. It was going to be a fucking pain to get a cab or trudge through all that snow to pick up his car, but he'd remember this lesson for next time. Like he'd told his son many times over the years, mistakes were regrettable but even worse would be not to learn from them. Luke would learn not to get so invested.

Right now, he was tempted to go home and burn the dress pants and expensive sweater Zach had made him buy for the play, since he'd been adamant Luke couldn't attend in his customary jeans and T-shirt combo. Stupid, yes, because just as he'd rationalized when he purchased it, there were other places he'd be able to wear the outfit, like Zach's upcoming graduation.

He raked his fingers through his hair and took a deep breath. This uncertainty was ridiculous. Even if he'd misread the situation, the only one who'd know it was him.

Didn't stop him from noting the nice, homey touches Jimmy had made to his bedroom. Jimmy's place wasn't much better than the concrete bunker masquerading as Luke's apartment, and yet, Jimmy's didn't seem quite as dreary. It wouldn't kill Luke to buy a couple of paintings and a few colorful blankets.

With one last look around the room to make sure he hadn't left anything behind, Luke drew in a deep breath and opened the door.

Music spilled out, cheery and bouncy. Luke wasn't sure if the tune was familiar because it was something Zach and Ryan listened to in his presence or if he'd maybe just heard it on the radio. Frowning, he walked down the hall. He still needed his coat before he could leave.

Standing in the entryway beside the radiator where Jimmy had hung his jacket last night, Luke had a perfect view into the kitchen.

Shaking his lanky body, Jimmy stood by the stove and sang along to the fluffy pop song. No wonder he'd assumed Jimmy was so much younger. Between the guy's energy and his upbeat and positive attitude, it was like he hadn't aged past twenty, and Luke could only admire that.

Jimmy wore nothing but a pair of tiny red briefs and the ass beneath... one night wasn't nearly enough time to have properly worshipped it. He salivated at the thought and ran his tongue along his teeth. Maybe just one last bite before he left?

Without taking his eyes off that firm ass, Luke reached out a hand for his coat and ended up knocking an umbrella to the floor. Both he and Jimmy jumped from the sudden clatter.

Jimmy whirled, and a huge smile split his face. "You're awake. I was making breakfast. We can eat out here or we can...." The smile fell away, and his eyebrows drew together. "You're dressed. Why are you dressed?"

With those few words, Luke's insecurities melted away. Jimmy hadn't been expecting him to leave. Hadn't expected him to leave the bed even. Luke hadn't misread things the previous night. But Jimmy's frown deepened as the silence lengthened, and he had to answer Jimmy somehow. Please let him figure out how to answer without fucking this up any more than he'd done already.

He dropped his gaze to the floor, but raised it again when Jimmy sucked in an audible breath. Jimmy looked... crushed. There was no other word for it. Without any thought for himself, Luke closed the distance between them. Despite knowing Jimmy for less than twenty-four hours, one undeniable fact had lodged itself in the depths of Luke's soul—a sad Jimmy was something that shouldn't exist in this world.

Like they'd practiced for years, Jimmy flowed into Luke's arms, fitting against him perfectly, solid and warm.

Jimmy pressed his face to Luke's neck and mumbled something.

"What was that?" Luke asked gently.

"I thought you were... trying to sneak out." Jimmy still wasn't looking at him but had pulled back enough so his words were audible.

If Jimmy hadn't turned around, yeah, he might have snuck out, like the coward he apparently was when it came to guys. "I thought you wanted me to go."

This time, Jimmy did raise his head. "Why would you think that? I mean...." Jimmy breathed deeply. "I thought we'd agreed last night we were going to spend the day together."

Luke slid his hands up from Jimmy's waist and cupped that narrow-boned face, so unlike the broad planes of his own. Stereotypically, men didn't like to talk about their feelings or weren't willing to commit. He might even scare Jimmy off, but he'd spent so much of his life concealing his innermost thoughts and desires. So much time afraid of being himself. The spike of uncertainty when he'd woken alone had only cemented his resolve to stop hiding. If it scared Jimmy off, so be it, but he was too fucking old to play games.

"I was scared. You scared me."

Jimmy's eyes widened, and his mouth opened. Luke had a feeling if he didn't scare Jimmy off, he'd have to get used to how quickly and how often Jimmy opened his mouth to talk, but for now, he wanted Jimmy to listen. Luke slid a gentle forefinger under Jimmy's lower lip and coaxed his mouth shut. Jimmy subsided, lips pressed together, but Luke could see in his eyes the reprieve was limited.

"You scared me. When I woke up alone this morning, I thought I'd imagined our connection last night."

Trying to let Luke have his say, Jimmy kept his mouth closed but shook his head, and Luke smiled and continued.

"I thought I'd mistaken a one-night stand for something more. Embarrassing, yes, but mostly disappointing. Because I like you, Jimmy. I want to get to know you better, in and out of bed. I don't want to play mind games or worry about power struggles." God. He'd read an article about how to get and keep the "power" in your relationship, and even though his only relationship to date had been his unromantic one with his ex-wife, he'd thought it an utterly depressing way to conduct a relationship. It didn't have to be about love, but it sure as shit shouldn't be about power.

"I want that, too."

"You do?" It couldn't be that easy, could it?

"But just so you're aware…."

Sudden tension knotted the muscles in Luke's shoulders. Was this where the bomb dropped?

"I talk. A lot."

Relief crashed over Luke.

"Just so long as you realize I don't. Not usually."

"See?" Jimmy's voice had dropped. "We're getting to know each other better already."

Relief instantly gave way to lust, and Luke couldn't resist those lips so temptingly close to his.

The kiss wasn't a frantic explosion like their first kiss last night, but it held so much promise that it made Luke tremble and tighten his grip on Jimmy's head. How would Jimmy feel about sex in the kitchen? Probably wasn't sanitary, but there weren't kids in the place, and Luke had never had dirty gotta-have-you sex in the kitchen.

A blaring alarm doused them like cold water, and Jimmy sprang out of his arms to rescue the blackened smoky mass of whatever in the fry pan. Burnt food wasn't a first for Luke, and he snatched up a dish towel to circulate the air below the smoke alarm.

Within a few moments, the piercing noise had ceased, but a smoky pall hung in the air. Luke had to smile. He'd never been so caught up in kissing that he'd missed something burning on the stove. They could save the kitchen sex for later. Luke was quickly realizing that sex with Jimmy was more vital to him than any sex had been before, and he didn't care where they had it.

Jimmy turned from the blackened pan, an impish expression on his face. "I knew you were hot, Luke, but no need to set off my smoke alarms."

Luke chuckled. "It's probably not sexy of me to say I'm glad that they at least work." When he'd been looking for apartments he'd seen far too many that hadn't been up to code in so many respects. His apartment might be a shithole, but it was a structurally sound, well-maintained shithole.

Jimmy swayed toward him, bringing that cotton-clad ass closer. "I dunno. It's pretty sexy having someone worry about my safety."

That wouldn't be any trouble. Between having a kid and being responsible for dangerous work sites, that instinct had been hardwired in him a long time ago. Caring for Jimmy would only make it stronger.

Once Jimmy's hips were in range, he snaked out a hand and grabbed a handful of that ass. Jimmy groaned, and the heat between them flared up again, hotter than the flames on the stove.

Luke's stomach growled, making Jimmy laugh. "Maybe I'd better start on breakfast, so we've got enough energy to lie around in bed all day."

"Good idea." He gave Jimmy a quick kiss. After all, it had been a long time since he'd had two orgasms in a twenty-four-hour period, and now he was prepping to get his third. His balls might never recover, but he wasn't sure he cared. "Can I help?"

Jimmy pursed his lips and looked him over from head to toe. "You can start by getting out of those clothes. We've got no reason to leave here until…." A faint blush colored Jimmy's cheeks. "I guess I was sort of hoping we could laze about all weekend, but that's not really feasible. I've got to be at the playhouse by five, and we've got a matinee and evening show tomorrow."

Laze about all weekend with Jimmy. Mostly naked. Luke had maybe died and gone to heaven. But he certainly understood about responsibility and obligations, and he'd seen enough of Jimmy's euphoria over the play to know that acting was more a labor of love than an obligation for him. Standing in the way of that wouldn't be right, and if he'd given that advice to Zach or Ryan, then he needed to heed it himself.

"That's okay. I understand. I'm meeting my son for brunch tomorrow anyway, so as much as I'd love to spend the entire weekend with you, we both have commitments." At least he'd had the good sense to park in one of the long-term parking structures near the playhouse. He didn't have to worry about digging his car out. "But maybe I could see if there's a ticket available for tonight. I could watch the play again."

"You… you'd see it again? Why?"

"Well, first of all, you were great." Luke had begun to suspect that the reviews might have been what drove Jimmy from bed before Luke had woken up. For someone so incredibly talented, he had absolutely zero arrogance about his ability. "And secondly, I might have lost track of the story a bit as soon as you came on stage."

If Jimmy had to be at the playhouse at five, that would give Luke time to buy another expensive sweater. He could wear the same pants, and if need be, go commando, although that might not make it any easier to concentrate on the play.

Jimmy laughed and kissed him. "If you're sure, I can get you a ticket. I'll just have to make a quick call. You don't have to buy one. And maybe... afterward...."

"I could come back here?" Luke wanted to cheer. It seemed they both wanted to spend as much time as they could with each other, and given their schedules, this was the best way to accomplish that.

"Exactly. Now, let me get you fed. If you pass out from hunger, I'll never be able to drag your carcass into the bedroom."

Luke left enough room between him and the counter that Jimmy had to slide against him on his way to the fridge. Teasing like this he could quickly get used to.

JIMMY COULDN'T let Luke go without giving him one more kiss. That reddish brown hair, still rumpled from Jimmy using it as an anchor while he'd thrust into Luke's enthusiastic mouth, turned him the fuck on. He didn't know if it was the color, the texture, or simply that the "style" had Jimmy's stamp all over it.

Threading his fingers through the soft strands, Jimmy tugged Luke back to his mouth and dove in. They'd kissed so much Jimmy was going to have to buy some lip balm or he'd be chapped and hideous.

He couldn't quite lose himself in Luke's mouth this time. Not when he was already going to be late. Last night's play had gone just as well as Friday's, as had sex with Luke. But he had a matinee to perform, and he was going to be performing on a sex high because he sure as shit hadn't slept enough.

"I wish...." Jimmy had so many things he wished. The weekend had been weird but wonderful. There was something about Luke. Something that made him feel comfortable and safe, but at the same time sexy as all hell. It was like they'd known each other forever.

"I know. Me too. I wish this weekend didn't have to end."

A shiver of pleasure raced up Jimmy's neck. Luke already knew what he was thinking. If Jimmy believed in a divine being, he'd consider that a sign. What he did believe in was love at first sight. He'd never expected it to happen to him, but could this be anything else? He'd never had a one-night stand extend the whole weekend. Other men sneaking out after sex wouldn't have bothered him a bit, but when he'd thought Luke was doing it, it was like he'd lost his best friend. Unfortunately, the theater was calling, and when it came to new—dare he hope—boyfriends, she was a cruel, cold mistress.

"I'd love it if you could come back tonight, but I'll probably be too exhausted to do anything but sleep."

"You get your sleep. We've both got early days tomorrow, and I haven't managed to get my laundry done for the week." Luke grinned, clearly not upset at Jimmy for wrecking his weekend schedule.

"What about tomorrow? I don't have a performance again until Thursday. Did you want to meet for dinner? Maybe catch a movie at the second-run theater?" Oh God, he was pathetic. Surely he could go one day without seeing this man. The last thing he wanted was for Luke to think he was some clingy barnacle who didn't know when he'd worn out his welcome.

But he didn't have to find out, because Luke nodded. "Sure. I'd love to. Um… this is where I'm supposed to say break a leg, right?"

"You are so adorable." Jimmy pressed his lips together. Really, he did talk just a bit too much. At least Luke didn't get that panicked look like a cat backing away from an unwanted cuddle. Instead, Luke tilted his head to the side.

"I'm forty-three."

"So?"

"Forty-three-year-olds aren't adorable."

Jimmy snorted. "You're fucking adorable if I say you're fucking adorable."

The corners of Luke's mouth twitched.

"You sure you're a teacher? Because you swear like you're on a construction site." There wasn't any censure in Luke's tone, or Jimmy would be pissed off.

"It's a release valve. I have to keep it bottled in all day at school, so it just kind of…." Jimmy waved his hands around. "Explodes everywhere when I'm not."

He narrowed his eyes at Luke.

"You sure you're a construction worker? Because your lack of swearing makes me think you're a teacher."

Luke laughed. "Habit from having two young kids around the house."

One single unexpected pluralization kicked Jimmy in the teeth, knocking the breath from his chest.

"Two kids? I thought you only had the one son. Grown."

The unconcerned shrug should have made Jimmy feel better, but it didn't. Had Luke been lying to him? It wasn't like they were boyfriends—yet—but lying would definitely start them out on the wrong foot.

"Oh, only Zach is mine. But his best friend, Ryan, didn't have it so good at home. Spent tons of time at our place over the years. I got used to watching my mouth, and my temper, because Ryan was super sensitive to raised voices, but I understand the release valve. Mine's at work and yours is at home."

"Fucking adorable," Jimmy said again, mostly for effect. And he got what he wanted, with Luke's blinding smile.

"Seriously, though, let me know how the performance goes, okay? Not that I have any doubts."

Jimmy bit his lip to avoid asking Luke to watch the play again. He didn't want to hang the anvil of "good luck charm" around Luke's neck. Nothing good came of that superstition, as he'd seen more than once after a fellow actor had broken up with their good luck charm.

"I will. And I'm looking forward to tomorrow."

After one last quick peck on the lips, Luke pulled his rainbow scarf around his neck and walked down the hallway. Before getting on the elevator, Luke waved. The man was so gorgeous and sweet. Jimmy had lucked the fuck out, as long as he didn't screw things up.

With a little sigh as Luke disappeared, Jimmy pulled back into the apartment and shut the door. Last night had been just as good as the first night, although they hadn't talked much. When Jimmy had found Luke after the performance and Luke had confessed to having lost track of the story again because of Jimmy, well, he should have probably been offended on the part of the playwright and his fellow actors, but he'd found it unbearably adorable and dragged Luke back to his place. They'd fucked, then talked a bit over pizza, but as much energy as Jimmy had, he put a lot of it into his roles and the euphoria of a good night only lasted so long, especially combined with the unexpected and enthusiastic sex.

He was exhausted. He needed his sleep. But that didn't stop him from wishing Luke would be back tonight, even if all they did was sleep together.

Jimmy sped through the apartment to finish getting ready. Tomorrow he had an early staff meeting, and it was just as well Luke wasn't staying. It was a smart decision, if not a very welcome one. Besides, maybe they both needed some distance to put things in perspective. Maybe they were drunk on pheromones or something.

One last look in the mirror had Jimmy groaning. A hickey. Nearly fucking a stranger in the dressing room and leaving with him—twice— so hastily he'd never said good-bye to anyone was one thing. A hickey was going to get him teased by just about everyone. He'd also have to make sure he dug out a turtleneck for school tomorrow.

He shook himself as he realized he'd been stroking the bruised skin on his neck while smiling like an idiot. If he was the only one feeling this connection, he might lose his mind.

But there was no time left to worry about it. If he didn't leave now, Damian would be too busy chewing him out for being late to even notice a hickey. When his friend wore his director hat, he was a stickler for punctuality, and no one was exempt. Jimmy had no interest in being read the riot act like he was one of his own unruly high school students.

One last tap at the spot on his neck for luck, and Jimmy headed for the playhouse.

LUKE HAD lingered way too long at Jimmy's, but just as he sensed Jimmy didn't want him to leave, neither had Luke wanted to go. The pull between them was magnetic and impossible to fight, even if Luke had any inclination to do so. He'd had enough time to stop at home, change his clothes, and wash his face before getting back in the car to meet Zach.

He was fucking exhausted—Jimmy was right about that—but his narrow bed was going to feel very empty tonight.

Narrow bed.

Shit.

The laundry could wait a couple more days. After brunch, he was going to go bed shopping. There was enough room in his apartment for a bigger bed and although his apartment was dull and dreary, Jimmy would liven it up. No way could he have a relationship with someone and never invite him over. Although he was sort of new to the whole dating scene and being openly gay, he was 100 percent sure that a relationship should be entered into on equal footing.

He pulled into the parking lot. The Wheelhouse had been a staple when Zach was a kid and they frequently had Sunday brunch here as a family. It was a little old and a little run-down, just like Luke was. It also attracted a large number of elderly folk, who likely gravitated to it for the same reason he and his little family had been regulars: tasty, filling food that was reasonably priced and prepared by someone else.

Not that Luke was particularly extravagant now that he had a financial cushion, but The Wheelhouse was so average, he'd never bothered going back on his own. Zach loved it, though.

A quick scan of the parking lot confirmed Zach was already here. Luke was only a few minutes late. He had no intention of explaining to his son that he'd been on his knees blowing someone rather longer than he intended this morning. Not that he'd minded. Once he got up close and personal with Jimmy's dick, it had seemed such a shame to rush things. Jimmy's dick was....

"Excuse me."

Luke blinked and stepped out of the way of a stooped, white-haired man with a walker. "Sorry."

An unexpected chuckle threatened to escape. He wondered if Jimmy would find it funny that he'd almost gotten run over by an octogenarian on his way to Sunday brunch with his son because he was too busy fantasizing about Jimmy's dick. But that was yet another thing he wasn't going to explain to Zach. Hell, he wasn't even sure he wanted to mention Jimmy at all. It was too new, too perfect, a soap bubble ready to burst if he did the wrong thing.

No, he'd wait and see how things went before he mentioned Jimmy to his son.

Once he stopped daydreaming, he made it to the door before the guy with the walker, and stood for a few minutes, holding the door open, until the old guy made his way along the heavily salted sidewalk to the entrance.

"Dad!"

Luke glanced around and saw Zach waving at him over a sea of blue hair. The Wheelhouse was busier than normal; there must have been some special church function that brought the oldsters out in droves. Luke refused to go for brunch—at The Wheelhouse at least—on any major holidays for that very reason.

Zach was tall enough that Luke was able to follow his progress across the room. When the sea of people parted, Zach hugged him.

"Hey. How are you?"

The moment Zach moved away, Ryan appeared and hugged him, too. "Oh, hey, Ryan."

This wasn't the first time Ryan had shown up to one of his and Zach's weekends, but it had been happening more of late. Luke got the sense that Ryan was under some sort of stress and being around him and Zach eased it. He didn't mind. Ryan was a good kid, for all the roadblocks his parents had put in front of him.

"You sure you want to stay? It looks like it could be a long wait." Luke didn't have any objection to spending time with his son, but now that he'd decided he needed to go bed shopping, he didn't want to spend precious time simply waiting around in a room filled with too much echoing conversation to even talk to Zach.

"Nah, we got here like twenty minutes ago. We should be getting a table soon."

"Kid, you've got an unnatural love for this place."

Ten minutes later, Luke had a plate in hand, staring at the buffet offerings. He wasn't a huge fan of buffets either, but the unlimited nature helped fill up a boy with a hollow leg. Or a young man. Zach's metabolism hadn't slowed a bit, not like Luke's had.

Waffles. Had he burned off enough energy with Jimmy to have waffles? Meeting Jimmy gave him even greater incentive to not overeat, but he did love waffles. With real maple syrup. And chocolate chips. Whipped cream. Strawberry compote. All together.

"Hi, LJ." Ryan had come up behind him, standing close enough to touch. But then, there wasn't a lot of room to maneuver with all the people. If he wanted waffles, he should probably get in line or he'd be here all day.

He rubbed at his stomach with his free hand. Didn't feel too plush, and Jimmy hadn't minded, not based on how often his lips ended up there.

"Are you feeling okay?"

Luke snatched his hand away from his belly. "Uh, fine. Just trying to decide if…." So embarrassing. "If I should have waffles. Fruit might be wiser."

"But not as much fun." Ryan's tone was playful.

"True." Luke's hand found his belly again and patted it. "But I gotta watch the waistline."

"Oh, no you don't. You're in great shape." Ryan's emphatic tone held no doubt, and he turned his head to smile down at Ryan.

"Thank you. I appreciate that. Maybe a couple of waffles wouldn't hurt." Especially not if he was seeing Jimmy again tomorrow.

"Do it. I know you want it."

Luke frowned. Jimmy had said almost the same thing this morning when feeding him his dick. Hearing those same words in almost the same tone of voice from Ryan was just wrong.

"Dad, I can't believe you're not all over those waffles. They even have chocolate ice cream today at the dessert station." Zach strode over, plate overflowing with cholesterol-laden bacon and sausage while Ryan stepped back.

That solved that dilemma. Luke didn't have much of a sweet tooth, but he loved throwing just about everything on his waffles, especially chocolate ice cream.

"Then I'm going in."

Zach and Ryan headed back to the table while Luke moved into line. While he waited his turn, his cell phone buzzed.

Enjoying brunch?

Luke smiled. He didn't know why Jimmy thought he was fucking adorable. Jimmy was the cute one of them. He hadn't expected Jimmy to contact him while he was busy with preparations for the matinee performance, but he was glad Jimmy had felt the need to connect. He set his empty plate down so he could reply; he'd never quite managed the knack of texting one-handed.

Waffles. Syrup. Ice cream. It's all good.

Together? Yuck.

Don't knock it until you try it.

I couldn't eat that. Not unless you want a very fat Jimmy.

I think we could find a way to work it off.

Luke's cheeks heated. It was one thing to think it, but quite another to see it on the screen.

Naughty, naughty. I'll hold you to that. Tomorrow.

Tomorrow.

"If you're just going to admire the waffles, move aside. I'm not getting any younger."

Luke almost dropped his phone at the admonishment. He thought it might be the same old gent he'd held the door open for, but he couldn't be upset. He *was* blocking the way, and the texts from Jimmy had put a smile on Luke's face that wouldn't easily be removed.

LUKE SLID into his chair, plate piled high with waffles.

"That's more like it, Dad." Zach stole a chocolate chip from his plate, and Ryan smiled at him. "So, how was the play you went to see with Bennett? That was Friday, wasn't it?"

Both Zach and Ryan had gotten along well with Bennett during their "man Christmas." Zach had been thrilled to find out Luke made a friend at the Rainbow Blues and had been smug as shit once he realized his gift to Luke had paid out dividends. If things worked out with Jimmy, Zach would probably take credit for that as well, since Luke wouldn't have met Jimmy if it weren't for Rainbow Blues and Bennett.

"It was great. A lot of fun. You should go see it." He glanced at Ryan, including him. He wasn't sure if either of them could appreciate the core story. It had resonated so well with him, since it mirrored his own life, but maybe a pair of straight twentysomethings wouldn't have the same visceral reaction.

The vibration in his pocket signaling another text made Luke's smile even wider. It probably wasn't from Jimmy, but the possibility that it might be made him feel as giddy as a teenager.

Ryan smiled back, before slowly biting into a strawberry. Zach, on the other hand, tilted his head.

"You look different today. Happier."

Luke lifted a shoulder and tried to appear nonchalant.

"Are you seeing someone?"

Both he and Ryan froze, food partway to their mouths.

"Uh." He didn't want to lie to his son, but neither did he want to talk about Jimmy yet.

"Dad, it's okay, you know. If you want to start dating, I'll be fine with it. Honestly, I'd worry less about you if you were."

Zach worried about him?

A memory of him on his couch right before Christmas flashed into his mind. Maybe his son had good reason to worry about him.

"I am happier, Zach. And I have you to thank. That Rainbow Blues group... well, it's nice having friends I've got something in common with."

"But what about a boyfriend? Bennett is good-looking and has a job."

"It's too soon to talk about boyfriends, and Bennett and I are friends only. Rainbow Blues isn't a dating service." Luke chuckled. Although he didn't want to outright lie to his son, as a parent he had a hell of a lot of experience at half-truths.

Zach rolled his eyes. "I know it said that on the flyer, but c'mon. It seems ideal for meeting potential dates."

Little did Zach know, Luke's tastes in sexual partners didn't run toward men like himself. Until he met Jimmy, he didn't have a clear idea of what exactly his taste was, but he knew now, and it was a lithe, talkative actor.

"Maybe for some, but... but... I *was* thinking about dating again."

Ryan gave him a wide smile. "And so you should. You're still in your prime, LJ."

"Thank you, Ryan."

"You won't have any trouble finding a man, Dad. I know it. And when you do, I want to meet him."

Luke nodded. Zach had been supportive when he'd come out, but being supportive in the abstract was different than being confronted with the reality of a boyfriend.

"I'll make sure I introduce you to any man I'm serious about." Once again, dancing around the truth a bit. As soon as he was sure he and Jimmy had a future, he'd introduce them, and if this past weekend was any indication, it would be soon.

He scooped up a big bite of waffle and ice cream so he wouldn't be tempted to set up a meeting with Jimmy now. Amazing, really, how ready he was to dive into a new relationship. Then again, he'd waited a long fucking time for the chance to be himself. There was no sense in waiting any longer to seize what he wanted out of life, and he got the idea Jimmy felt the same.

The conversation moved on to less sensitive topics, although Luke's mind was never far from Jimmy and his planned shopping trip. Once the two boys went to the buffet for another round, Luke pulled out his phone and checked his texts. There were a couple from Jimmy, which he lingered over, pleased the matinee performance had gone well.

The one from Bennett was simply one word: *Details!*

He laughed. He wasn't quite ready to be that open with his sex life, but maybe Bennett could meet up with him after brunch, because he might not be able to easily set up his new bed on his own. King mattresses were big suckers.

Generalizations only! Can you meet up this afternoon?

Nope. Sister in town. Dinner/drinks tomorrow?

Nope. Date.

Details!

Later this week?

No matter how well things went with Jimmy, even if they found themselves wanting to spend every day together after such a short acquaintance, Luke suspected he'd be on his own most performance nights. Even Jimmy's seemingly inexhaustible energy had to flag after a few days at his current frenetic pace.

Nope. Out of town job. Going to RB next Thurs?

Luke had only been to the one Rainbow Blues event, and he didn't quite know what to expect, but they were indirectly responsible for him meeting Jimmy. More friends would be good, and he liked hanging out with Bennett. He'd played poker several times before but never attended a tournament.

Yeah. Prepare to lose.

Ha! I'm a shark! Let's grab dinner together first.

Sure.

Luke didn't want to give up the idea of a new bed to bring Jimmy home to, though. Maybe IKEA had some sort of service he could pay for to help set it up.

Zach and Ryan returned to the table, plates piled high, although Ryan's food was far more health-conscious than Zach's. Luke eyed them. Maybe he had some free labor right here.

"Say, if you guys aren't busy, I was going to buy a new bed today. Maybe you could help me set it up, take the old one to the dump."

Ryan wiggled an eyebrow. "A new bed?"

Luke tried desperately not to flush. Ryan hadn't missed the connection between this errand and the earlier discussion about Luke dating. At least his own son still seemed oblivious.

"Dad, sorry, I've got another paper due. Can it wait?"

"Oh, don't worry, Zach. I don't have any plans this afternoon. I can help your dad." Ryan smiled at him conspiratorially.

By sheer force of will, he refrained from rolling his eyes. The idea that his son's friend was helping him get laid freaked him out a bit, but that wasn't enough to prevent him from accepting Ryan's help. Ryan wasn't as strong as him or his son, but Luke was pretty sure he'd just need another set of hands, not Hercules.

"Thanks, Ryan, I appreciate it."

After his date tomorrow, he'd be able to bring Jimmy over to his place.

CHAPTER 5

JIMMY ENDED up having to stay late after work, so he met Luke at the restaurant instead of picking him up. As soon as he saw Luke, he wanted to kiss him or hold his hand, but they hadn't discussed Luke's stance on PDAs. Jimmy suspected a man who'd spent most of his life in the closet wouldn't want an obviously gay man to even stand too close in public, no matter how enthusiastically he sucked Jimmy's cock in private. Jimmy sighed and suppressed his natural exuberance.

"Luke," Jimmy called.

Between the wide smile on Luke's face and the rainbow scarf he was wearing again, maybe it wouldn't take too long before he'd let Jimmy touch him in public.

"Jimmy." Luke approached, his gaze hot and focused solely on him. Jimmy's skin got tight. He hadn't been lying about wanting to get to know Luke better out of the bedroom, but he wasn't sure he could wait until they'd seen a movie as well.

Not unexpectedly, Luke stopped far enough away to put them firmly in the friend category. Jimmy sighed. At least he didn't think Luke was embarrassed by him, just closeted. Closeted was better, although Jimmy longed for the day a man he liked would just kiss him in public and damn the consequences. At least Luke had the closet door open and was peering around, which was an improvement over a couple of guys Jimmy had… certainly not dated. Even dinner out with his obviously gay self made them worry about gay by association.

"How was your day?" In Jimmy's experience, Luke's genuine interest was rare. Most guys he dated just didn't care.

"Good." Better, now that he was with Luke, even though he had to control his impulses to touch the man. "You?"

Luke shrugged. "Same old, same old. Working sites in the winter sucks, but I'd rather be working than not."

A work ethic. Jimmy had suspected it was there, but he was still pleased by its existence. More than once, Jimmy had ended up with guys who were looking for a sugar daddy, even if he was younger than them, assuming his acting made him rich. What a laugh. But they always got pissed at how much time he needed to devote to the theater on top of his day job. He just prayed Luke would understand.

The hostess interrupted, and they followed her to the table.

The service was great and in a few minutes, they'd put their order for dinner in, had bread on the table, and were sipping drinks—a strawberry margarita for Jimmy and beer for Luke.

Luke gave him a bashful little smile and brushed his fingers deliberately over Jimmy's hand on his way to the bread basket.

A little of his apprehension melted away, and he smiled back. This was new for Luke, and at some point, Jimmy was going to have to find out just how new, but he didn't want to talk about his own previous sex partners and boyfriends just yet. He'd rather dazzle the somewhat inexperienced Luke with his bubbly personality before slamming him with that information, and it was a bit heavy for….

"Is this our first date? Third?"

Luke crinkled his nose and tilted his head. Jimmy just wanted to eat him up. And do other things with his mouth and hands that were substantially dirtier.

"I don't really know. Definitely not the first. I think Chinese food and sex counts as a first date for sure."

"And you went home Saturday during the day. I think we can call Saturday after the play another date."

Luke bit into the roll he'd just buttered. "Me, too," he said after swallowing his mouthful.

Jimmy leaned back in his chair. "So, third date. Three dates is the sex date. It's a rule."

Luke laughed and crumbs flew out of his mouth. He clapped a hand over his mouth, but it didn't hide the fiery blush that heated his cheeks.

"I'm sorry." The words were muffled behind Luke's hand, and Jimmy couldn't stop a giggle from escaping.

"I'm sorry, too. I should have waited until you'd finished swallowing." Jimmy couldn't help it. He emphasized the last word in such a way that Luke would have no trouble recognizing the innuendo. Based on Luke's suddenly darkened eyes, he'd definitely picked up on Jimmy's intent. Jimmy just grinned back at him, waiting. He liked that Luke not only got his humor but also the inflections in his tone.

"I bought a new bed."

That… wasn't what Jimmy had expected. "What?"

"Yesterday. I thought we could go to my place tonight after the movie, and my bed was too small to spread you out on."

The breath fled Jimmy's lungs as his cock hardened instantly. Apparently Luke hadn't been lying when he said he believed in saying what he meant, and his simple words evoked an image of himself splayed across sheets, Luke between his legs, feasting on him before fucking him senseless. Goosebumps flared up on his arms, and he shivered, hard. He wasn't sure he was ready for that tonight, but soon.

"Are you cold?" Embarrassment forgotten, Luke didn't wait for Jimmy to reply but leapt up to wrap that soft, wide rainbow scarf around his shoulders. Jimmy stopped him. He wasn't cold, at all, and the sweet gesture heated him up even more. He grabbed Luke's shoulder before he could sit down again and whispered in his ear.

"Not cold, Luke, but I'm now imagining me on your new bed and you sucking my cock."

Luke gasped and stared down at Jimmy, pupils blown. Oh, fuck. They'd be lucky if they managed to finish dinner.

With an awkward shuffle, and his scarf bunched near his groin so he wouldn't reveal his raging erection to the other diners, Luke returned to his seat and cleared his throat.

"We could…." He coughed. "Maybe we could see a movie another night."

Jimmy smiled. "You are a smart man."

The happy glow on Luke's face dimmed, just a bit.

"What's wrong?"

The shrug said Luke didn't really care, but Jimmy had seen that same stance in many a teenager over the years. Luke didn't want to care, but he did.

"Nothing. Just… you've got degrees. You're a teacher and an actor. I never went to college." Luke ripped off a big bite of his bread and refused to meet Jimmy's eyes.

"Luke. Dammit, look at me."

Huh. Jimmy could add another thing he'd learned about Luke. He could be a stubborn idiot. No way did he want Luke to think of himself as stupid, though.

"If you don't look at me, I'm going to kiss you right here in the middle of the restaurant."

Jimmy could be stubborn, too, and it wasn't as though kissing Luke would be any hardship at all.

Shocked, Luke lifted his gaze to Jimmy's.

Oh. Fingers trembling, Jimmy pressed his palms flat on the table in an effort to keep from actually doing what he'd threatened. The want in Luke's eyes… gave him hope. Hope that one day, kissing Luke in a restaurant wouldn't be a threat. Hope that one day, Luke would be comfortable shutting the closet door behind him.

But if he truly wanted a relationship with Luke, this wasn't the way to go about it.

"I'm sorry, that wasn't fair." Jimmy clenched his hands into fists and tried to smirk, although he was sure he failed to produce anything other than a grimace. "Apparently the third date is also for getting into some deep waters."

Luke frowned, and Jimmy hated to see it. "What kind of deep waters?"

The server set down a plate of gorgeous fried calamari, but as tense as he was, they were about as appealing as chewing on old tires.

"Enjoy!" The twinky little server, named Toby, swung a hip along Luke's shoulders, his smile much warmer for Jimmy's date than for him. Not surprisingly, Luke didn't appear to notice, and Jimmy didn't know if that was a simple lack of attraction or unawareness of his hotness. "Is there anything else I can get you?"

There wasn't a doubt in Jimmy's mind that the server's "you" was singular and directed at Luke.

"Thank you," Jimmy answered with an edge in his tone. "Another beer for him and strawberry margarita for me."

Jimmy barely got a glance, which wasn't a surprise. He'd probably be lucky if he got the right drink.

"I'll be right back."

"No rush." Jimmy hated servers who always seemed to interrupt at exactly the wrong time. At least Luke was still looking at him.

"Deep waters?" Luke prompted.

"We haven't really talked about it, but I feel like you're still in the closet. At least partially. You... I couldn't even tell you were gay at first, and usually my gaydar is exceptional. I don't know if that's just you or if you're still actively hiding it." A gay man didn't have a kid and stay married to its mother for years without hiding his sexuality.

"Ah. *Those* deep waters. I'm not used to being out, that's true." Luke laughed, a little bitterly. "My ex-wife... she's a great woman. We got along great and as a parent? I couldn't ask for a better partner. But as soon as Zach was on his own, I couldn't take the deception any longer. I thought we both deserved more fulfilling lives than the half-life we lived with each other. The divorce was amicable, and Kelly almost immediately fell in love with a great guy."

Luke gulped back the rest of his beer, and Jimmy was glad he'd ordered them both another drink, although he suspected their infatuated server was going to return at another inopportune moment.

"I'd never cheated on Kelly." Luke bit his lip and looked down. Jimmy recognized those signs. Luke was either lying or embarrassed.

"Did you have any experience with guys before Kelly?"

"High school stuff. Enough to know I was queer, and enough to realize my parents would have died. Or disowned me. They were... very religious. When rumors started circulating about me, I latched on to Kelly." Luke paused and rubbed at the bridge of his nose, broadcasting his unease. "Anyway, when we divorced—"

Jimmy held up a hand. He wasn't letting Luke gloss over this.

"Whoa, back up there. I'll admit, I'm not a huge fan of cheating." Certainly not after he'd caught both his first and fourth boyfriends with cock up their ass. "But there's a big difference between my boyfriend getting pissed about how much time I spent in rehearsals and getting himself porked by one of my friends, and you, married with a kid trying to be straight. I won't judge you."

Luke went to grab more bread, but the uncomfortable discussion had made him devour it all already. Instead, he picked up the end of his scarf and began twisting his fingers into the thick knit.

"We got married within weeks of Kelly discovering she was pregnant. The weekend before, I was… crazy. Afraid. I thought maybe if I…." Luke waved his hands slightly. "If I went all the way, maybe I wouldn't like it. Maybe I could stop thinking about it, and settle in as a straight guy and soon-to-be dad. The weekend before our wedding, I hired a rent boy."

Jimmy's eyes widened. He'd almost been expecting a horrific story about him approaching the closeted captain of the football team and getting beaten or raped or something. Not a rent boy.

"And?"

Luke's eyes were haunted. "He was older than me, and sweet. I was awkward, and the whole thing was uncomfortable. It wasn't great, but it cemented one fact in my mind. I was gay and about to get married."

"You could have called it off."

"I couldn't, not really. Kelly—and my son—needed me."

"Was that it?" If Luke told him the rent boy had become a regular part of his married life, Jimmy might judge, just a little bit. Deception like that over years… hell, he was amazed Luke's ex didn't clock him over the head with a frying pan for keeping the gay thing a secret for like, two decades.

Luke shrugged. "After we were married, I wasn't with anyone except Kelly. But, I did have some porn."

A surprised laugh sputtered out of Jimmy. "Porn? Of course you had porn. That's not cheating, that's probably the only thing that kept you sane and kept your dick from withering away."

Luke's shoulders sagged as his fear and tension dispersed.

"And after?"

"After… I was a forty-one-year-old man trying to figure out where to even find other gay men, never mind ones who were the same age as me or had the same interests. I didn't have anyone to talk to, anyone to mentor me. I ended up at a few clubs, had a few one-night stands, but mostly I wanted to find something… more."

Again, Luke's gaze drifted away.

"I want something more, too, Luke. I think you might be my something more." Jimmy kept his voice low, but his words were enough to have Luke looking back at him.

"I'd like to be your something more," Luke whispered. "I'm not out at work. And I'm not sure I even know what I'm supposed to do as a mostly out gay man. I don't like… I'm not comfortable…." The furtive glance at the rest of the restaurant told the story. Despite the strides forward he'd made, Luke wasn't about to get up on the table and proclaim that he was here and queer. Rainbow scarf notwithstanding.

Jimmy smiled. "You're a good man, Luke Jordan. You only need to be yourself. Whatever stereotypes you see on TV or in the movies… there's no unifying gay law that says you need to conform to those archetypes. You just be you, I'll just be me, and I think together, we can be something better."

"I think I can do that."

"I know you can." Jimmy hadn't forgotten what had prompted this whole deep discussion. "As I said, you're a smart man."

Luke opened his mouth, ready to object again, but Jimmy held up a hand to forestall him. There were so many things about Luke he already knew without asking. So many things that spoke of a down-to-earth personality, responsible and ethical.

"No. University degrees aren't always all they're cracked up to be. Let me guess… you're not in debt, you've got some savings socked away for a rainy day, and you've already told me you've got employees reporting to you."

Eyes wide, Luke nodded.

"And your son… he's a good guy, right? Responsible, about to get one degree, and going to grad school next year."

"Yes." Luke smiled, full of sweetness and love, and Jimmy's heart melted just a little bit more.

"You've got nothing to be ashamed of, Luke. I mean, you could go back to school if you wanted to, but considering you started out with some pretty substantial barriers, it's clear you've made a lifetime of good decisions. That takes brains, and degrees aren't the only way to measure brain power."

A tiny nod and a smile were Luke's only responses, but Jimmy thought he'd gotten through to the man.

Twinky waiter boy, hips swinging to draw attention to his pert little butt, approached the table with two enormous gourmet burgers, and Jimmy was suddenly starving.

The server put the burgers on the table, then frowned and rested his hand on Luke's shoulder. Jimmy rolled his eyes but no one noticed.

"Was there something wrong with the calamari?" Neither of them had touched it, getting too deep in their discussion for food. Not that Toby cared if *Jimmy* had issues with it. Getting involved with Luke probably meant he'd be habitually ignored by gays on the prowl. Jimmy didn't mind; he got plenty of attention after performances, and it wasn't like he didn't understand. A sexy man unaware of his own attractiveness was like catnip, and if Luke became more overt about his sexuality, Jimmy would be beating off the twinks with a stick. Not just twinks, either.

He snorted at his double entendre, but Luke was too busy reassuring the kid that there was nothing wrong. They'd just gotten distracted. Jimmy sure as shit wasn't eating cold calamari; that would literally be like chewing on old tires.

"I'll just take this out of your way," Toby said with another squeeze of Luke's shoulder. Jimmy narrowed his eyes a bit, but Toby whisked the calamari away and was gone without making eye contact.

With the first minihurdle out of the way, Jimmy's appetite returned with a vengeance. Judging by Luke's attack on his burger, he wasn't alone, and aside from a few innocuous comments, they focused on eating.

Stuffed full, Jimmy sat back in his chair and sipped at his margarita. He wasn't going to finish it because he still had to drive.

Little Toby returned with a swish. "Something sweet for you tonight?"

This time, Jimmy held in a snort… barely.

"Jimmy? Dessert?"

"I'm full, but get something if you want it."

"Yes, do get something if you want it. On the house, because of the calamari," Toby purred with another touch to Luke's shoulder.

Jimmy glared at the back of Toby's head. He was pretty sure slutty twinks weren't on the menu. God. Did no one have manners anymore?

"No, thanks, the burger was great."

So polite and so oblivious. Jimmy's irritation with Toby faded. Luke was coming home with him tonight and didn't appear to be craving "something sweet."

With a flourish, Toby placed the check in its black faux-leather folder right at Luke's elbow. One last squeeze of Luke's strong shoulder—*bitch*—before he sauntered away, hips swinging in such a way to draw attention to his bubble butt. Jimmy didn't even rate a second glance, but then, neither did Luke bother following Toby's pert ass with his gaze. How did he get so lucky?

If Luke were comfortable with PDAs, Jimmy would have jammed his tongue down Luke's throat in that moment. Instead, he snatched the check away from Luke before he reached for it.

"I can get that. We're on a third date, right? If I want to get lucky, I should pick up the tab." Luke smirked at him, and Jimmy laughed.

"What if I want to get lucky? Doesn't that mean I have to pick up the tab?" Not that Jimmy was going to let Luke anywhere near this check. That skank of a waiter had to have put his phone number in the folder somewhere.

Luke pulled out his wallet. "We could split it, so we both get lucky, but that doesn't seem very date-like."

"I know you wanted to show me your new bed, and believe me, I want to see it. But maybe we should go to the movie first." Their serious discussion had intensified Jimmy's feelings for Luke but had dialed back some of the sexual urgency. Oh, there would be orgasms tonight, but if Luke wanted a proper date, he was getting one. Not many guys were content with weeknight dates while Jimmy spent his weekends at the playhouse, and he was pleased Luke didn't seem to mind.

"Uh-huh." Luke licked his lips, making Jimmy almost change his mind.

"Totally date-like. Put your wallet away. I'll pick up dinner, you can get the movie. Then after, we'll take a detailed tour of your new purchase."

"Perfect." Luke leaned in, almost like he was going to kiss Jimmy. Nope, shoehorning him out of the closet wasn't going to be that difficult after all.

"Just promise me one thing." As tempting as it was, Jimmy refrained from taking a quick kiss anyway.

"If I can."

With one finger Jimmy pulled down the neck of his turtleneck. "Marks below the collar, please. Makeup teased me for *hours* yesterday."

Attention riveted to Jimmy's neck, Luke's eyes darkened, and more goose bumps sprang up on Jimmy's skin. Luke liked the look of that hickey, and Jimmy suspected he'd be wearing more before the night was over.

"Anywhere below the collar?"

Pulse racing, Jimmy stared at Luke. Oh, yes, he'd be wearing more marks. "Anywhere."

"Good." The smug tone heated Jimmy up in all the best ways. And if he had to go to the movies and be all date-like, he was going to do his best to make sure Luke was insane with lust by the time they got back to Luke's new bed.

Jimmy pulled out some cash, and left enough for a generous tip, despite twinky Toby trying to hit on his date. He palmed the slip of paper with Toby's phone number on it, and when Luke's back was turned to put on his coat, he crumpled it up and dropped it in the dregs of his margarita.

As they passed their waiter on the way out, he scowled fiercely at Jimmy. He hadn't intended for the kid to see him toss the number, but he sure wasn't torn up about it. It was fucking rude after all.

With a huge smile and a full-on erection hidden by his peacoat, he followed Luke out into the frigid winter night.

"IT'S NOT much," Luke said as he ushered Jimmy into his apartment. He might have been more apologetic, but his place was clean, and it wasn't much smaller than Jimmy's place. Had a lot less character, though.

Jimmy didn't say a word but took off his wet boots and handed over his coat when Luke held out a hand.

Since his apartment wasn't much more than a couple of concrete boxes squished together, the tour took about three seconds.

"As you can see, here's the kitchen, dining room, living room. The first door is the bathroom, the second is the washer and dryer, and the third is the bedroom."

Luke couldn't keep from emphasizing the last word. Jimmy had spent the whole movie taking advantage of the dark, trailing his fingers along Luke's thigh. Luke had spent the entire movie with a raging erection and had completely lost track of the plot about halfway through. But he'd had a good time. He'd never been on a date like that, so charged with sexual tension. If asked, he would have assumed he'd hate it, that he'd be too worried about people seeing anything to enjoy himself. But that wasn't the case, at all.

Once or twice, the sheen of butter on Jimmy's lips had tempted him to lean in and kiss the man, regardless of who might be watching, but he wasn't quite ready to kick open his closet door. Not that publicly, at any rate.

"We'll get to the bedroom, don't you worry."

Luke wasn't worried, he just wasn't sure he could wait. He turned on a couple of lamps while Jimmy wandered over to his bookcase.

"Did you want something to drink?"

"Water would be fine, thanks."

Jimmy ran his long fingers over the spines of a few books before picking up a framed picture.

Luke handed him a bottle of water from the fridge.

"Wow, this must be your son."

Luke smiled. "That's my Zach."

"You guys could be twins."

"Uh-huh. Not hardly, but thanks for the compliment."

"Who is the other guy?"

"Zach's best friend, Ryan. I think I told you about him. Calls me LJ."

"LJ? How come?"

"I don't know. He had a dad, so wasn't going to call me that, even though he was at our place whenever he could be. He called me Mr. Jordan for a long time, but at some point just started calling me LJ. Less formal I guess."

"Cute."

Luke thought Jimmy had been going to ask something else, but instead, he turned and stepped close to Luke's chest.

"Ready to show me around your new purchase?"

Luke groaned. "Since the opening credits of the movie. C'mon."

He guided Jimmy into the bedroom.

AFTERWARD THEY lay together, sweaty bodies rubbing skin to skin. Luke fucking loved the sensation of Jimmy's masculine body next to his. He couldn't stop touching it, even though there was no way he was getting it up again anytime soon.

One day, they'd get around to actual penetration. Now that Luke had a more mature understanding of the male body, he wanted to try it out again. It hadn't been terrible with the escort, but none of those orgasms had come anywhere near to the mind-shattering ones he shared with Jimmy. No reason to believe getting fucked by Jimmy, and fucking Jimmy, wouldn't be just as good. He'd have to remember to get condoms, though. Jimmy had teased him for forgetting to buy some, and although he had lube, Jimmy gave him a few pointers on ones that worked best with condoms. Luke was nothing if not a fast learner. Especially with motivation like Jimmy's dick.

Jimmy didn't seem to mind the gentle caressing, since he stretched and squirmed closer like a cat.

"Your parents call you Jimmy, or is that a stage name?"

"Why?" Jimmy laughed a little, as though he thought it a weird question.

"No real reason. Just don't meet many people named Jimmy, I guess."

"My birth certificate says James, but no one calls me that, except my mom when she's pissed. I kind of hate it. I guess I'm a little old to still be Jimmy, but James just sounds so… serious. Buttoned-up. I've never thought it suited me."

No, that made sense. Luke ran his fingertips over the barely visible blond hairs on Jimmy's chest.

"My turn," Jimmy said and shifted so he could stroke Luke's hair. "No offense, but why haven't you decorated this place? It looks like a wasteland of despair. Uh, except for the bed."

Luke laughed. He was pretty sure no one could call the bed a wasteland of despair. Best fucking purchase he'd ever made.

"I'm not a decorator. At all. Besides, this place is hopefully only temporary."

"Temporary?" Jimmy's expression got more intent as he shifted onto his side, propping his head on his hand. "How so?"

Luke stroked the length of Jimmy's torso from pit to hip, and back again. The goose bumps he brought forth were like a prize.

"Kelly and I were able to buy a house after my parents died, which we sold once the divorce was final. I really liked owning a house, and now that I don't have to worry about raising a child, I might have time to plant a garden. I love to cook, and I think it would be cool to cook with things you'd picked out of your yard."

Jimmy blinked and squirmed. "That sounds awesome. I've always wanted my own house, too. For different reasons, of course."

"Yeah? What are those?"

"I want free rein to paint a place however I want and not worry about security deposits or rules or having to leave it behind because an apartment is just rented."

"So why haven't you bought a place? Gone crazy with decorating?"

Jimmy ducked his head into Luke's shoulder, hiding his eyes. "You'll think it's dumb."

"Probably I won't, but tell me anyway."

"I've always associated a house with family. My parents still live in the house me and the sibs grew up in. I want… I want to buy a house with the guy I'm going to be with forever."

Luke cleared his throat, but it didn't change the fact he felt all clogged up. Jimmy had articulated exactly why Luke had never bothered moving out of his concrete bunker, aka the wasteland of despair. He'd been hoping for the same thing, although he'd never put it in so many words.

"I don't think that's dumb."

Jimmy lifted his head. "No?"

"No. That's why I've lived here for two years. It does the job… for now."

Luke could see him and Jimmy in a house together. Someday, hopefully soon. He was falling fast and hard, and he didn't want to stop.

Jimmy gave him a warm smile and kissed him, gentle and sweet, just enjoying the press of lips together without any particular goal in mind.

CHAPTER 6

COMING IN to school from Luke's apartment on Tuesday morning was a little surreal. Jimmy had planned for it, sure. He was showered, in fresh clothes, nary a rumple in sight, and yet it all felt deliciously naughty. He was also exhausted, but it was the good kind. The kind that came with aching muscles from contorting limbs around another person, lassitude from the orgasm endorphins, and a jaw just a little bit tender from the blow jobs. He'd sucked Luke's cock more times since they'd met on Friday than he'd sucked cocks all of last year. Maybe even the last two years.

Then there was the simple comfort of sleeping next to someone. A lot of guys he knew found the actual act of sleeping the night with someone the hardest hurdle to overcome when starting a relationship. It certainly required a lot of trust, but Jimmy just loved the warmth and the skin-on-skin contact.

Jimmy smiled, remembering the springy texture of Luke's hair. Maybe it made him unusual, but he liked how natural Luke was. Took a lot of stress out of the encounters.

Without having any conscious recall of traversing the parking lot and the warren of hallways, Jimmy found himself at the staff room. He had time for a cup of coffee before his first class, and he suspected he would need it.

Karen Harper strode into the room as he was doctoring his coffee.

"Congrats, Jimmy! I saw the reviews. They loved you just as much as I did."

"Thanks, Karen. Everything just really clicked with this play and this cast." He'd only seen her in passing the previous day.

"And I noticed you slipped out of the theater Friday night without saying good-bye, didn't call, and pretty much ran out of here yesterday. Got anything you want to tell Aunt Karen?"

Jimmy shuddered. "Oh, for God's sake, Karen, don't ever call yourself that again."

Karen laughed wickedly. "I notice you're wearing a turtleneck again today. The new boy a bit of a Hoover, is he? When do I get to meet him?"

"Never, if you don't stop teasing me about it." Jimmy looked around. He was out at work, yes, but it had been so long since he'd had an honest-to-God boyfriend—and he thought maybe he could call Luke that pretty soon—that he'd forgotten how weird it was talking about sex in the vicinity of his coworkers. Luke's apprehension about coming out at work made a lot more sense. After all, he probably worked with guys who could break Jimmy in half. The most Jimmy had to fear was if Coach Patterson decided to run him over with his oversized, overcompensating penis-mobile, otherwise known as the biggest fucking pickup truck Jimmy had ever seen. Not like that would happen, though. Coach Patterson's wife thought he was cute. The rest of the staff were mostly apathetic.

"Did you finally cave and take Damian to bed? You know I'd pay money to see that."

"Jeez, Karen, hush! And no, not Damian."

Karen thought Damian was hot, and had been rooting for the two of them to get together for years.

"Not Damian what?" Damian spoke behind them, making them both jump.

"Hey, Damian. Who are you in for?"

Karen answered, "Mary's out again, poor thing." Mary was the English teacher, and subbing for English was a good fit for Damian, since he'd minored in English.

"Yeah, looks like there's the possibility of it turning long term." Damian shook his head sadly. He'd been subbing for the district long enough that he was friends with most faculty in the school. This year, he'd been subbing for Mary an awful lot, and although she'd been discreet about the reason, her number of absences told a tale all their own. "But enough sad talk. You were talking about my fine ass for a reason."

Jimmy rubbed at the hickey on his neck. True to his word, Luke had kept the other marks below the collar, but Jimmy had a few more days of high necks in his future until this one faded.

"I was wondering if you were the reason Jimmy's wearing a turtleneck today and yesterday."

Damian laughed. "Turtlenecks two days in a row? That's not my fault. But the three of us are having lunch together. Today. Get the scoop on the neck sucker."

"I don't know, Damian. I've got a bunch of tests to grade." Because he'd done sweet fuck all the past weekend... except fuck a sweet man, and of course, give his all to the character of Gary.

"No. If we don't get the dirt on whoever put that smile on your face, and presumably a hickey on your neck, I'm going to come ask you about it during the pep squad class." Karen glared at him, and Damian rubbed his hands.

"You wouldn't." The pep squad class was one of his senior biology classes. Any senior girl taking biology who was also a cheerleader had been scheduled for that class. Had something to do with their practice schedule. There were a lot more cheerleaders taking senior biology than you might expect, and half of them treated him like one of those fluffy accessory dogs rich women carried around in Burberry bags. The other half thought if they flirted hard enough, he'd first become straight and second, lose his ever-fucking mind and become fixated on a student. If Karen or Damian came in asking about Luke, it would be like setting off a firecracker in a methane factory.

"Then we're going to have lunch and you're going to tell us everything."

"Fine, fine." The tests could wait another day if it meant not fanning the flames of the pep squad class. But his two friends would be sadly disappointed. He wasn't about to share graphic details about Luke with anyone. Luke was too special for that, and if he wanted Luke to be his boyfriend, he didn't want the shy man to be embarrassed when he met Jimmy's friends.

BENNETT PULLED the car into a parking space behind a squat industrial-type strip mall. A couple of teenagers slouched against the wall, smoking. Luke itched to tell them to butt out, but he doubted they'd appreciate a total stranger attempting to parent them. He had one kid and another pseudo-kid who turned out pretty good, but parenting was more than some sage advice in passing.

"This is the place, eh? Thanks for driving." Going to the first Rainbow Blues event by himself had taken a lot of willpower. Until he knew more people, he was just as happy to share driving duties with Bennett.

"Happy to have the company."

They walked around the building to what presumably was the front door.

A few more teenagers, somewhat more socially awkward in appearance than the smokers, pushed past them and entered the same door that Bennett was heading for.

Through the silvered over windows, Luke could see shadows like people seated around a table, but he was surprised by how young these guys were.

"Are we in the right place?"

"Yeah, we have events here all the time."

They did?

"Aren't these guys awfully young? I thought the minimum age for joining was twenty-one."

It wasn't like the social group intended to indulge in illicit activities or even sexual ones. But there had been booze at the Christmas party and aside from confirming his identity as a member, no one had checked IDs. Not that Luke had been carded in years, but not all the guys in Rainbow Blues were as old as he was.

"There's private function space that we rent out on a regular basis. It wasn't available for the Christmas party, but most of the events are here."

Bennett opened the door and ushered him inside. The acrid scent of unwashed bodies and musty clothes hit him like a slap in the face. And he spent all day with guys on construction sites.

"Uh." A throng of teenagers—mostly male—gathered around a number of tables. On the tables were miniature figures, cards laid out in intricate patterns, or board games far more complicated than Monopoly. Most of the words that reached Luke's ears were completely incomprehensible. He'd at least heard of a Hopping Vampire, but what the hell was a Shaolin Monkey? Even worse, what was a Melting Flesh Squad?

The smell bordered on eye-watering. Zach and Ryan had gone through a phase where they'd smelled like goats, followed shortly by a period where they smelled like goats drenched in body spray before they discovered showering regularly worked better. Here, the goatlike stench was concentrated because there were so many kids. Luke wasn't sure if body spray would make things better or worse.

The kids didn't pay any attention to them, and Bennett led the way past the tables to another door.

Once through, the noise and stench from the main room was cut off. In this room, there were eight large tables covered with green felt and stacked with poker chips. Like the Christmas party, snacks and coolers filled with beer sat on tables along a wall.

The poker games hadn't started yet, since they were a little early, so they dug through the coolers for a beer.

"It's okay to have beer here?" Because Luke would bet his next year's salary that more than half the kids in the other room weren't of age.

"Sure. Private event space. The gamers aren't allowed in here when the space is rented out."

"Makes sense. What is this place?"

Bennett jabbed a thumb toward the door. "Nerd nirvana. Or so I assume. There's another room attached to the main one, stacked to the rafters with games that they sell—shit I've never heard of. But mostly they make money holding tournaments for various games and from overpriced snacks and soft drinks. Kids and adults show up to play all sorts of games. Board games, card games, and role-playing games mostly. And they've got this self-contained event space. Doesn't have a proper kitchen, but it's got banquet heaters, a fridge, and its own bathroom. There's even a little enclosed patio out back for the smokers."

"If it's got a fridge, why the coolers?" Luke asked.

"Pain in the ass to load and unload the beer. This is easier."

More men filed in and began milling around the poker tables, not exactly impatient, but clearly ready to start playing as soon as possible.

"So, I've been to a holiday party and now a poker tournament. Is there always a planned activity?" Not that Luke cared one way or the other. It was nice to get out and socialize. Jimmy was awesome, and Luke would be happy spending all his time with Jimmy, but he did miss having friends to just hang out with.

"Yeah, sometimes it's a movie night, or there's a speaker, but usually it's something to do that encourages us to talk to each other. After all, it's not like we're going to stand around and do those weird icebreaker exercises they do on corporate retreats."

Luke shuddered. He'd never had the "pleasure," but Kelly had gone on a few and told him about them. They would have sent Luke screaming from the room.

"Makes sense. I mean, it would send a weird message to meet in a church basement like an AA meeting, a banquet hall would cost a lot of money, and a library might not have suitable hours. It's not a sex club either. But who the hell found this place? Don't get me wrong, it seems ideal for Rainbow Blues, but it's a little obscure."

Obscure was the most neutral word he could come up with. Luke couldn't picture any of the older guys on his crew ever setting foot in a place like this. Even the younger guys… he hated to resort to stereotypes, but he doubted any of those kids out there were now or were going to be construction workers.

Bennett laughed, clearly knowing what Luke was thinking. "Let me introduce you to the guy who started the Rainbow Blues. He wasn't around for the Christmas party. His partner is an event planner and knows everywhere he can get event space for cheap. He's actually the one that plans most of the events. I think, after hearing some of the weddings and shit he's done, planning RB events is almost an afterthought. C'mon, I think we're ready to start. We'll grab the same table as Peter. He's also a manager like you."

Steering him to the farthest table, Bennett sat next to an older man, probably in his early fifties, who Luke had no trouble imagining in a hard hat.

"Peter, let me introduce you to a new member. This is Luke."

"Luke. Glad to have a new member. We're growing far faster than I would have expected."

They shook hands and took their place at the table, along with Graham, a drywaller, and Hector, a roofer.

"I understand your partner was the...." Luke didn't quite know how to ask the question without sounding like an ass.

Fortunately Peter didn't mind. "Oh, Scotty was absolutely the driving force behind RB. Mind you, this was about ten years ago and Scotty's business was starting to take off. I was in the closet at work— still am—but he hated that I was basically sitting at home alone while he had to work such long hours. He came up with this as a way for me to find guys I'd have something in common with, someone I could hang out with while he was busy. It grew well beyond either of our expectations, but it's good, you know? Good that all these guys have someplace to go and be themselves."

"It's a great thing you've done. Thank you." Luke couldn't express how much this group had already come to mean to him. "And taking dating out of the equation made it a lot less intimidating to join."

"Well, we do certainly see some relationships come out of it, and there's an alley around the corner where a few guys have had quickie hookups, but yeah, we definitely encourage the social, not the romantic. We all need friends, don't we, Luke?"

Over the course of the tournament, he learned that he wasn't the only one who tried to fake a heterosexual life, and discovered that some of the guys, although none at the table, were still married and in the closet with just about everyone.

The guys at his table, though, were great, and he could easily see meeting up with them outside of RB. Hell, next time he was putting together his own construction crew, he'd be tempted to recruit members from RB. Not having to constantly monitor every word and action on a job site would be such a relief. Nice dream, but maybe not feasible.

CHAPTER 7

LUKE'S PHONE rang, and he snatched it up. Jimmy had only been over a handful of times, but already the place was almost unbearable on those nights when he knew Jimmy wouldn't be there. The weeknight performances were too draining. Still, Luke waited up, because Jimmy would text him when he got home.

The caller ID said it was Jimmy, but he rarely called in case Luke had gone to sleep early. It had been only three weeks since they'd met, but they'd slipped easily and painlessly into a routine. Dates on Monday or Tuesday, texting the rest of the week, and on the weekend, when Jimmy wasn't at the playhouse, they were together, whether it was at Jimmy's or Luke's. Mostly Luke's, though. He'd made a wise choice when he bought the bed.

"Hey there. Is everything okay?"

"Yeah." If a voice could slouch, Jimmy's was doing it. "Just tired. Wanted to hear your voice."

"How'd it go tonight?" If Jimmy had had a bad performance yet, he hadn't shared that information with Luke.

"Fine. Just…." The silence lengthened while Luke waited.

"Jimmy?"

"I forgot to go shopping. And I'm hungry, but too tired to go back out. Pathetic, right?"

Jimmy ate very lightly before performances, but was usually ravenous afterward. Still, the past three weeks had to have been grueling.

"You've got nothing? Jimmy, you've got to eat something. You'll make yourself sick." Luke rolled his eyes. That was the sound of a man who'd spent years as a dad. But he'd seen firsthand how hard Jimmy pushed himself, and not eating was only going to weaken him. In fact, the last time he'd gotten Jimmy naked, Luke wondered if Jimmy had lost some weight, but he was still learning Jimmy's body and might have been mistaken.

"Eh. I'll grab a danish or something on the way into school tomorrow."

A danish. If that was Jimmy's idea of food that would stick with him all day, no wonder he was running on fumes.

"Order a pizza. They should still be delivering."

Jimmy let loose a loud sigh. "Not sure I'll be awake that long. Maybe we can do some grocery shopping on the weekend? You won't mind going with me, will you?"

The weekend? That was still two days away. Luke was going to make sure Jimmy had something to eat before then. "Sure, be happy to."

"You sure? I can do it on my own."

"Jimmy, I like spending time with you. It doesn't have to be dates or sex or some sort of organized activity, you know. Just you and me, doing everyday things." Luke liked the everyday things. They spoke of commitment and stability and maybe, just maybe, forever.

"Luke, I lo—" Jimmy cut himself off, and Luke held his breath, waiting. "I like spending time with you, too. You make everything better."

Had Jimmy been about to drop the L word? Excitement fizzed through his veins. Maybe it was stupid of him, but the word had formed in his mouth more than once in recent days, and wanted to escape out into the world. He'd never felt like this before, and he could only attribute it to being in love. Yes, it was fast, but he'd already done the traditional marriage thing and failed miserably. The timeline didn't need to conform to anyone else's rules but theirs, and he knew his own mind and what he wanted.

He wasn't quite ready to say it yet, either, but soon. Soon, the urge to say it would be stronger than his fear that Jimmy didn't feel the same way.

"When the play is done... we'll make a date for you to meet my son, right?"

Jimmy gasped. "Really? You've told him about me?"

Oh. "Well, no, not yet. I mean, it's not like I need his approval, but... we're together right? Just you and me, seeing where this goes?"

"Yeah, Luke. Just you and me." Jimmy's voice was high and tight, like he was trying not to cry. Maybe springing emotional stuff on him wasn't a good idea when he was exhausted and starving.

"Then you need to meet my son."

"Okay. Yeah, that's good." Jimmy cleared his throat. "I'd like you to meet my family, too."

Luke smiled. Just him and Jimmy, seeing where it went. And it looked like it was going somewhere serious.

LUKE STOOD in the foyer near where he'd first spoken to Jimmy. He just hoped that coming out to speak with lingering audience members was something the cast did every performance and that it wasn't something special for the opening weekend shows. Otherwise, he'd wasted money on yet another ticket for *Walking Wounded*. Jimmy had been great, again, but Luke knew him so much better now. Jimmy's indefatigable energy was gasping its last.

He understood why Jimmy had felt the need to agree to supervise the girls basketball team during another teacher's sick leave, but evidence of the strain on Jimmy was clear to him, even if no one else saw it. The sad thing was, his friend Damian was the substitute teacher covering, but he couldn't even help share in the duties because of the school's policy about faculty advisors for extracurricular activities. Damian didn't qualify, and if Jimmy hadn't said yes, they would have had to cancel the basketball team for the year. Jimmy didn't want to let that happen, but the extra responsibility was taking its toll. Luke saw it in Jimmy's eyes and heard it in his voice.

Luke cleared his throat and shifted back and forth. A couple of men caught his eye and smiled. Luke smiled back but didn't hold eye contact. It was possible that coming to a play by himself, intending to ambush one of the lead actors with food like a fretful Italian momma, was just a little bit pathetic. After he'd hung up with Jimmy last night he'd thought it was perfect. A little romantic, and a way he could take care of a man who was coming to mean everything when he wasn't around. Now that he was here by himself, he felt conspicuous and possibly stalkerish.

Before he could completely lose his nerve and leave, Jimmy burst out into the waiting audience with a wide smile. Luke couldn't take his eyes off him, and the sheer joy that had made Jimmy glow that first day... well, it wasn't gone, but it was muted. Unless Luke was just imagining things.

Then Jimmy laughed at something one of the men said to him. The brittle, tight edge to his laugh, one Luke had only started to hear the past couple of days, was unmistakable. His lover needed a break, but Luke didn't think Jimmy would take one until this play was done.

Regardless of his concern for Jimmy, the guy was still stunning. Luke smiled and leaned back against the wall, content to watch Jimmy do his thing.

As though he could feel the weight of Luke's stare, Jimmy cocked his head and looked around. Do-or-die time. Jimmy's reaction, unprompted, was going to tell Luke whether he'd made the right decision or not.

Jimmy turned his head, gaze finally landing on him. Jimmy's eyes widened, before a huge smile brightened his face. Luke let out a breath he hadn't realized he was holding. There was no hesitation, no anger. Like that first night, Jimmy arrowed in on him to the exclusion of everyone else, and this time, Luke didn't have any fear of the unknown. Anything he didn't know about Jimmy yet, he was eager to learn—nothing to be afraid of.

"Luke. What are you doing here?" Jimmy leaned in as though he was going to kiss him but glanced around and stopped like he'd hit an invisible wall.

"I missed you." Fingering the rainbow knit of his scarf, Luke realized he'd let fear govern too many of his actions. The audience members of this play had to be gay friendly; this was a safe place. A place without judgment. Luke was here solely because he wanted to see Jimmy, wanted to make him feel better. Stupid to pretend otherwise, because each time he saw Jimmy the temptation to touch and kiss him got stronger.

Luke took another glance around the room. He wasn't the only one with eyes on Jimmy. It wasn't like he wanted to put a stamp of ownership on him—he was more mature than that—but he couldn't deny he wanted to claim Jimmy as his own. Which was a completely foreign feeling for him, and he wanted to revel in it.

Setting his bag down, he stepped into Jimmy's personal space. Then he cupped Jimmy's face in his hands and kissed him. Shock vibrated through Jimmy for a split second before Jimmy slid his arms around Luke's waist.

Luke couldn't let go of his lifetime of reticence to lose himself as completely as he did when they were alone in the dressing room, but resisting these urges had been so damned hard, the relief of letting go was almost orgasmically beautiful.

Jimmy pulled back, eyes reddened but smiling. He sniffed. "Hi."

"Hi. Why the tears?" Luke kept his voice low, because he didn't want to embarrass Jimmy.

With fists clenched in Luke's sweater at the small of his back, Jimmy looked at him as though he were the only man in the world, and there was no denying Luke liked it. Loved it.

"I just thought... I wasn't sure...." Jimmy closed his eyes for a second and took a deep breath. "I wanted, so badly, for you to just kiss me. Just because. I thought, eventually, you'd be ready but I... it's much sooner than I expected."

Gales of laughter from across the room burst the little tiny bubble that had encased them for a few moments, buffering them from the rest of the world.

"But seriously. What are you doing here? How'd you get in?"

Surely Jimmy didn't think he'd snuck in or anything. "Bought another ticket, of course."

Since the other options were limited to breaking in or bribery, Jimmy's obvious surprise should probably offend him.

"To see the play again?"

He lifted a shoulder. "Nope. To see one of the cast members. And to bring him a little gift."

There was no mistaking the surprise and pleasure on Jimmy's face. "A gift?"

Reluctantly, Luke pulled out of Jimmy's arms and stooped to grab the handles of the paper bag he'd set down earlier. He pulled out a single red rose.

"This is for you. Well, what's in the bag is, too, but this you can have now."

Jimmy took the rose with tentative fingers, and sniffled again. "A flower."

Luke shrugged. "I'm not much of a flower guy, but I thought you might like it."

Jimmy's smile was tremulous but happy; Luke was pleased he'd given in to the temptation. He'd seen other people give the actors flowers that first day, but none for Jimmy, so he'd been afraid Jimmy might not like it.

"I love it. Thank you."

A theatergoer moved behind Jimmy, jostling him into Luke. Clutching Luke's biceps, Jimmy smiled at him. "You have no idea how badly I want to see what else is in that bag, but maybe this isn't the place. Can I introduce you to a couple of my friends before I take you backstage again?"

Getting hot and heavy in the dressing room again was out of the question, and Luke knew it. Now, without the stage makeup on, the signs of Jimmy's exhaustion were even more visible. He was still the most gorgeous guy he'd ever spoken to, but the bubbly veneer was cracking like frozen asphalt. Luke wasn't going to do anything to make Jimmy worse.

His momentary pause put shadows in Jimmy's eyes. "It's okay if you're not ready. I mean… I just thought when you mentioned me meeting your son…."

"I'm ready." And surprisingly eager. He'd kissed a man in public. He was going to introduce him to his family. The terror and confusion and paralyzing uncertainty weren't entirely gone, but finding the Rainbow Blues, Bennett, and now Jimmy were rapidly banishing those isolating forces. He still had half his life before him, and this time he wanted to live for himself. With Jimmy.

"Can I... should I...." Jimmy pursed his lips then huffed, although Luke didn't know which of them he was exasperated with. "Can I introduce you as my boyfriend? I'm okay if you just want to—"

Luke pressed a finger over Jimmy's lips. "Yes, of course. I mean... that's what we are, right? It's just you and me? Exclusive?"

For his part, Luke had been exclusive since he'd laid eyes on Jimmy, and he'd thought they were both fully invested in a serious relationship, but they'd never actually come right out and said so in those exact words.

"Oh yes." Jimmy's lips moved under Luke's finger, his voice breathy as his eyes darkened and glittered. The tip of Jimmy's talented tongue slipped out, touching Luke's skin and shocking him back into full arousal. His cock and balls were going to mutiny if he kept getting riled up and then having to settle down without sating them both, especially since Jimmy was running on fumes. And if they found themselves anywhere with a bed or couch, Jimmy was going to pass the hell out. He'd love to tell Jimmy he needed to quit the substitute coaching job, but this wasn't the time or place to even broach that discussion.

"Hey now. Cut that out. I don't want to meet your friends with a raging erection."

Jimmy smiled wickedly but thankfully stepped back so Luke could breathe. "They wouldn't mind, and you'd make a fantastic first impression."

Luke rolled his eyes, hoping to distract from the heat in his cheeks.

"C'mon, boyfriend. Let's meet some people so you can give me my present."

Boyfriend. It was a good word, and in Jimmy's honeyed voice? A great word. Stupendous.

TWENTY MINUTES later, Jimmy led Luke—his boyfriend—backstage. Luke showing up had been such an incredible surprise, making a long, stressful day much more bearable. But a public kiss? A red rose? Introducing Luke as his boyfriend? The thrill of it was still sparking in his veins, giving him a better buzz than a piña colada with a rum runner chaser.

That Luke had brought him a gift as well? It was certainly better than Christmas, especially since he'd spent Christmas being wildly jealous of his siblings' families. Not that he wanted kids himself, but he'd rather not have his nieces and nephews grow up wondering why their weird Uncle Jimmy was a lonely old queen.

They sat down on a scruffy couch that Jimmy had napped on more than once. He'd probably fall asleep in a Pavlovian response if it weren't for the fact he'd miss out on Luke's gift.

Reaching out to the bag, he noticed his fingers trembling, and he grabbed at the handles before Luke could notice.

"I can't remember the last time a boyfriend brought me a gift just because." He crumpled the top of the paper bag in his suddenly clenched fists. Christmas and birthdays, yes, he got gifts, and ones without much thought behind them, too. Out of the blue, I was thinking of you? Never. Not once.

"Well, that's not right."

Maybe it wasn't, but that only proved that his instinct about Luke being the "one" was spot on. Weirdly, he was almost afraid to look in the bag, though. And if he'd been looking in the bag, he would have missed the look of consternation on Luke's face.

"It's not much. Nothing to get too excited about."

Too late. He was excited. "Out of the blue, I was thinking of you."

Luke crinkled his nose. "What?"

"This." Jimmy held up the bag. "It's… that's just what I call these gifts, in my head, when I see other people get them. Gifts—and it doesn't matter how big or small—that aren't attached to some commercial occasion or celebration. But, I've never had a boyfriend who gave me one."

"Out of the blue, I was thinking of you." The faraway look in Luke's eyes as he repeated Jimmy's words said he was storing that away somewhere in his brain. "I like it. And I hope you like your first one, because it's seriously not much."

Inside the paper grocery bag was a silvery thermal bag. Could it be? Food? Now that tonight's show was over, he was fucking starving, but like many performance nights, by the time he got home, even his grumbling stomach wouldn't be enough to keep him from going right to bed.

Past the insulation was a little cold pack with a.... Jimmy pulled it out. "Giraffe?"

Luke laughed. "I've got a whole set of safari themed cold packs from when Zach was a kid. Now I use them to keep my own lunches cold."

How many times would this man prove over and over that he was so fucking cute?

Beneath the cold pack were a bunch of disposable food containers and sandwich bags.

"What's all this?"

"Just, some snacks that don't require any preparation for you. Crackers, pitas, veggies, cheese, salsa, hummus. Stuff like that. Filling and good for you, but fast."

Never mind the cute, he was fucking undone by the sweet. Not even one of his Christmas or birthday gifts from past boyfriends had been even close to this thoughtful. His eyes started burning again, and he took a deep breath. He wasn't going to start crying over hummus, for God's sake. That'd scare a solid man like Luke away in a heartbeat.

"Thank you. This is... just perfect. And I love hummus, especially."

"Oh, good. It's one of my specialties."

What? Jimmy glanced up from his perusal of the care package. "Wait. You didn't make this, did you?"

Luke shrugged like it was no big deal. "Sure. I used to cook a lot. Haven't done it as much since it's been just me, but I like it. Cooking was the only way to make ends meet after Zach was born, and I was better at it and enjoyed it more than Kelly did."

Jimmy set the bag down carefully and flung his arms around Luke, kissing him thoroughly and deeply.

When they separated to grab a breath, Luke asked, "For hummus?"

"You can cook for me any time. I can't tell you how awesome that is. I love to eat, but I'm shit at cooking anything more elaborate than spaghetti."

A wave of red colored Luke's cheeks. "So, yeah, about that."

Jimmy bit his lip. This sounded like a shoe about to drop. Luke dug in his pocket and pulled something out but kept it hidden in a tight fist.

"I… well… I'd prefer if you didn't have to work so hard."

Oh, fuck. This was where all his previous relationships had fallen apart. The guys just couldn't handle his long hours and while he understood, he loved acting. Loved it. He also enjoyed teaching and it paid the bills. Stomach twisting, he wrapped his arms around his middle. Was the gift, the kiss, the new title of boyfriend a bribe to get him to quit the play? Guilt him into spending more time with Luke? The shitty thing was, this was the first time he wanted to spend more time with a guy and couldn't. Not with the extra responsibilities that had been dumped on him at school.

He couldn't speak past the constriction in his throat, which wasn't like him, but he'd really wanted to keep Luke longer than this. Staring at Luke, waiting, he ignored the little niggle of guilt that wanted to make this easier for Luke who was clearly struggling to find the right words. But shit. Helping Luke only meant losing him that much faster. Why did every man he met assume he'd be the one to sacrifice everything for their relationship?

Luke rubbed at the bridge of his nose with his free hand while staring down at his lap. "But I know it's important to you. And I also know that sometimes you just need to be home alone. Downtime. I understand all that, but I also hate thinking about you being by yourself, stressed and hungry. So, I want you to have this. Use it whenever you want, whether I'm there or not."

What the hell was going on?

"I'll cook, make sure there's food there you can eat. You can help yourself to anything. Or you can just sleep in my bed. If I'm there, no pressure for anything. Just a… refuge. If you want one."

Not wanting to speculate anymore, because he was afraid his hopes would be dashed on the rocky shores of misunderstanding,

Jimmy reached out with cold, bloodless fingers and opened Luke's fist. Two shiny silver keys attached to a simple key ring lay within Luke's palm.

Jimmy wasn't sure he could talk yet. If those were what he thought, this was big, and he wasn't sure he was ready.

"I'm not going to lie, Jimmy. I'd like to see us moving in together someday. Maybe soon."

That was his Luke. Blunt as all hell, just laying out everything on the table.

"And yes, these are keys to my apartment. But I'm not asking you to move in. Aside from the fact that I think both our places are too small for both of us to be there full-time, it's still early. We don't have to rush it. But like I said, you can use this as a refuge. If you want. My place is closer to the school than yours is. You can... maybe even nap during lunch or before you go to the theater if you need to. We can still have our regular date nights, but if you're too tired to go out and just want to hang out and watch TV, I'm good with that."

The band of fear that had squeezed at Jimmy's chest released with a snap, and he could breathe again.

"This is the best present anyone's ever given me."

Luke peered at him as though assessing the truth of his words.

"Seriously, Luke. This is so thoughtful, and I've been missing you. I'd like to see you more, and maybe this will help. At least until the end of February, when I've got a bit of a break and we can go out on weekends like a normal couple."

At his words, Luke smiled.

"I know you don't talk much, but when you do, it's all good. I'll run out tomorrow and get a key made for my place."

While he was still talking, Luke was already shaking his head, although the smile never disappeared. "Nope, I don't want it."

There hadn't been any objections to his place before. At least his place was cozy and lived in. The only things going for Luke's place were Luke himself, a great bed, and proximity to the school.

Luke laughed and squeezed his shoulder. "Hold on there. I like your place just fine."

God. How had Luke been able to read all that on his face?

"Then why?"

"You spend a lot of time doing things with and for other people. There will be times when food or sex or companionship will be the last thing you need. Which means having me drop by unexpectedly will just be one more stressor. You invite me over? I'm coming. But I want you to have what you need in order to come out of this with your health and sanity intact."

Normally, Jimmy would scoff at the implication he wasn't able to handle things; he thrived on the attention, on being busy. This time was different, though, and he wasn't sure if it was simply a desire to see more of Luke, or the additional responsibility of the basketball team, or even just that he was getting older, but he was slowly breaking, and Luke had picked up on that even before Jimmy. He wasn't a young kid anymore. In fact, lately all he'd wanted to do was scream or cry, to the point Damian had asked if he was going through menopause. Bitch.

"When we move in together, we'll make sure it's big enough so you'll have a sanctuary."

And there went his damned watery eyes again. He sagged into Luke, nuzzling into his neck, and Luke wrapped a comforting arm around his shoulder.

"You must think I'm a crazy, emotional idiot."

"Nope. Just a crazy, exhausted idiot."

Jimmy snort-laughed into Luke's collar. If it was too soon to talk about moving in together, it was too soon for talking of love, even though it had almost slipped out a couple of times. It had been fucking fast, but God, he loved this man.

"What about you? Don't you need a sanctuary, too?"

Warm lips pressed a kiss on the top of his crunchy, styled hair. "I've been living alone for more than two years now. I don't think I'm really suited to be on my own."

No, his Luke really wasn't. Sure, he didn't talk much and was a solid, practical man. But he was also the most charming companion, and that would be wasted all by himself.

"Want to come back to my place tonight? Uh, despite the kissing and stuff earlier, I don't think I'm up for anything besides sleeping."

He shoved his face back into Luke's neck, not wanting to see the disappointment.

He wasn't expecting the earthquake shaking Luke's chest as he laughed.

"What's so funny?"

"You don't have to put out just because we kissed, you know. I like being with you, and kissing you. We don't have to go *all the way*. I won't dump you for the slutty cheerleader."

Laughing, Jimmy was reminded that they still had a few other sexual avenues to explore. He'd have to show Luke some of what he may have been missing when he was married to a woman. After he'd slept for about ten days.

Jimmy curled his fingers around the keys as though he were holding precious gems. "I have one more question about your keys. What if I walk in, and you're watching porn and jerking off?"

"I don't know. What if you walk in and I'm jerking off?"

As tired as he was, his cock gave a little throb at the mental picture. "I'd probably get naked and help you out."

"I knew you were perfect for me."

THE RICH smell of tangy tomato-based meat sauce filled the kitchen. The music station on the TV had switched over to one of the early songs by The Killers, and Luke sang along to it, swinging his hips as he cooked. His mood had steadily improved the closer they got to the end of *Walking Wounded*. Watching Jimmy drag was killing him, and he feared Jimmy was going to break. But the end was in sight. The lasagna he was making would feed them for the next couple of days until the cast party on the final night of *Walking Wounded,* and then they could relax for a bit. In a week, Jimmy was going to be done with his coaching duties, and then Luke didn't know what they were going to do with all that free time. More sex, for sure.

The Killers were followed up by Duran Duran, and Luke smiled, remembering the intense crush he'd had on John Taylor. Still singing, he began layering cheese, noodles and sauce into a pan.

A sharp knock at the door interrupted him. Couldn't be Jimmy. He'd gotten used to walking in like he lived there, something Luke loved. And yes, he'd walked in once on Luke beating off. Jimmy's help had been… much appreciated, especially since Luke hadn't been watching porn but fantasizing about his boyfriend.

But tonight was a performance night, and Jimmy would be on stage about now.

Luke danced to the front door and opened it.

"Ryan. What are you doing here?"

"Can I come in?"

Stepping aside, Luke gestured for Ryan to come in. He stuck his head out into the hallway, but there wasn't a sign of his son. As much as Luke considered himself a backup dad to Ryan, their relationship was more reserved than that between him and his son. Dropping by randomly without Zach wasn't common.

"Hang on a second." Luke put the last layer of cheese on top of the lasagna before sliding the pan in the oven.

"Smells great. You expecting company?" Ryan looked agitated.

"Nope, just preparing meals a couple days ahead. If you want to stick around for dinner, you can. It'll be about forty-five minutes until it's ready."

Ryan grinned at him. "Sure thing, LJ. Glad to see you're cooking again. I love your cooking."

Luke lifted a shoulder in a halfhearted shrug. "It was time." It was time he crawled out of his self-pity, and Jimmy had been the catalyst. But he wasn't going to tell Ryan that. Not when he hadn't told Zach. Midterms had kept Zach busy enough that they hadn't been able to see each other in person since the brunch the day he'd bought his new bed. He needed to tell his son about Jimmy, have them meet, but he didn't want to break that news over the phone. He'd be more comfortable gauging Zach's reaction when he could see his face.

"I know Zach was getting concerned."

"He worries too much." Although he'd have to make sure he gave Zach kudos for signing him up for Rainbow Blues. In one fell swoop, his son had given him friends, a boyfriend, and a social life. "You spoken to him lately?"

"We're both pretty busy with classes."

If Luke was reading the subtext correctly, either Ryan had a problem that Zach couldn't help him out with, or he was just missing Zach and Luke was a reasonable substitute. Luke couldn't imagine any other reason for him to drop by like this, but Ryan required a different approach. He and Zach were very different people and the best way to coax information out of Ryan was to get him comfortable enough to talk. Asking outright never worked with him, for some reason. Probably had something to do with his family life, as much as Luke had tried to be a supportive stand-in parent over the years.

"Want to find something on the TV to watch?"

"Sounds good." Ryan stopped at the fridge and grabbed a beer. "Want one?"

"Yeah, I could use a beer."

Beers in hand, they sat on the couch, and Ryan turned the TV on. A little company sure didn't hurt.

AFTER DINNER, Luke didn't bother cleaning up the dishes from the table. He could do it later. He was enjoying just relaxing with Ryan. During commercials, they'd talked a bit about Ryan's classes, and Luke gave him an update on Bennett. It was difficult avoiding mention of Jimmy, but Luke thought it would be disrespectful to tell Ryan about his new boyfriend before he had a chance to tell Zach. Jimmy was too important to him, and he didn't want Zach to have any reason not to like Jimmy.

Through it all, Ryan hadn't touched once on whatever had brought him over here. Luke could be patient. Besides, maybe all Ryan needed was company tonight, nothing more sinister than that.

The movie ended predictably, with a monstrous explosion and the guy getting the girl. As soon as the credits rolled, Ryan turned the TV off. Luke turned to him, wondering if he was getting ready to go or if he wanted to talk, but before he could say anything, he suddenly had a lapful of young man, lips on his, and Ryan's tongue pressing insistently for entrance.

Shock paralyzed Luke for a couple of seconds before he managed to grab Ryan's shoulders and push him back.

"Ryan? What the…." Ryan was gay? Since when?

Looking flushed, Ryan tilted his head to the side.

"What? You said you were ready to start dating. We went and bought the bed together. But you never called. We can go slow, but not that slow."

"Ah." Luke had no words. None. This was a misunderstanding of epic proportions, but he couldn't figure out how to reject Ryan without humiliating him.

"Jerking off is one thing. Threesomes are quite another."

Luke's vision grayed at the edges at the sound of Jimmy's voice, who'd let himself in as Luke had told him to do.

Jimmy was not amused. Not even a tiny bit, a fact that was confirmed by looking up at Jimmy's pursed lips and narrowed eyes.

"It's not a threesome." Oh by all that's holy, that was what Luke managed to say? He was stroking out. That was the only explanation.

Judging from Jimmy's devastated expression, it had sounded even worse to Jimmy than it sounded to Luke.

"Who the hell are you?" Ryan bounced off Luke's lap—thank God—but proceeded to get in Jimmy's face like he was spoiling for a fight.

"I'm his boyfriend."

Jimmy's glance took in the dirty dishes still sitting at the table, the empty beer bottles, and even though he hadn't done anything wrong, Luke felt as though he'd cheated on Jimmy. Which was also what Jimmy clearly thought.

This time, Ryan turned a hurt look on him. "It's been just over a month since you decided to start dating, and you've already got a boyfriend? What about buying the bed together? Didn't that mean anything?"

"You bought the bed with *him*?"

Luke gasped. What the hell was Ryan doing?

"Correction." Jimmy's voice was icy enough to drop the temperature in his apartment to almost freezing. "I am his ex-boyfriend."

Jimmy turned and walked out. Luke had to fix this, because otherwise, his heart might never be whole again.

"LJ, I'm sorry." Ryan's face was pinched and white and panicked. "I... I... you gave him a key. Even Zach doesn't have a key. I'm sorry."

Luke pointed at the couch. "Sit. Stay. We need to talk."

Since Zach moved out on his own, Luke hadn't had occasion to use his disappointed-dad voice, but it came back as naturally as Ryan obeyed it. Which was good. Because he couldn't worry about Ryan until he'd talked to Jimmy.

Running while it felt like he was having a heart attack was probably not recommended, but he couldn't let Jimmy go. He couldn't leave this appalling misunderstanding festering between them. Not for a minute, not for a second, did he want to be the cause of Jimmy's pain.

At the elevator he caught up to Jimmy, who stood stabbing the button, apparently hoping it would bring the elevator faster.

"Jimmy."

"Please don't, Luke. I can't take it." His voice cracked, and Jimmy wouldn't even turn to face him, just hunched his shoulders protectively, like Luke was going to add physical hurt to the emotional one.

"Jimmy, please listen to me. It was nothing, I swear. That was Ryan, my son's best friend. I didn't know he was going to come on to me. I didn't even know he was gay."

"Wait, that's your son's best friend?"

Jimmy finally turned to stare at him, and Luke's heart wrenched. His beautiful boyfriend's face was ravaged by tears, eyes red, face wet, and nose shiny.

"Yes. I swear, nothing's going on."

"He's young. Handsome. And now you know he's gay."

"It doesn't matter that he's gay. He's practically my kid. I don't know where the hell that in there came from...." Luke flapped a hand toward his apartment. "But I swear to you, I never put out any signals. I wouldn't."

Taking a chance, he stepped closer and placed his palms on Jimmy's cheeks, gently tilting his head back to make Jimmy look at him.

"Jimmy, I gave you a key, and said you could come by whenever you wanted. Whenever."

"What about the bed?"

"Good Christ, I don't know." Luke thought back to the day he'd shopped for the bed, and the brunch before. "I was going to have Bennett go with me, just because I thought I'd need an extra pair of arms to set it up. But he was busy, and I was out for brunch with Zach and Ryan. I asked them both to help, but Zach couldn't. Ryan could, so he came with me."

Fuck. Had Ryan been putting out signals he'd been too oblivious to notice?

"There's really nothing going on? How come he didn't know about me?" If it had been anyone else, Luke might have been annoyed at the implication that he was lying. But Jimmy had been burned by cheaters before and… there was no "and." Luke would get down on his knees and grovel. Anything to keep Jimmy from walking out of his life. To be fair, it had to have looked just terrible. He couldn't blame Jimmy for remaining uncertain.

"I haven't told Zach yet."

Jimmy flinched like Luke had stabbed him. "I thought…."

"I'm not hiding you. I just haven't actually seen my son since I gave you the key. I haven't seen him since the day I bought the bed. And it's important enough I didn't want to do it over the phone. So there's no way Ryan could have known."

"No? Has he been by before?"

"Apart from helping with the bed, no. Usually he's an extension of Zach."

His words had Jimmy frowning. Jimmy just had to believe him.

"I swear to you, Jimmy. I would never do that to you. I love you."

Jimmy sucked in a breath, his lip trembling, and looking more vulnerable than Luke had ever seen.

"I love you too." Jimmy hiccupped and wracking sobs gripped him. Burying his face in Luke's neck, he cried. Luke's own eyes burned in sympathy.

Relief and joy liquefied the bones in his legs, and he crowded Jimmy back so he had a little support as well.

The elevator door opened, and Jimmy stumbled back, Luke following. He hadn't realized the solid wall he'd pushed Jimmy against was the elevator door.

Jimmy laughed, and if the sound had a hint of hysteria in it, who could blame him? Sliding his hand down into Jimmy's, Luke pulled him back out of the elevator. No way was he letting Jimmy leave now. The elevator doors slid closed again.

"What you must think of me." Using the sleeve of his jacket, Jimmy swiped most of the tears away.

"I think you're an incredible, wonderful man."

Jimmy snorted. "Who cries at the drop of a hat. I'm sorry I'm so emotional."

"Don't be sorry. It's honest. I like honest. I like knowing what you're thinking, even if it's not good. And your ability to express your emotions is probably why you're such a great actor."

Luke pulled his boyfriend close, lowered his head, and kissed the salty traces of Jimmy's tears before placing a gentle kiss on his lips.

Jimmy clutched him close and returned the kiss, but it wasn't carnal. It was simple, sweet, and filled with perpetual sunshine.

But he couldn't make out with Jimmy all night. There was some unfinished business waiting in his apartment.

"I have to go talk to Ryan. Clear up this mess." Even if he had no idea what to say or how it all started.

"Can I go with you?"

"Of course you can. This affects you too. Just don't be too hard on him. I think he realizes what a bad mistake he made."

A sharp tug on his sleeve kept Luke from striding back down the hall.

"Um… is your son gay?"

"If he is, he hasn't told me. My gaydar is terrible, but honestly, I don't think so. Why?"

"Okay, I could be way off base here, but you and your son look an awful lot alike. You're gay and your son isn't."

That was it. The key he was missing. Finally this whole weird fucking night made sense. "You think he's got feelings for Zach that aren't strictly friendly? The poor kid."

"Yeah, I did that once—fell for a straight guy. It sucks."

"Well, at least that gives me a hint about how to deal with this. I wonder if he's even told Zach he's gay. I'm sure he wouldn't have told his parents."

Jimmy shrugged. "Depends on when he started feeling like this, I guess. If it started shortly after puberty, my guess is no."

"Right. Well, let's get back there and sort this out with the least embarrassment for all concerned. After, you and me are going to get some sleep in the bed I bought only thinking of you. Got it?"

"Yes, sir!" Jimmy mock saluted him, and Luke couldn't resist taking just one more quick kiss. He'd have to ask Bennett if Rainbow Blues ever did any dating type events. He'd bet a cutie like Ryan would get snapped up in seconds, and it wasn't like the entire membership were older guys like Luke.

CHAPTER 8

LUKE SMILED as he entered the sushi restaurant with Jimmy. Sushi wasn't his favorite, but both Jimmy and Zach loved it, and he wanted them to have some common ground.

It had been over a week since Ryan had made a play for him, and this was the earliest Zach had been free. He hadn't told Zach about Jimmy, and while he wasn't sure surprising his son was the best way to break the news to him, he hadn't been able to come up with anything else.

He glanced over at his sexy boyfriend, and realized Jimmy's smile was frozen. "Are you okay?"

"Just a little nervous." Luke grabbed his hand and squeezed, touching Jimmy in public getting easier every time he did it.

"Don't be. Zach's a great kid."

Jimmy's smile thawed a bit. "I know. I can't believe you'd have raised a bad kid."

"I love you," Luke whispered. It felt so damned good to say, and he loved the heated look it put in Jimmy's eyes.

"I love you, too."

Luke scoped out the restaurant and saw his son. Alone. "Surprise. Ryan didn't come with."

Jimmy snorted, but he squeezed Luke's hand. "Not a surprise. Poor kid. He'll get over the embarrassment sooner or later. It sucks, but we've all made passes at the wrong person."

"I haven't."

"You don't count. You were in the closet most of your life, then I snatched you up before anyone figured out how great you are. And there better be no making passes at anyone but me."

Oh, Luke could easily obey that edict. He led Jimmy over to Zach.

"Hey, Dad. You never want to come to this place." Zach smiled up at him, momentarily oblivious to the sexy man attached to his hand.

"Zach, I want you to meet Jimmy."

Shock passed over his son's face, but he held out his hand to shake. Jimmy had to disengage their fingers to reciprocate, a fact which Zach did not miss.

He smiled at them both. "Jimmy. Are you my dad's boyfriend?"

"I am." Jimmy sounded so fucking happy, just the way Luke liked him.

Once he and Jimmy had sat down and ordered, they covered all the major bases like how he and Jimmy had met, what Zach was doing in school, what Jimmy did for a living.

"What about your family, Jimmy? Do they know about my dad?"

Jimmy nodded before snaring a California roll with his chopsticks. "Yes. Haven't met him yet. My parents are snowbirds, and aren't back home yet. I introduced them on the phone earlier this week. And to my brother and sister, who don't live here anymore."

Biting into his tempura, Luke had to congratulate himself on how well that had gone. He'd been more nervous talking to Jimmy's parents than Jimmy was meeting Zach. Probably because Luke's own parents had been so rigid, unyielding, and not particularly loving. He hadn't wanted to be that way for his son, but he was a little wary of Jimmy's parents, afraid they might be too much like his own.

"They loved me," Luke teased his son. He wasn't lying, though. Jimmy's parents had been as sweet and welcoming as Jimmy was.

"Oh really. Jimmy, I guess you share that same hereditary blind spot?"

Jimmy snorted. "Your dad is awesome, but you know that."

Zach rolled his eyes but smiled at Luke.

Yeah, they did okay.

While they were having their mutual little compliment exchange, a couple walked past their table behind the hostess. The guy stopped abruptly.

"Luke?"

Luke inhaled sharply and coughed. "Oh, hey, Sean. How are you?"

"Good. This is my girlfriend, Cindy. Cindy, this is Luke."

A pretty blonde woman smiled at him and held out her hand. Luke shook it, all the while feeling like he was speeding madly toward a crossroads he wasn't sure he was ready for. But he couldn't just ignore Sean. They'd worked too many jobs together.

"Uh, Sean, this is my son, Zach. Zach, Sean and I started working on the same construction crew together, back in the day, and we've worked many jobs together since."

Zach smiled and greeted Sean while Luke quietly panicked. He hadn't expected his personal life and work life to collide. Not this soon.

The crossroads was here. Jimmy smiled at him, just a bit sadly. In that moment, Luke realized Jimmy was giving him permission to lie to his coworker. That simple understanding gave Luke courage he never thought he had. Because he didn't want to lie about who Jimmy was. He shouldn't fucking have to. And if anyone wasn't going to judge him, or make a big thing about it at work, it would be affable, easygoing Sean.

An expectant pause told Luke the time had come.

"Sean, this is my boyfriend, Jimmy."

The shock and joy and huge bubbly smile on Jimmy's face made it all worthwhile. Zach gave him a proud thumbs-up.

"Aren't you Jimmy Alexander?"

Luke froze, and exchanged a confused look with his son.

"Yes, I am."

"Saw you in *Much Ado About Nothing* last year. You were great."

"Oh, thank you. I appreciate that."

Sean turned back to Luke. "He's your boyfriend? No wonder I haven't seen you with anyone since Kelly. You aim pretty high, don't you?" He jabbed an elbow into Luke's side and grinned. "See you at work Monday."

The pair left, and Luke fell back in his chair.

Jimmy nudged his chair closer so their shoulders were touching.

"Thank you," he whispered. "How are you doing?"

"I'm still shaking, but I'm glad I did that."

"I'm glad, too." They smiled at each other, hands brushing together, until Zach cleared his throat.

"Guys? I'm still here, you know."

Luke cleared his throat. "Uh, right, sorry. It's just that… this is the first time I've come out to a coworker."

Zach's eyes widened. "Good for you, Dad. That calls for a drink. I'm buying."

Luke let out a shaky breath and smiled at his son, who seemed genuinely pleased.

Jimmy's hand crept onto Luke's thigh, and he sighed. This was the life he was supposed to be living.

JIMMY GOT off the elevator and stared down the hall toward Luke's apartment, a headache stabbing red-hot knives into his temples. His cold, sodden socks and squishy shoes only made him more miserable, although at least the foot soaking hadn't happened until he'd gone out to the parking lot at the end of the day. Not paying attention, he'd stepped in an enormous slush-filled pothole, cleverly disguised by a thin layer of ice covered with a light dusting of snow. He knew the pothole was there, just too sunk in his own misery to watch where he was walking. Freezing feet turned the red-hot knives into razor-sharp icicles. March sucked.

As utilitarian as Luke's apartment was, the attraction of Luke's presence outweighed the appeal of everything in his own apartment. Having a key to Luke's place had saved his life or at least his sanity.

He'd been half-afraid of Luke's motives when he'd offered a key to his apartment as a refuge during one of the most grueling months of his life. It hadn't taken long to realize that Luke didn't assume Jimmy's presence meant he had the energy for sex. Embarrassing a bit, because they were new enough that according to romantic fiction standards and Damian's judgment, they should be bonking like hormonal bunnies on Viagra and speed. Instead, Jimmy had been battered by his obligations and while they'd had a few sex-crazed-bunny moments, they'd spent a lot of time since *Walking Wounded* ended making up for lost time.

Not tonight, though. The headache had started during first period and hadn't let up all day. He'd taken the prescribed dosage of ibuprofen, but it hadn't made a dent in the pain.

Dogged steps kept Jimmy going, but Luke's apartment was so far away. He and Luke had been dating just over two months, and Jimmy had spent less than half that time at his own apartment. Probably he'd never go home again, just move right in, but Luke was right. Neither of their places could easily accommodate two of them full-time. As it was, Jimmy mostly went home for clothes. He'd left a couple of changes at Luke's, but there wasn't space for much more than that.

With numb fingers, Jimmy turned his key in the lock, opened the door, and slunk into Luke's apartment. The scent of cooking meat and vegetables hit him in the face. Most times, coming home to Luke's cooking was cause for joy, but the pain stole his appetite and left his stomach jumpy.

"Hey. Dinner will be ready soon."

Jimmy didn't have it in him to respond. He just shucked off his water-logged shoes and socks and hung up his jacket before shuffling toward the bedroom. A shower might help.

"Jimmy? Are you okay?"

Luke followed him into the bedroom, and zombie-like, Jimmy turned.

"Well, you're definitely not okay. What's wrong?"

Speaking took so much effort. "Headache. Stepped in a puddle. Bad day."

"I saw your shoes. Are you sure it wasn't a lake?"

Jimmy shrugged. He didn't want to cry in front of Luke again, but it had been a shitty, shitty day.

"Come here."

Wrapped in Luke's strong, warm arms, Jimmy let himself sag. He didn't know how he'd gotten so lucky to find Luke, and he had no idea why Luke stayed with his normally manic self, but Luke took such damned good care of him.

A few minutes later, Luke guided him into the bathroom.

"Let's get you warmed up and clean first."

JIMMY HAD very little recollection of the shower itself, aside from an overwhelming impression of tenderness from Luke. It hadn't been dragged out, and there were no sexual overtones. Now, he was curled up on the couch, snuggled in another of Luke's "out of the blue, I was thinking of you," gifts. The food Luke had prepared the day he'd given Jimmy his key hadn't been the only one of those, by a long shot, but after Jimmy had told him the little name, Luke had found it amusing to incorporate the color blue into them whenever he could. The plush robe he was wearing, for example, was a pale blue that might be a little girly but suited his fair coloring better than the navy one Luke had.

The first time they'd showered together after Luke gave him a key, Luke had made him wear the navy robe, but by the next time Jimmy came over, there was a light blue one hanging from the back of the bedroom door, softer and fluffier than Luke's. Jimmy didn't mind. Not only was he fluffier than Luke, he suspected the robe was a woman's, but that was okay. A lot of the time women's stuff was softer, like it detracted from a guy's manliness quotient if he appreciated something soft against his skin.

Luke returned with a bottle of water. Jimmy frowned.

"Water?" He had to admit, he'd been expecting tea. Or hot chocolate. He held back a snort, because he didn't want to aggravate the knives in his brain, but he was maybe getting the teensiest bit spoiled.

"You might be dehydrated. Drink this while I work on your shoulders, and after, I'll make you a cup of tea."

Tea was another little present. Luke didn't drink it, but he'd bought a tiny kettle and some of Jimmy's favorite tea bags to keep at the apartment.

"I love you." How could he not? Luke was the sweetest, sexiest, most adorable man, and Jimmy couldn't imagine his life without Luke in it, and not just for his pampering skills, which were admittedly excellent.

"I love you, too." Luke kissed his cheek and coaxed him around so he could get behind. The second those strong hands started kneading the knots in his neck, the pain receded.

Jimmy drank his water and concentrated on relaxing his muscles.

"Want to talk about it?"

His eyelids dropped closed. Funny how all his problems receded when he was around Luke.

"First day of fetal pig dissection for the senior class. It's always a nightmare."

Luke's fingers stilled. "Fetal what now?"

"Didn't you ever do dissection in school? It was worse then, because, gah, formaldehyde, but it's certainly not new."

The firm massage started up again. "Yeah, I guess I remember hearing about frogs, maybe. Not pigs. But I never took biology. I'd been planning to be an engineer, remember?"

An engineer. One unexpected pregnancy and a set of stern parents changed the course of his life. Jimmy knew without asking that even if Luke might still prefer to be an engineer, he wouldn't change the circumstances that gave him Zach. Jimmy wouldn't change anything either because then a lonely Luke might not have needed a social group who might not have gotten discounted tickets for Jimmy's play. Jimmy's life was immeasurably richer for having met Luke, and he only hoped he did the same for Luke.

"Well, there are always some kids who feel it's against their morals to dissect real animals. It's a grand argument every year. This year they picketed my classroom."

A splutter of laughter sounded behind him before Luke choked it off. "Sorry. Pickets? Really?"

It had been funny. "Yeah, it wasn't as bad as the year they graffitied the room like they were rabid animal activists, but the arguments were intense. And in the case of the cheerleaders, a little shrill."

The cheerleaders had given cogent arguments, which he might have given them extra credit for, but the two classes following had more or less the same arguments, and each successive class had gotten louder, which put him in a foul mood. A mood that only got worse when the picketing prevented him from eating his lunch.

"I'm not trying to take their side or anything, but surely there are computer programs or simulations or something. I mean, how many of those kids are going to need to get up close and personal with pig anatomy?"

Jimmy sighed. He had this fight with the principal and parents in addition to students; he dug in his heels every year. But Luke genuinely wanted to know, he wasn't trying to influence him either way.

"Yeah, there are simulations. But here's the thing. Some of these kids, and maybe they're in the minority, sure, but some of them want to be doctors and veterinarians. There's only so much you can learn without getting right in there. Wouldn't it be better if they find out now if they can't stomach it or have no aptitude for it, when they don't have to worry about paying for classes or destroying their GPA because the point when students figure out they should drop the class is always about a month after they'll let you."

"Huh. I never thought of that."

"And there are a few kids who finally click with the learning. Develop a love of biology, realize what they want to do with their lives." Jimmy did love that. He loved seeing that moment when his kids connected to something he was teaching them.

"From cutting up a pig? You sure they aren't developing an aptitude for serial killing?"

Jimmy gasped and twisted around. "What the fuck?"

Hands up in supplication, Luke grinned. "Just kidding. Seems reasonable. But it also seems a little gross, too."

"Well, yeah. And if the kids are gonna puke from a sanitized, embalmed fetal pig, then they probably should rethink their career choice as ER physician, you know? The earlier the better, so they can focus on something they do have an aptitude for."

Like magic, Luke's fingers had smoothed away the tension causing his headache.

"Okay, okay, seems reasonable. But surely no one actually pukes. Like you said, it's all sanitized."

"And no formaldehyde. That shit smelled foul. But speaking of puking... what's for dinner?"

"Beef stew... oh."

This year there were two pukers. Better than last year.

"Yep. Can I take you out? Treat you to steak or something?"

"How's the headache? Are you sure you don't want to order in?"

Jimmy grabbed Luke's hand and kissed the knuckles. He wanted this every night for the rest of his life, and he didn't care if anyone thought it was too soon. "You fixed me up. And I'm hoping to be celebrating tonight."

"Celebrate what?" Luke looked confused.

Maybe it wasn't the most romantic conversation, but the epiphany had been several days coming, and Jimmy didn't want to wait any longer, no matter how fast anyone thought it was. He was going to take a page from his blunt lover's book.

"I want us to move in together."

Luke peered at him as though trying to decipher a code. "Where would we live?"

A slightly disappointing response. Jimmy didn't know why he was expecting a more excited reaction. It wasn't like he'd asked Luke to marry him, and even then, his boyfriend wasn't the most excitable man. Exciting, yes. Excitable, no.

But they'd talked about things they wanted in a home. Granted, it hadn't been in the context of living together and what they wanted together. Maybe Jimmy had been extrapolating that data all on his own. Somehow, he didn't think so.

"I think we should buy a house together."

Luke blinked at him. Jimmy began to fidget. The silence lengthened. Palms sweating, Jimmy couldn't take his eyes off Luke's, but he couldn't read Luke's face. Was Jimmy scaring Luke right out of his life, or was Luke simply considering all angles? Anxiety danced in his belly like fire ants.

"Is this a theoretical discussion?"

Jimmy swallowed heavily. When Luke actually spoke up about what he wanted, which still took some effort, he was blunt, open, and straightforward. His boyfriend preferred if people dealt with him the same way, and Jimmy was going to do his best to comply, no matter how terrifying.

"No. I want to come home to you every night. I want to sleep next to you every night. I want our clothes to mingle in the closet and washing machine. I want to quibble over which brand of toothpaste we'll buy, bemoan the politeness of the neighborhood kids, and argue about who used the last of the toilet paper without changing the roll. I want to curl up to you every night and wake up to you every morning."

Luke laced their hands together. "Then I'll call a real estate agent in the morning."

"Really?" It couldn't be that easy, could it?

"I want that too, Jimmy. Everything. We've already talked a little bit about what we'd like in a house, let's go find one, the sooner the better. Right now, you don't have to worry about rehearsals, and we can maybe move in and settle during the summer."

Jimmy's pulse picked up, Luke's excitement crackling in the air, and suddenly a dreary evening at the end of March had become filled with color and energy.

"Okay. Let's do it." Jimmy wiggled in his seat. "I'm great with color schemes. I can pick out paint and fabrics and matching upholstery."

Luke laughed. "Don't get ahead of yourself. We might only be able to afford something that needs a bit of work. You'll have to let me do my thing before you can do yours."

Jimmy held in an unmanly squeal of delight. Luke was going to let him decorate. Although he'd accessorized his apartment like a fiend, he'd never had a place where he could truly let his instincts take over. Bit of a fucking stereotype, but he loved acting, and he loved decorating. At least he had the whole biology teaching thing as a foil. Then again, maybe that just made him a nerdy stereotype.

But he was happy, and Luke loved him. Didn't matter how anyone else labeled him. Amazing how it felt like all his dreams were coming true even though this was a completely different dream than the one he'd had twenty years ago.

CHAPTER 9

"You sure it's okay that I'm here?" The first meeting with Luke's son had gone well. Zach had seemed genuinely happy his dad had found a boyfriend. Jimmy had even tagged along for a couple of their father-son dinners since. Getting to know Zach was important to him, but that didn't change the fact that he thought he might have been intruding a little. If Zach wanted more alone time with his father, he really hoped he would say so and not let any resentment toward Jimmy build up and fester.

"Of course it is. Besides, this is as good a time as any to share our news."

Jimmy couldn't stop the wide grin that stretched his face. The answering grin on Luke's face warmed him inside. Three weeks after deciding to buy a house together, it was a done deal. The contract had been accepted yesterday, and they'd be taking possession of their house in June, just after school let out for the summer and a week before rehearsals started for Jimmy's next show. When he wasn't rehearsing, he'd do what he could to help Luke fix up the place, and then he'd have carte blanche to decorate.

He wanted to be living there with Luke already, settling into a domesticity he'd begun to think he'd never find. No more lonely Uncle Jimmy at family functions. No more pitying looks when his siblings asked if he was seeing someone. No more cheating. He'd never had the faith and trust in his previous boyfriends that he had in Luke. Lying and sneaking around just wasn't in his nature, and Jimmy loved him even more for it, because he knew he was maybe a little sensitive on the issue.

"I can't wait to live there with you." Jimmy wanted to kiss Luke, but didn't want to shock the plethora of little old ladies in the lobby of The Wheelhouse. Luke was getting more comfortable with PDAs, but for the most part, Jimmy let him initiate them—the last thing he wanted to do was make his boyfriend associate kissing with embarrassment or fear.

"Me neither." Luke grabbed his hand and held on, and Jimmy thought he might just burst from happiness. The fact that they'd pretty much given up all pretense of living apart didn't change the fact that a place of their own, bought together, was a significant milestone worthy of the expensive bottle of champagne they'd drunk last night, courtesy of Bennett.

Jimmy wasn't much of a wine snob, and Luke didn't drink much besides beer, but Bennett came from a much more refined background than either of them, and when Luke called to tell him about the house, he'd showed up on their doorstep with two bottles of champagne. Jimmy couldn't read most of the French on the label and didn't think he'd heard of it before. But it had slid down their throats like silk, attesting to the quality, and as soon as Bennett had taken his leave, they celebrated in a much more carnal way. In fact, Luke was the one wearing a turtleneck today. At least the spring weather was still cool.

If Jimmy spent too much time dwelling on the specifics of their celebration, he would end up with a raging erection in a room full of octogenarians, waiting for Luke's son to arrive. Seemed inappropriate on a number of levels. With some effort, he turned his mind down a different path. Like their current location.

"So, is the food here really good?" This seemed an odd place for… anyone without dentures to choose.

"It's not bad. They have great waffles. We used to bring Zach here as a kid, because, well…." Luke made an apologetic hand gesture with his free hand. "It's not expensive. We didn't go out much to eat, and it was one of the few places Kelly and I could afford. Zach's attachment to the place is probably more sentimental than anything."

"That's a nice reason to come." Jimmy looked forward to making their own traditions, but he was more than happy to share in the ones Luke had already created with his son.

"Hey, there he is." Luke waved, but then his fingers tightened around Jimmy's hand. Jimmy turned and froze. Ryan stood beside Zach, the blue streaks in his black hair not distracting from his reddened ears and uncomfortable expression.

Neither of them had seen Ryan since the night he'd tried to get in Luke's pants. They'd agreed to keep Ryan's secret, but Jimmy knew Luke wasn't happy about it. Considering he'd kept the secret of his sexual orientation for so long, Jimmy wasn't a bit surprised that Luke didn't want to keep any more secrets.

AFTER FILLING his plate with food, Jimmy sat next to Luke. "What the hell is that?"

Luke's cheeks took on a rosy hue that lately Jimmy had come to associate with desire, since there was very little Luke had to be embarrassed about.

"Waffles?" Luke didn't sound sure, and yet he must have gotten the plateful of waffles himself.

"Waffles? It looks like ice cream soup. Or Picasso's interpretation of a dessert trolley." Was that pineapple peeping out from underneath the chocolate soft-serve ice cream and syrup? A shudder rippled through him.

Luke shrugged. "I like it."

Jimmy had already figured out his boyfriend had a sweet tooth, but he'd never witnessed Luke eating waffles before.

"Disgusting, isn't it?" Zach commiserated with him. "He's loaded his waffles up like that forever, though."

"Huh."

Ryan's expression didn't change, but then, aside from a mumbled greeting, he hadn't spoken nor had he looked either Jimmy or Luke in the eye. Poor bastard. He'd like to say something, because he really hadn't been as level-headed as he could be the last time he'd seen Ryan, but he sure as hell wasn't about to out Ryan to his best friend Zach.

"You'll just have to get used to it." Luke's words held a hopeful defiance, as though he was hoping Jimmy wasn't going to push.

"Just as long as you don't make me try to eat that, you enjoy your sugar coma."

Luke grinned at him and stuffed a huge bite in his mouth, only to promptly wince and clutch the bridge of his nose.

"Brain freeze? Poor thing." Judging from Zach's guffaw, Jimmy hadn't been quite able to pull off "sympathetic."

He did, however, squeeze Luke's knee under the table. Getting used to everything about Luke sounded like the best job in the world.

After gulping down half a cup of coffee to combat the cold, Luke cleared his throat. "Actually, we have a bit of news."

Zach's gaze popped up from his omelet while Ryan simply flinched.

Luke paused, but no one said anything, not even Jimmy for a change, although he couldn't hold in a wiggle of excitement. Luke had to be the one to share this, and Jimmy wanted to shout it from the rooftops.

"Okay, then. Well, Jimmy and I… we bought a house together. It's… it's perfect."

Luke put a hand over Jimmy's and stroked his fingers, and the bubbly excitement they'd shared since first seeing the place arced between them.

"It is perfect." Jimmy couldn't keep quiet any longer. "Three bedroom side split. It's got two fireplaces and a huge kitchen for your dad. The windows in the kitchen are enormous, and look out onto a cute yard. Your dad wants to plant a garden, and there is a ton of room for that."

Luke spoke as soon as he took a breath. "It'll need a bit of work, but nothing I can't take care of on the weekends."

"And then it will need some decorating help, but, oh, it's got such potential. The backyard will be great for barbecues, and if we're feeling adventurous, there's even room for a pool."

"Seriously, Dad?"

Uh-oh. Zach didn't sound pleased at all. Even Ryan gave him a weird look.

Luke's grip tightened on his hand, and Jimmy shifted his hand so they could clutch at each other.

"What do you mean?" Luke asked.

"You bought a house together? You've known each other for, what, three months? Have you lost your mind?"

Each word licked a stroke of fire across Jimmy's heart. It was true, he and Luke hadn't known each other long. If it came down to it, Luke would choose Zach—as it should be—but he'd thought Zach hadn't minded sharing Luke with a boyfriend. If he lost Luke, his heart might never recover.

"Of course not. I know spending twenty plus years in the closet might indicate I don't know how to make up my own mind, but that's not the case. I've been at loose ends for a couple of years, and Jimmy's the man I want to be with, forever. I have no doubts."

"And what if it all goes tits up? Remember when you and Mom broke up? Even I know that your divorce was probably one of the smoothest on record, but you were both still miserable. Odds are, this time, it'll be an ugly breakup."

"Wow. Your lack of faith in my judgment is astonishing." There was no doubt Luke was a dad, not when he spoke in that tone. "And the assumption that one, Jimmy and I will inevitably break up, and two, that we can't be trusted to be adult about it should it happen, is a bit insulting. Even if you don't know Jimmy well enough, you do know me well enough to know that's not very likely."

Zach rolled his eyes. "If I told you I wanted to move in with a girl I'd known for three months, you'd have a shit."

"Zach." Luke's voice was sharp. "Jimmy's the man I love. He loves me, and we're both at a point in our lives where it would be stupid to play games or wait on someone else's rules. We've both got plenty of life experience, and we know what we want. A house and life together. You, on the other hand, might need more time to make the same decision."

"Are you sure you're not just blinded by the chance to get laid regularly? Your boy toy has you thoroughly snowed. He's an actor, after all."

"Boy toy?" Jimmy had done his best to keep his mouth shut and let Luke handle things, but really. Boy toy?

Zach sneered at him. "He's not rich, you know. If you want a sugar daddy, you should look elsewhere."

Jimmy gasped at the venomous and unexpected attack. Zach knew he was a teacher. Luke, on the other hand, growled.

"You are out of line, Zachary Joshua Jordan."

"No, Dad, you are. You're making a fool of yourself over this guy who is way too young for you."

Ryan glared at Zach as well. Not surprisingly, since Ryan had once thought he'd be happy dating his best friend's father, and that age difference was rather more extreme.

"Dating is one thing. Buying a house? No way. You're an idiot if you think you can keep a guy like this happy. He's probably got a half dozen of you on a string. People are going to laugh at you, dating a guy young enough to be your son."

Jimmy smothered a laugh, but Luke sputtered in anger, furious in a way Jimmy had never seen. He didn't want Luke to say anything he'd regret, because the last thing Jimmy wanted was to be responsible for a rift between Luke and Zach. And really, a lot of the accusations were ones he should be answering anyway.

"Just how old do you think I am, Zach?"

Zach's ire faltered. "Uh, you're around my age, aren't you? Or only a few years older."

Jimmy sighed. Most times he enjoyed how youthful he appeared, but this time it wasn't working in his favor. "It's sweet of you to say so, but I'm thirty-eight. I'm going to be thirty-nine in the fall."

This time, it was Ryan smothering a laugh while Zach was rendered speechless.

"And while some gay men have the faithfulness of a tomcat on the prowl, I am not one of them. I value fidelity and loyalty. I also love your father very much. More than I've ever loved another man. I will take good care of him, and I'm confident we can build a good life together."

Zach's face flushed red, making him and Luke look like a matching set, before he pushed back from the table and ran.

Luke and Ryan both stood, but Jimmy grabbed Ryan's arm and held him back, letting Luke follow Zach out of sight.

"Let them talk."

Ryan sank back reluctantly into his seat.

"I take it you haven't told him yet."

Jimmy's comment prompted Ryan to look at him for the first time, wariness in his eyes.

"No, I can't."

Jimmy signaled for a server.

"Can we get a couple of mimosas please?"

"Of course, sir."

"A mimosa?" Ryan's lips pursed in a little pout like he didn't know what to make of that.

"You're old enough to drink, and a mimosa is the flagship drink of gays at brunch everywhere."

"But...."

Jimmy patted Ryan's hand. The poor kid acted so much younger than Jimmy had at the same age. But then, by the time Jimmy had reached Ryan's age, he'd already come out of the closet, had his dreams of being a Hollywood actor broken, and was well on his way to his second career path. Normally, he looked back on his youth and thought he was a fool, but maybe he'd been fortunate. His choices had let him grow up.

"You're a gay man. Start drinking like one."

Ryan let himself smile, which was Jimmy's intention. He was the last one to encourage gay stereotypes, mostly because he hated that everyone saw him as one. Just because he was one didn't mean he thought they should all be the same.

"And maybe a mimosa or two will ease Zach into the notion that you're gay."

The little smile on Ryan's face disappeared again.

"I can't tell him. And I don't know what to do. Everything's all weird now."

"It's only weird because of your perception. I know for a fact Luke doesn't want you to feel uncomfortable. He doesn't like keeping secrets, especially from his son, but he considers you a son, too."

Ryan covered his face with both hands and groaned. "I can't believe I did that. I'm such an idiot." Ryan's words were muffled by his hands.

The mimosas arrived with startling swiftness; the server must have recognized that the tension at the table needed a little alcoholic diversion. Jimmy glanced at the melted, soggy mess on Luke's plate and handed it to the server to take away.

"C'mon. Have a sip."

Ryan sniffed at the glass before taking a sip. "Oh. That's pretty good."

"Yeah, it is." Jimmy took a sip of his own. The champagne wasn't anywhere near the quality of the stuff he'd had last night, but that's what the orange juice was for.

A glance around the restaurant confirmed Luke and Zach weren't anywhere about, which meant Jimmy was safe to offer what little wisdom he had available to him.

"I've been there, Ryan. I've fallen for a straight guy before, and it sucks. Now, I would never presume to speak for another guy, and I haven't spent a lot of time with Zach, but I'm almost certain he's as straight as the horizon."

Ryan's shoulders sagged, and he huffed out a sigh. "Yeah, I know. And I know Zach won't care if I'm gay, but I'm just afraid if I admit I'm gay, he'll know that I... well, anyway, I'm worried *that's* what will drive him away."

"A little distance might not hurt, you know. Help you move on."

"No. No. Zach's pretty much the only reason I survived puberty. I can't lose him."

Oh, this pain was so much deeper than Jimmy's foolish crushes on straight men. Jimmy understood even more than before why Ryan had been so desperate to substitute Luke, a gay man who already cared for him, into the role of lover. Because it was clear that no matter the status of their romantic entanglement, Ryan would always love Zach. What they needed was to find a way to separate out the "in love" part.

"I still think you need to be honest with Zach, at least about being gay. But have you tried meeting other guys? Guys who maybe could fall for you, too?"

Ryan shook his head sadly. "Not really. Zach and I are roommates, and most times we go out together. Although I have more time on my hands now than he does, since he's going for a postgraduate degree."

"Good. Then between me and Luke, maybe we can at least introduce you to some other guys, ones who can become friends even if nothing else comes of it. Because, kid, I think you're headed for a serious meltdown if you can't figure out how to fall out of love with him."

Ducking his head, Ryan dabbed at his eyes. Poor kid. When he lifted his head, his eyes were still shiny, but otherwise there was no hint he'd been near tears.

"Thanks," Ryan whispered and began to nibble at his food.

Jimmy wolfed down his food before it got completely icy.

"Congratulations on the house." Ryan picked up his half-empty mimosa and lifted it in a toast. Jimmy grinned, hiding his discomfort over Zach's reaction, and picked up his own to clink against Ryan's.

"Think Zach will come around?" Because if he didn't... would Luke change his mind? The papers were signed and all, but getting out of the contract wasn't impossible, just expensive. Jimmy didn't care about the money, but the house was perfect, and he could see growing old there with Luke.

"Yeah, I think so."

Jimmy hadn't thought there would be any opposition from Zach, since he was a grown man, but he didn't think it would be appropriate to discuss the reasons why with Ryan. If things didn't clear up, Luke would tell him what he needed to know.

A few minutes later, Zach and Luke returned to their seats, Zach appearing abashed but no longer spitting venom.

"I'm sorry, Jimmy. I shouldn't have said what I said. I mean, about you. I still think you guys are rushing it."

"Zach." Luke's tone was sharp and masterful. Jimmy might try and copy it in the classroom, although he usually managed to keep the ravening hordes under control.

"Dad, I'm allowed to have an opinion on this. And I'm an adult. I don't have to agree with you. I think you should wait. But I know my opinion isn't going to carry any weight. But I was wrong to attack you, Jimmy, and I'm sorry."

"Thank you." Not what Jimmy hoped for, but it could be worse. Luke wasn't thrilled either, but he bit his lip against another outburst. Besides, Zach's words only proved he was his father's son, blunt and honest as possible. No game playing.

"Where'd my waffles go?"

Luke's plaintive question eased the tension, the laughter a little more raucous than the question deserved, Jimmy laughing the loudest. He was an actor, for God's sake. He could make the rest of the world believe he wasn't teetering on the edge of panic, because Luke wouldn't appreciate a public scene.

The rest of the meal passed without incident, but Jimmy couldn't stop worrying that Luke's eagerness to live with him had been tainted by Zach's reaction. Couldn't stop turning scenarios over in his mind, none of which seemed to end well for their relationship.

IT WASN'T often that Luke was glad to see the back of his son, but brunch had been more tense than he'd anticipated. They'd had spats before—almost impossible not to—but this one had blindsided him. He'd thought his son, the one who'd told him he needed get on with his life, would have been happy for him. And as far as he knew, Zach was happy that he'd found Jimmy, and liked Jimmy, but something about buying a house together put a hair up his butt, and only time would get him over it.

One look at Jimmy in the passenger seat was enough to know he'd been bothered by it, even though he'd seemed almost normal in the restaurant. One slender finger picked at a ragged piece of vinyl that had curled up beside the door handle as he stared out of the window. Worse than that, though, the entire car ride to Luke's apartment had been silent. Jimmy was so rarely silent. Or still. Aside from those grueling few weeks at the beginning of their relationship, Jimmy was almost like a live electrical wire, bouncing and spitting with all that untapped energy. Made the sex hotter than hot, and it was probably the only reason he'd survived Dramageddon, as Jimmy had taken to calling that vortex of hell when he'd been working, performing, and coaching.

They were supposed to start packing nonessentials today. Do a little bit of celebrating in between packing the boxes. With Jimmy in this funk, Luke had no idea how the rest of the day was going to pan out. He couldn't fault his son for having his own opinion, but he was more than mildly irritated that his son wasn't supportive of one of the biggest milestones of his life, and definitely the biggest one since divorcing Kelly. Disheartening, in fact, when he'd assumed Zach's support after finding out he was gay wouldn't ever waver.

In silence, they parked the car and rode the elevator up to his floor. Luke spent the whole time wondering if he should pretend everything was okay or if he should just rip the bandage off, damn the hairs and skin.

Outside the apartment, they paused. Luke had hoped Jimmy would use his key like he lived there, like he'd been doing for weeks now. Instead, he stood there in a daze, a million miles away.

Luke reached around him to open the door. After hanging up his coat and the rainbow scarf he loved wearing, even though it was going to be too warm soon, he turned to take Jimmy's jacket, only to see Jimmy standing at the kitchen counter, still bundled up and looking as disconsolate as he'd been the whole ride home.

Nope. No pretending everything was okay. He walked over and gently coaxed Jimmy out of his coat. He didn't move a step while Luke hung up the coat.

"Jimmy." Luke didn't know what to say.

"Luke. We can still back out. We'll lose some money, but we don't have to buy that house."

The words were like a fist in his stomach, and yet, they weren't entirely unexpected.

"Is that what you want?" Luke could barely spit out the words, but it was only fair he ask. After all, it was his son who'd put a wrench in the works. Luke should have known happiness of this magnitude was too good to last.

Jimmy twisted his head away and didn't answer. Luke's breath came fast and shallow, making his head swim. He swayed, and brunch threatened to make a return trip. Breaking the contract on the house and losing money was nothing next to the thought that Jimmy might be throwing in the towel on the two of them entirely.

Forcing himself to breathe deeply and slowly, Luke's equilibrium returned, and with it, some of his logical faculties. If breaking up was best for Jimmy, Luke would do it in a heartbeat, without a single grudge, even if it flayed his soul to pieces. But they were good together, better as a whole than they were apart and separate. Giving that up didn't seem logical or wise.

He hated not knowing the answers, he hated that he was exploring uncharted waters and most of all he hated how uncertain that made him.

"Jimmy?" His mouth was dry as dust, the word cracked and crumbling.

Jimmy grasped the counter, his fingers as pale as death, and Luke knew they'd be freezing cold. Jimmy's discomfort was enough to snap him out of his trance. In one swift move, he spun Jimmy around and held his icy hands to his chest, using his own bigger hands to warm them. The shock of the maneuver was enough to get Jimmy to look at him, eyes filled with pain and tears.

"I don't want to cause problems between you and Zach." Jimmy's voice wobbled, and Luke squeezed his hands tighter. His vibrant, frenetic lover, who felt things so intensely.

"I love you, Jimmy. So much. My son will get over this, and even if he doesn't, it's not his decision." Luke bit his lip for a second. Was his son the only issue, or had the foundation of their relationship cracked and Luke hadn't noticed? "I may never have been in love before, but there is no doubt in my mind that we're solid, and we can make it through whatever comes our way. But if you don't feel the same way… then, yes. It's better we know now."

If Jimmy said they were done, Luke was going to have to find the strength—somehow—to loosen his grip on Jimmy's hands.

Jimmy's eyelids dropped, and a couple of tears escaped. He sucked in a great, shuddery breath and opened his eyes again.

"I love you, too, Luke. I want to live with you in our perfect house that we picked out together and—"

Jimmy slammed their lips together and pushed Luke back against the fridge.

The sudden aggression stunned Luke for as long as it took his cock to fill with blood. Opening his hands became a simple matter when the alternative was to fill his grip with the solid, muscular cheeks of Jimmy's ass.

And once they'd recovered from this, they were going to tell the rest of their friends and family, hope they took it better than Zach had.

CHAPTER 10

THE TOPOGRAPHY of both their apartments had changed to a mountainscape of boxes over the past month. It was a pain, for sure, but worth it. Jimmy couldn't fucking wait. Aside from Zach, the rest of their friends and family trusted that even after a short time dating, they were old enough to know their own minds. It still bothered Jimmy a bit, but Zach had been very adult about it, thankfully, and Luke was determined to plow on regardless.

The timing of the move couldn't be better either. He'd have all summer to putter around the house, helping Luke get it ready and decorating it. Sure, he had rehearsals for his next play, but this wasn't the first time he'd be playing Hamlet, so it shouldn't even be that stressful. Even though Luke said summer was a lot busier for him, Jimmy knew they'd be fine. Maybe Jimmy would figure out how to cook for Luke. Or at least find better delivery food than Chinese and pizza.

He'd moved a few times in his life, and he much preferred their plan of packing together, instead of tackling each of their apartments alone. Then he realized Luke was no longer singing in the living room but had moved into the bedroom.

"Oh, no. No way." Jimmy left his half-packed box in the kitchen and ran into the bedroom. He skidded to a stop in the doorway. "Whatcha doing?"

"Nothing. Just looking for a change of pace."

"Uh-huh. I bet you were packing your embarrassing stuff."

Luke laughed. "I told you, I don't have any embarrassing stuff."

Jimmy stamped a foot. "You have to have embarrassing stuff. Everyone does." Jimmy had thought he'd been beyond embarrassment until Luke had unearthed a box of sex toys. Toys themselves weren't so bad, but one year Damian had decided to throw him a dildo birthday party, and everyone had brought the most outrageous dildos they could find. It had seemed a shame to throw them away, even though he was never, ever going to use any of them. Plain and simple, like the ones in his bedside table, were more his style, toy-wise. He'd boxed them up and shoved them in the back of his closet.

Once Jimmy had convinced Luke he wasn't interested in test-driving the foot long "ass rammer" on either of them, Luke had found them utterly hilarious, and Jimmy found out he wasn't quite as world-weary as he thought.

"Not me." Luke's grin, though, was decidedly naughty. And he'd just realized Luke had a hand behind his back.

Jimmy advanced. "What are you hiding?" If it was something embarrassing, he was going to tease Luke for months after all the comments about how Luke could never measure up to Jimmy's box of boyfriends.

He pounced and tried to wrestle Luke's arm from behind him, but even laughing his ass off, Luke was way stronger.

"Damn it." Jimmy backed off with a theatrical pout—might as well go with what he was good at. "Show me. It's embarrassing. It's got to be."

Luke licked his lips, eyes darkening, and now Jimmy really wanted to know what he was hiding.

"It's not embarrassing. I think you'll have to demonstrate how best to use it before it'll be embarrassing."

With a magician's flourish, Luke was suddenly brandishing a slender glass dildo with a bright ribbon of royal blue swirled through it.

Jimmy's breath caught in his throat and blood raced south.

"Out of the blue, I was thinking of you...." Luke's wicked smile kicked Jimmy's pulse into the stratosphere. God, he loved this man more than life.

"You want to test it now?" Between the throb of his cock, the insistent bulge behind Luke's fly, and the thought of showing Luke how a toy like that could add another dimension to their already spectacular sex life, Jimmy was amazed he could put together a coherent sentence, but they'd both been working hard for a few hours.

"I'm a little sweaty."

Luke advanced with purpose.

"I like your sweat." He tossed the dildo on the bed, yanked Jimmy's T-shirt over his head, and licked him from nipple to ear.

"I like you dirty."

Jimmy had no breath to speak, his cock pulsing in his pants, and he shivered, hard, at Luke's words.

"Now, get me sweaty and show me what a dirty boy you are."

An unmanly whimper escaped Jimmy as precum dampened his briefs. How the fuck did he get so lucky?

FRESHLY SHOWERED, Luke lay on the bed dozing while Jimmy continued to putter around packing. They'd made good progress, and they still had another month before closing. Although they'd both had to break the leases on their apartments, they'd arranged to keep their apartments for two weeks after closing to give them plenty of time to move stuff out.

Luke wasn't sure he was going to be useful for anything for the rest of the day. If he'd known how much fun dildos could be, he'd have bought one sooner. Then again, having Jimmy showing him and sharing with him made it special and so fucking hot they should have charred the sheets.

Jimmy's phone rang, and drowsy, Luke listened to the soothing cadence of Jimmy's voice. The discussion was rather lengthy, or at least it seemed so in his drowsy state. Until the tone changed, became sharper and harder. Luke sat up in bed. This wasn't a regular phone call.

By the time he found his boxers and pulled them on, Jimmy had returned, face pale like he'd seen a monster.

"What's wrong?" Luke bounded over to Jimmy and gripped his shoulders with both hands. "Who was that? Are your parents okay? The family?"

Jimmy shook his head. "No, I mean, they're fine. It's not that."

Luke was going to shake his boyfriend if he didn't spit it out. "Jimmy, you're killing me here. What's wrong?"

"Uh, that was a director."

"A director? Damian, you mean?" Damian often cast Jimmy in the plays he was directing, including the upcoming *Hamlet*, and despite Damian's penchant for calling Luke the "throat-sucker" in the few times the three of them had met for drinks, Jimmy swore up and down he could be a vicious taskmaster. Luke didn't see it, but he didn't know Damian well. Jimmy's friend from school, Karen? Karen, Luke could see as a strict disciplinarian.

"No, a Hollywood director."

"Okay. I have no idea what that means."

"I need to sit down."

Luke knew what that meant, at least. He led Jimmy into the living room, cleared the sofa of the half-packed boxes, packing tape, and box cutters. The second he was done, Jimmy flopped bonelessly into the cushions.

"Jimmy, you're freaking me out." He tried to keep his voice level, but it wasn't easy.

"Sorry. Sorry. It's just sinking in, you know?"

His nostrils flared in annoyance. "No, I don't know. You haven't told me." Another few minutes of this, and he'd just grab Jimmy's phone and dial the last number.

Jimmy took a deep breath. "*Walking Wounded* was optioned for a movie. I think I remember telling you that."

Luke nodded. Jimmy had been pleased that the playwright was getting well-deserved recognition, and he'd been thrilled that he'd had a chance to play the role before future productions were shut down in favor of the movie option.

"Apparently, the director got ahold of the recorded version we did, and they want me to play Gary."

A movie role? "Seriously? They want you to act in a movie? That's awesome." Luke hugged Jimmy, who didn't move, who remained stiff in his arms like a bundle of sticks.

"Yeah, I guess so."

This didn't make any sense. The pieces of this puzzle weren't falling into place. A movie role was something Jimmy had always wanted. He'd already played Gary to wild critical success. Why wasn't he bouncing around like he'd been electrified?

Jimmy sighed. "I'd have to be in Los Angeles two days after closing on the house, at the latest. Production's expected to take two months, but they want me to be there another two months for publicity and in case there are unexpected delays in filming."

Oh. Two days after closing. "Okay. So, yeah, the timing sucks."

"Maybe the universe is trying to tell us something."

Luke frowned. "The universe? What are you talking about?"

"Zach still doesn't think we should be buying this house. Now I got this opportunity. Maybe it's a sign."

"A sign we shouldn't live together? I don't think the universe gives a fuck, and when did you start believing in signs?"

"I'm an actor. We're a superstitious lot."

Luke snorted. "You're also a biology teacher. A melodramatic one, to be sure."

Jimmy gave him a hard look. "Why aren't you upset about this?"

"Upset because you're going to be able to fulfill a dream? What kind of shitty boyfriend would that make me? You'll be gone four months, we can probably visit each other if our schedules allow, we can definitely call, and I'll keep myself busy getting the house ready for your extraordinary decorating skills." Summer was a busy time for construction, and Luke wouldn't find it easy to take time off, but maybe Jimmy would have chunks of time in the shooting schedule where he could come back home.

The brittle bundle of sticks began to soften into the Jimmy he was more familiar with. "You'd be okay with that?"

"Of course I would." He'd hate every second away from Jimmy, but how fantastic that Jimmy was getting a second chance at a dream? "What about your job? The teaching one, I mean."

Because that was a lot less flexible than the playhouse, even if Jimmy liked the theater better.

"I'd have to take an unpaid leave of absence. Probably just a semester."

"Unpaid?"

Jimmy shrugged. "Amazingly, the pay I'd be getting for the movie will be more than enough to cover my salary, plus getting a short-term apartment in Los Angeles, plus my half of the house expenses, and leave some left over."

Luke couldn't help it. He started laughing, and Jimmy's confused stare only made it all funnier.

"I can't wait," he gasped out, "to tell Zach I'm going to be your boy toy."

It took a second for Jimmy to absorb the joke, but he laughed, sweet and happy, and the last of his worry seemed to melt away.

When they were both recovering, Luke wrapped an arm around Jimmy's narrow shoulders. "I'm not lying, it will be hard. But we're strong. Four months out of the rest of our lives is nothing, right?"

Jimmy smiled at him. "Right. Guess I'll call them back and tell them yes."

LUKE AND Jimmy stopped by the house the day before Jimmy's flight. Since they didn't have to leave their apartments on the same day as closing, Luke had suggested they leave the house empty for a week so he could easily work the most pressing tasks. Which meant there wouldn't be any furniture in their new house before he left for Los Angeles.

Jimmy's bags were packed. He'd been on the edge of crying for days, even when they'd signed the final paperwork to make the house theirs. In a week, Luke would supervise moving their stuff in, and then sleep alone in their home. It was fucking killing him that they weren't going to share that experience, that first night in the home they'd bought together.

Luke had wanted Jimmy to come by, see it before he left, maybe give Luke a few pointers for things he wanted done. Make notes, maybe. It was times like this that Jimmy wanted to shriek in frustration about how logical and practical his boyfriend—his partner—was. It made sense, it really did, but Jimmy had never done this before, and this was so not how he imagined it. Sometimes, he even dreaded the thought of getting on that plane.

Many times, he'd picked up the phone, intending to call and say he couldn't do it. But then Luke would tell him how proud he was, how wonderful it would be, how talented Jimmy was. Maybe it made him a bad person, but the praise gave him the courage to keep on with the plan. And it was only four months. Four months would be over in the blink of an eye, and Jimmy could erase that niggling shame of having failed so absolutely when he was younger.

Jimmy sighed.

"You okay?" Luke gave him a hug and kissed him on the temple as they stood in the driveway.

"I guess. This just isn't how I imagined these first few days. You'll send me pictures of stuff you're doing, right?"

Luke shrugged. "I can. Most of the stuff won't be too interesting. Not at first."

"I don't fucking care. I want to see." Jimmy already had the pout, all he needed was a shrill whine and a foot stamp before he was officially in childish tantrum territory, but this was their home, and he was leaving Luke to deal with all the hard work.

"Then I'll send you pictures."

"Are you sure? I can still cancel."

"I think this is what's called cold feet. You'll be fabulous, everything will be fine, and we'll be just as strong in four months as we are now. Besides, don't tell me you wouldn't make some of these repairs harder." Luke lifted his eyebrows, because they well knew he might be able to deftly wield a scalpel on a fetal pig, but he didn't know the first thing about power tools. The odds of him fucking up while learning were pretty damn good.

"C'mon. I've got a tape measure and a pad of paper. We'll start in the basement and work our way up." Luke laced their fingers together and pulled him into the house. If he hadn't been so despondent, he might have assumed Luke was being deliberately provocative with the innuendo.

A couple of hours later, they were ready to head up to the bedrooms, and despite the fact he hadn't had much of an appetite since taking the so-called role of a lifetime, he was getting a little hungry.

"There wasn't anything in the bedrooms, was there? I mean, just painting, right? We could head out and grab some dinner."

Honestly, Jimmy wasn't sure if he'd be able to keep from crying if he had to wander through the bedroom he wasn't going to be able to share with Luke until some nebulous future visit, assuming he was even able to return for a visit before his four-month commitment in Hollywood was up. This should be the most exciting time in his life, and all he could focus what he was missing out on at home.

"Just a quick run through and then we can get some dinner." Luke gave him a little swat on the ass with his notebook, and Jimmy mock glared before sucking it up and going upstairs. He headed to the master bedroom first, to get it over and done with, give him a little time to recover before he'd have to be a functioning dinner companion.

He stood on the threshold, the evening sun lighting dust motes in the air.

"Go on," Luke said softly, and pushed him gently into the room.

Jimmy stumbled into the room and immediately his eyes welled up. Luke had set up an air mattress with blue bedding, flanked by a pair of electric hurricane lanterns. A cooler and picnic basket sat on the floor by the closet.

He turned to Luke. "What?"

"We have to spend our first night in the house together."

Jimmy sniffed and did his best not to let the tears fall. This was why Luke was perfect for him. They weren't carbon copies of the other, but the important things? Those were the same.

"I'm sorry." Jimmy's voice wavered, and he scrubbed his cheeks with the back of his hands. "It's perfect. Thank you. I'm not crying again, I swear."

Luke's eyes were a little shiny, and he drew Jimmy close. "I don't mind you crying, you know. You know I like honest, and I like that you feel as intensely as I do about us."

Yeah, he felt things intensely. So much so that he'd been afraid the past few days he was going to crumble into jagged shards every time he thought about getting on that plane and leaving Luke behind.

"Is that dinner in there?" Jimmy pointed at the cooler and basket. Luke smiled and let him change the subject, although he hoped Luke's preparations had included tissues, because he suspected there would be some ugly crying sandwiched between eating and sex.

"Yep. Nothing fancy, but I didn't think either of us would be up to dealing with a lot of people."

"Thank you." He teetered on the brink of sobbing his eyes out just about every other minute; not worrying about making a scene would make these last few hours with Luke a lot less stressful.

Jimmy frowned. "Where the fuck did you get a picnic basket?" Even if he hadn't spent the past month helping Luke pack up all his shit, he'd never have taken Luke as a man who owned a picnic basket. The cooler he'd seen before, and was more in keeping with the Luke he knew. Unless it was some weird holdover in storage from having a kid, like the safari ice packs.

"Bennett had one. I borrowed it from him."

That made more sense.

They sat on the mattress, and Luke began pulling dinner out of the two containers, all of it homemade. Jimmy was going to miss Luke's cooking, too. His eyes started burning again, so he drew in a deep breath and did what he did best—talk.

"Bennett's a weird dude, isn't he? I mean, he's an electrician and all, total blue collar, but he's still got the air of a rich guy clinging to him."

"Yep. His parents have money. He knows all kinds of 'society' people, politicians, high-powered lawyers, all that, but he's just not interested in that life. He says his family didn't have any trouble with him being gay, but choosing to be an electrician was difficult for them."

That drew an unwilling laugh from Jimmy. "I can't hardly imagine that conversation, can you? Coming out as an *electrician*. Oh, the shame."

Luke laughed. "I know. He does a lot of independent work, but when he takes jobs on big sites, he feels like he has to keep the gay *and* the rich under wraps."

Jimmy could almost see a skit, where being an electrician had the same stigma in certain circles as being gay. Of course, in this case, it was Bennett's choice, but Jimmy suspected part of the choice was the chance to metaphorically flip the bird to his folks. Probably he shouldn't judge, but he couldn't imagine being particularly passionate about working with wires all day.

"So, you know, this stuff will all keep," Luke said. "We could stop talking about Bennett and christen the new place. In here at least. We can wait until you're back to work our way through the other rooms."

Sex first? Jimmy could agree with that. He stood and began slowly stripping. If nothing else, he was going to make sure Luke didn't forget him.

CHAPTER 11

JIMMY SAT in a chair in the corner, hoping no one would see him. He was utterly overwhelmed and thoroughly humiliated. How was it possible that he felt more out of place now, as a mature man and accomplished stage actor, than when he'd been knocking on doors for a year after high school?

He snorted softly to himself. Probably he was too stupid to know better. Picking up his phone, he checked the time. If he texted Luke again, his boyfriend would think he'd totally flipped his lid. But the bustle in this place was crazy. Just as in a play, there were far more people required for a production than the actors, but the vibe was completely different.

Then again, maybe he was in a rut. This was supposed to the role of a lifetime. He could enjoy it. Somehow. Soon.

He glanced down at the papers in his hand. His first interaction today had been to be belittled by an assistant who clearly thought he was a moron because he had no idea where he was supposed to be on his first day. She'd led him to a minigym where a fitness expert and a nutritionist delivered a scathing lecture on the evils of food, alcohol, and sitting down. According to the documents, the only things he'd be allowed to do aside from filming were work out and eat pocket lint. Or sawdust. Some plywood for fiber. While standing. Or jogging. Nothing with taste or calories, apparently, given the number of times "celery" had been emphasized. They'd set up a grueling workout schedule in the process of telling him, indirectly, that he was a fat-ass slug who would probably waste their time. Apparently the director, who'd called Jimmy "perfect" for the role had a somewhat different definition of perfect than Jimmy had.

The first two hours had been spent performing various fitness tests and enduring being poked and pinched and weighed and tsked over. Apparently, the trainer—Roland, a muscular man whose face was set in a permanent disapproving scowl—had worked on one of those weight-loss reality shows. Finding out he was personally taking on Jimmy's "training" as a favor to the director to "quickly whip him into shape" was probably the most terrifying thing Jimmy had ever heard. At least he'd updated his will when he and Luke bought the house. With nothing more than a lifelong nodding acquaintance with the gym as he walked past it to buy a latte, Jimmy was pretty sure he was going to die under Roland's tutelage.

At least he wouldn't have to worry about the celery overdose. Yuck.

They'd left him feeling fat, stupid, and utterly alone in the midst of an open sitting area positively bustling with people, and no idea what he was supposed to do next, or who he was supposed to see. Maybe he *was* stupid because he didn't even know how to find the front desk of the studio or the assistant's office.

Wiping his damp palms on his pants, he stood and shoved his "food journal" and schedule from hell into his back pocket. Food was a unifier; he'd head to craft services and hang out by the food. Surely he could meet someone that way, and hopefully they'd be someone he could latch the fuck on to as a guide dog. The playhouse was tiny by comparison, entire sets constrained by having to remain in a single stationary building, but here, everything was so big.

Jimmy groaned at the food offerings. Pastries weren't the only items available, but after the past few ego-demolishing hours, they took up, in his opinion, more than their fair share of table space. At the end of the table, he spied a few of the things on his depressingly short list of "can eat."

He snapped a quick pic of the assorted baked goods with his phone to text to Luke.

This is the first thing I saw after being told I'm fat and need to watch what I eat. Of course, I want to eat ALL the pastries.

The tone wasn't quite as light as he'd have liked, but he thought he managed to appear slightly upbeat and not one step from heading back to his rental and burying himself under the covers with a pint of ice cream and tears.

He only had to wait a few seconds for a response, and it was everything he could hope for.

You're not fat. You're gorgeous. Perfect. Who said that?

Trainer. Nutritionist. I'm on a "schedule" until filming is done. It's Hollywood. And getting in better shape is a good thing, right?

He didn't want Luke getting bent out of shape, but the unexpected blow to his self-esteem had him needing reassurance.

It is a good thing, but if anyone calls you fat, I'll come out there and punch them. :) Love you. Gotta run.

He grinned and gently stroked the words on his phone.

Love you, too.

"James Alexander?"

Jimmy turned at the unfamiliar address. He'd been told in no uncertain terms that he'd be billed and referred to as James, not Jimmy, and the name suited him about as well as purple skinny jeans on a leather bear.

"Hi, I'm Aaron."

"Aaron." Jimmy squeaked out the name. He didn't need an introduction to Aaron Young, his co-star. In a few short years, Aaron had made quite a name for himself in several action movies as a beta male turned accidental hero. It suited his willowy stature and almost pretty face. The character in *Walking Wounded* would see Aaron playing completely against the archetype he'd created for himself, but it was that very success coupled with his recent coming out that had been the impetus behind the film.

Although neither of them was particularly muscular, the differences in their coloring would provide a striking contrast. Aaron had dark everything compared to Jimmy's pale blondness. Dark brown eyes, black hair, black lashes that extended for miles, and smooth caramel skin. The age difference between their characters, with Jimmy playing Gary, the older, closeted man coming out for a younger man, was fifteen years. Jimmy wasn't quite that much older than Aaron, but he also knew he'd never have been chosen for the role if he didn't look damned good for his age. Hollywood could be a little ageist.

"It's great to meet you. I'm looking forward to working with you."

They shook hands, and Jimmy's breath came fast and shallow. *Aaron Young* had just shaken his *hand* and was *looking forward* to working with him.

"Whoa, slow down there. Don't want to hyperventilate on the first day. Let's save that for the days we're shooting naked scenes."

Jimmy nodded, and then Aaron's words trickled into his brain and took root. "Naked?" He didn't remember naked, but then, he'd let the entertainment lawyer Damian knew take care of everything. Probably he should have asked more questions.

"Yeah, naked. I didn't get a chance to watch your whole performance, but didn't you perform the love scenes nude on stage?"

Setting down the plate of food he'd just picked out, because he couldn't fucking concentrate on keeping it horizontal, Jimmy swiped a bottle of water and gulped half of it down, hoping to moisten his desert-dry throat.

Aaron stood with a kindly smile and allowed Jimmy the time to compose himself.

"Uh, no." Jimmy squeezed the half-empty water bottle. "I mean, we did the sex scenes, but very chaste. The nudity was implied. I take it the script calls for...."

"Haven't read it all the way through, have you?"

Jimmy shrugged. "They said it didn't deviate much from the play, actually, so I only skimmed it." Again, details he probably should have verified with Matthew the entertainment lawyer. The part of Gary was so poignant and could have so easily been him—and probably had been similar enough to Luke's life to make him uncomfortable—that he could get up on stage and perform the entire play from start to finish without prompting, even though it had been months since his last performance. He took another sip.

"Nude, you say?" His tone was far from nonchalant, but he hoped Aaron couldn't hear the terror.

"Well, not completely nude, no. They make sure we're not actually cock to cock."

Jimmy choked and sputtered, Aaron's blunt words making him inhale his water instead of swallowing it.

"Okay, good. That's good."

Aaron frowned. "Not that it matters, because you played the role so well, but I thought you were gay. A little cock between two gay men shouldn't be an issue."

"I don't know about you, but my cock's not little." Jimmy clapped a hand over his mouth. That was the sort of response he'd make if he were in a bar trying to pick up a guy, not at his work place for God's sake.

Fortunately, Aaron snickered instead of being offended, or even worse, thinking Jimmy had been trying to get in his pants. Aaron was gorgeous, no doubt, and so far he seemed super nice, but Jimmy was done with other men. Luke was it for him.

"I guess I walked right into that one."

Jimmy's star-struck social paralysis broke, and he put the water bottle down on the table so he could gesture properly. "I am gay, just newly in a relationship, is all."

"Oh, yeah?" Aaron grimaced and a flash of hurt crossed his face. "That's nice."

"I, uh, take it you're not seeing anyone."

Aaron shrugged. "It's not exactly a state secret that I just came out. But I'd been in a relationship before. He finally got sick of watching me pretend, seeing me on the television at events he felt—rightly—he should have been attending at my side."

This was a lot of personal information coming at him from a virtual stranger, and a famous one at that, but the easy camaraderie soothed Jimmy's nerves. Maybe that had been his intention, or maybe he believed getting to know each other would make the—oh, God—*naked* scenes more comfortable. Either way, Jimmy relaxed and asked the same question he'd ask of anyone who'd dropped that load of information on him.

"He broke up with you, I take it?"

The pain appeared to be a living, breathing monster inside Aaron, and Jimmy hurt for him.

"Yep. Getting dumped made me come out. Not right away, though, and by the time I did, it was too late. He's moved on, and I have to figure out how to deal with that."

Jimmy laid a comforting hand on Aaron's forearm, hoping that sort of casual touch would be acceptable. "I'm really sorry."

Aaron shook his head ruefully. "Thanks. Sorry, I guess you weren't expecting that upon our first meeting."

"Hey, this whole thing will be easier if we're friends, right?"

"Yeah. And I have to say, since I came out, I find I sometimes have a hard time harnessing my inner thoughts as well as I used to."

Jimmy laughed. "I guess you just broke the seal, and now everything's gushing out. My partner is exactly the same way. He was married for just over twenty years, came out a few years ago. Blunt as hell." Blunt was probably the wrong word, but close enough, since Luke didn't like prevaricating or mind games.

"Want to grab some lunch, somewhere else? I can show you around after."

Fucking amazing. Aaron Young was just a regular, friendly guy who didn't seem arrogant or stuck up at all. And Jimmy wasn't stupid. He immediately agreed, although, could Aaron Young just "go out for lunch" without getting mobbed by fans? Then again, maybe in LA he could.

Sighing, he pulled his paperwork from his pocket and brandished his new instructions, the humiliation still fresh. "Sounds good, but my lunch options are limited."

"Yeah, that can be depressing as hell, since the majority of the craft services stuff isn't on the list."

"How do you know?" Aaron Young was in great shape and probably didn't get lectured and shamed by a fitness expert and nutritionist together.

Aaron laughed. "I've got that list memorized by now. Don't worry, there are a number of restaurants we can eat at that will have plenty to choose from."

"Okay, then, lead the way."

They spent the next couple of hours walking around the set and the studio before grabbing some lunch, and then doing it again. By the time Jimmy stumbled back to his tiny sublet apartment, he didn't care what was on his list. The stress, full day, and time change made him too fucking tired to eat, and he had to get up early to meet the trainer anyway.

"CUT!"

Jimmy blinked. He and Aaron had each spoken one line of dialogue. One. From the middle of the play. Film. Whatever. He'd spent several preproduction days letting his trainer work him into a limp, broken thing in between rehearsals that seemed to little more than blocking exercises. Not that Jimmy's memory was all that clear on the matter. Between the lack of food and his screaming, knotted muscles, Jimmy's entire focus had been standing without assistance and not screaming every time he moved.

The only thing that had been clear through it all was his yearning for Luke. It wasn't just the sex he was missing, which quite frankly might be more agonizing in practice than in fantasy right now, no matter how often his cock hardened when he thought about getting naked with Luke. But Jimmy missed Luke's smile. The little brushes of his fingertips along Jimmy's nape. His encouragement. Kisses. Cuddling in front of the television or in bed. The way he lovingly soaped Jimmy up when they shared a shower. The way he worried about Jimmy eating properly and his cooking. Oh, God, the food. He wanted to lie down and wallow in pans and pans of Luke's lasagna.

And now, after waiting hours for makeup and getting cameras and set dressing and... he was so exhausted. It was all a blur, but he'd been here for hours today, after days of torture, and he managed to spit out one single line before the director stopped them. He should be grateful, he supposed. After all, Sam McKenzie, the director, had been the main reason Jimmy had the opportunity to pursue this dream. Only problem was that the director was a giant asshat. Damian had been a demanding director, but he'd never screamed obscenities at anyone. Jimmy found this more like a nightmare than a dream, and he hoped to God it got better than this.

With some effort, he pasted a smile on his face and turned to Sam.

"Too much, James. Gotta dial that shit back. You're going to be a movie star. Stop hamming it up."

Jimmy clenched his teeth together. Once again, he should be grateful that Sam hadn't devolved into a screaming, red-faced imp, but hamming it up? He'd never once had a critic accuse him of ham.

Aaron smiled sympathetically.

Jimmy took a few deep breaths, hoping to stave off this sensation of being so fragile he was going to shatter. He knew damn well stage and film were different. He just hadn't fully comprehended how difficult it would be to tone down every single line he uttered. Tone down every single movement and every single expression. He'd discussed it briefly with Aaron, but since Aaron had very little experience on stage and Jimmy had never done anything in front of a camera before, besides auditions, neither of them had any clear idea how to make the transition.

"Ready?" The director only had a faint sneer in his voice, and Jimmy nodded. He had to do better.

This time, Jimmy was ready, but it was fucking hard to be in the mindset of someone who already stifled their sexuality and desires deep in a closet. Blunting his movement and expression was like being in a crawlspace behind a secret panel in that closet. He was a good actor, for fuck's sake. He could do this shit.

This time, they got through a whole six lines of conversation before the director stopped them.

"What was wrong with that?" he whispered to Aaron, who smirked.

"Nothing. They're switching camera angles, setting up a new shot."

"Take two. James, that last time was good. Do it again."

Again. He could do it again. Somehow.

After an hour or so, they took a break. Jimmy had stopped counting how many takes they'd done of those same few lines. Hitting ten had been too damn depressing, since it was clear that sadist, Sam, wasn't ready to let them move on.

"What do we do now? How long do we have?" It wasn't like he could eat anything. Or more like, it wasn't like he should eat anything. The nutritionist was a weedy little lurker, and every time Jimmy even thought about sneaking a danish or even a fucking bagel, he was there, glacially disapproving without a word. Jimmy hadn't felt like a guilty kid this often since he'd *been* a guilty kid.

Aaron shrugged. "Mostly I just take a leak, find a comfortable chair and a cup of coffee. It won't be long enough to take a nap or for Roland to come find you."

Jimmy blanched. "For Roland to come *find* me?"

"Sure. This early on, he'll grab you during the longer breaks and make you do stretches or lunges or something."

Not if Jimmy locked himself in the bathroom, he wouldn't. Still, hitting the bathroom seemed like a good idea and then… "Hey! They let you have coffee?"

Aaron smirked and brought his arm up, fist tightly clenched to show off a bulging bicep. He flicked the hard muscle with his other hand. "I'm already perfect, baby. Coffee is my reward for good behavior."

Jimmy rolled his eyes. Suddenly, it wasn't difficult to understand why actors got hooked on drugs. Drugs had no fucking calories.

"Sometimes, I'll go over my lines for upcoming scenes."

Shit. Jimmy didn't need any help with his fucking lines. They'd practically burned themselves into his psyche. Maybe he could wander around some of the other sets during longer breaks. See other actors in action.

Before he knew it, they were back in the same position, with the same few lines.

AGAIN. JIMMY grew to hate that word over the next six hours. Each time the director uttered the words cut or again, it was like being flogged. Or flayed. He was pretty sure there were people who liked being flogged, even though he was not one of them, but he didn't think anyone enjoyed being flayed. That one had to be worse.

Over and over and over again. He could have run through the entire play three times in the time it took to slog through two pages of script. He was in hell. Or the *Twilight Zone*. Those were the only possible, logical explanations.

"Good job." Aaron clapped him on the back.

"Thanks. You, too." Jimmy said it, but quite frankly, he had no idea if either of them had done a good job. They'd gone through the same lines so often, they'd become complete and utter gibberish to Jimmy's ears. He'd put in a grueling day without even one smatter of applause, and having those great black eyes of the cameras on him wasn't the same as the admiring stares he got from an audience.

The only hint he had that they'd done a passable job was the director hadn't started any frenzied swearing. Luke made fun of Jimmy's constant swearing, but he had nothing on Sam McKenzie. Holy fuck.

"Want to grab some dinner?" Aaron asked.

Not even the prospect of hanging out with the famous, attractive, and successful Aaron Young could coax Jimmy away from his bed this evening. By the time he made it back to his tiny sublet apartment and showered the sweat of despondency away, Luke would already be asleep. Good thing Jimmy had a TV. He could flip it on and fall asleep in front of it.

"Uh, no, not really. I'm beat. Rain check? How do you still have any energy left?"

"You'll get used to the pace, trust me. In a couple of weeks, you'll feel different, I promise."

"By different, surely you mean 'dead.'" Jimmy still hadn't quite managed to start thinking in West Coast time.

Aaron laughed. "Get some sleep. I'm giving you another week, and then after that, I'm dragging your ass out somewhere. You can't come all this way to star in a movie and not get to see any of the sights."

"Sounds good." Jimmy did his best to sound upbeat, but inside he was cringing. A week's reprieve. It wasn't going to be nearly enough. He was too old to be changing his spots now.

LIVING IN limbo in a house meant for two made Luke edgy and uncomfortable, and he had to keep reminding himself it was only temporary. The house echoed less, now that Luke had all their furniture and boxes of stuff moved in. He'd only unpacked the critical stuff, partly because it would be easier to do his repairs but also because it felt weird to make decisions about where stuff should go all by himself. Deciding how to orient the couch and which wall to put the entertainment center on was a job they should be doing together, and Luke was willing to wait until Jimmy had a chance to come home. The bed was a necessity. That first night in their house, together, would live forever in his memory, but he wasn't in a hurry to sleep on the air mattress again. Not unless he wanted to be crippled on the job site for the next four months.

There was a time when he could pass out on the floor beside Zach's crib and still be mostly functional the next day, but that time was long past.

The kitchen was also an exception to his unpacking embargo. He had no intention of unpacking until the majority of the fixes to the house had been made, but over the span of their relationship it had become obvious that the kitchen was Luke's domain, so there was little reason to get Jimmy's input. Besides, he wasn't going to eat fast food or frozen dinners for the next four months. He'd done that plenty since his divorce, and he'd be damned if he was going back to that.

He had the whole weekend blocked off. Zach, Ryan, and Bennett were coming over to help out, and Luke was pretty sure they could get a good chunk of his list done. He had everything he needed stored in the garage, but it would take a while to get everything installed. One weekend wasn't going to do it. Not when he was replacing the kitchen counters and cupboards, the bathroom counters and cabinets, the water heater, and switching all the windows to double-paned ones. Just about every room needed walls primed and baseboards painted in preparation for either Jimmy's help or instructions. At least the plumbing, roof, and electrical were in good shape. The AC unit had a couple more years before he'd have to worry about replacing it.

A rumble of car engines pulling into the driveway made him smile from the small satisfaction of having friends and family show up at his house. He just wished Jimmy were here to share in it.

Luke walked out the front door to the porch to greet his friends. He couldn't call them guests since he was going to make them work like dogs.

Zach and Ryan climbed out of their car while Bennett was still getting out of his. What he hadn't expected were the additional cars pulling up and parking on the street. A battered white pickup, which looked a lot like the one Luke used on the job, parked, along with two other cars.

Peter got out of the pickup, while Graham and Hector emerged from the other two vehicles.

"What are you guys doing here?" Luke called out as they strode across the lawn.

Graham tugged at his worn, thinning jeans and tight T-shirt, both of which were spattered with the paint of long past jobs. "Obviously, we're the strip-o-grams."

Hector winked. "And I've got a big hammer in my toolbox, if you know what I mean."

Luke spluttered with laughter to cover the sudden trembling in his belly, knowing these guys, ones he'd only known a couple of months, were here to help him fix up his and Jimmy's new home.

As soon as Peter reached the porch, he clapped Luke on the shoulder. "You've got more friends than you realize, Luke. We're happy to help."

"Thanks, man."

By lunchtime, they'd gotten the cabinets and sinks ripped out from the kitchen and two of the three bathrooms, and Luke snapped a couple of pictures to text to Jimmy, as he'd promised to do.

Look what we did.

It had only been two weeks since Jimmy had left, and they'd learned pretty quickly that phone calls were next to impossible. With the time difference between the east and west coasts, Luke's early schedule on the job sites, and Jimmy's completely erratic film schedule, they had a hard time finding a time when they were both free to talk, even when Luke set up a calendar on his phone that he shared with Jimmy. Texting, though, had become his lifeline to his partner.

Holy shit. When did you start—yesterday?

Nope. Peter, Graham & Hector showed up, along with Bennett and the boys.

I should be there helping :(

I wish you were here, but helping?

Shut up! Can't wait to see what the new cupboards look like.

We're breaking for lunch now. Call?

The quick responses to Luke's texts had set off a glimmer of hope that maybe Jimmy was free for a few minutes for a mutually beneficial schedule overlap. They hadn't even managed to have phone sex since Jimmy had been gone, and Luke's recent immersion in regular, spectacular sex had left him feeling the lack. Luke shifted his stance and glanced around as his dick plumped at the thought of Jimmy talking dirty in his ear. Hell, he'd probably get a full-blown erection hearing Jimmy's voice, period. Not that this was the time for phone sex, even if Jimmy could manage to call him.

Can't. I'm supposed to be on set in a sec. Shouldn't even have my phone with me.

:(Love you.

Love you, too. Need more pics!

The doorbell rang, startling Luke. He started toward it, but before he got there, the front door banged open and Scotty marched inside carrying a couple of bulging paper bags.

"Lunch time, boys," Scotty sang out and strode into the mostly demolished kitchen with Luke following. Scotty set the bags on the drop cloth-covered table, and Peter wiped his hands on his jeans before wrapping an arm around Scotty's waist and kissing him.

"Pete, you're going to get me all dirty."

"Yeah, and?"

Luke had to look away, Peter's husky tone and Scotty's smug little smile only painful reminders of what he was missing. He started pulling food containers from the bag.

"Scotty? You didn't have to do this. I was going to order some pizza."

"Not a problem. They're leftovers from a swank corporate retirement party last night. No sense in them going to waste, and it's the only help I can offer this weekend, because I've got two more weddings to get through."

Luke thought he might tear up. Jimmy's emotional nature was apparently rubbing off on him.

"Thanks, I really appreciate this."

While they set out the food, the other guys filed in, dusty as all hell, the RB guys shirtless and sweaty, chests streaked with dirt.

Since Luke and Peter were the oldest guys there, and everyone was in good shape, he wondered if Graham had been totally joking about the strip-o-grams.

Ryan and Zach were the last to arrive, and Ryan's eyes bugged out as he took in the expanse of man chest. He didn't know where to look, and his gaze kept skipping from one man to the other, completely oblivious to the food on the table.

And there was so much food, beautiful and bountiful. Luke snapped several more pictures and sent them off.

Look what Scotty brought for lunch!

This time, Luke had to wait several minutes for a response.

I HATE YOU. How dare you taunt me with food porn when all I can eat is plywood and wallpaper paste?!?

Luke snickered. He'd forgotten for a moment about Jimmy's draconic diet. He hated that anyone thought Jimmy was less than perfect, but he guessed he had to accept Jimmy's assertion it was a Hollywood thing.

Sorry! Love you!

Pfft. I'm not so sure now ;) XOXO

Luke was tempted to start scrolling through his pictures of Jimmy, but last night Jimmy had sent him one, his head partially cut off, but his dick hard and ready. He knew damn well he shouldn't be looking at that in public, but if he started looking for pictures, he wasn't sure he could make himself avoid that one.

With great fortitude, he pocketed his phone and turned his attention back to grabbing himself some food.

After lunch, Luke pulled Ryan aside. "Kid, you know I think you need to come clean with Zach, and I also know how hard it can be. But if you keep ogling the guys, Zach isn't going to need you to say one word. Don't you get enough half-naked guys at the clubs?" Luke had only been to gay clubs a few times before deciding they weren't for him, but he'd been enough times to know half the guys seemed to be allergic to fabric.

He wasn't expecting Ryan's full-on fire-engine flush and the way his gaze dropped. Luke started to get an unwelcome suspicion that Ryan was maybe a little more innocent and virginal than either he or Jimmy suspected. Damn it. Now he was going to worry. Maybe Peter wouldn't mind if Luke brought Ryan to Rainbow Blues as a guest. At least he could meet some guys without Zach around.

"Sorry, LJ."

"Don't be sorry, kid, just be aware that if you don't intend to out yourself today, you'd better be careful."

He'd wait until Jimmy got home, though, so they could discuss it before Luke made things worse by coming between Ryan and Zach.

Luke went back to work, excited by the progress they'd made so far.

CHAPTER 12

OF ALL the scenes they'd filmed so far, none of them in order, the nude one had been the weirdest. Not that Jimmy wanted to get turned on in front of all those people, but he'd never been less turned on in his life. Mostly nude, in bed with a mostly nude Aaron Young, and he'd never felt less like having sex.

The only good thing about the nude scene was that they finished early. Jimmy pulled into the palm-tree-lined parking for his building while it was still light out. Amazing.

Inside his apartment, he glanced at the clock and made the time zone calculation. Shit. Luke might still be awake.

He pulled out his phone and pulled up Luke's name.

"Jimmy?"

Jimmy sank down on the bed, the sound of his partner's voice soothing the jagged edges of his nerves.

"Hey, Luke."

"It's so good to hear your voice." Luke's voice was low and husky.

"Did I wake you up?" Jimmy wasn't sure he cared, because he needed this touchpoint so badly.

"Nah, I was just watching TV. Are you doing okay?"

Jimmy tried to imagine Luke on their couch, watching TV in their home, but it was hard with only a few texted photos as a reference.

"The shoot today was difficult. It was the naked scene."

Luke cleared his throat. Jimmy had tried to prepare him, but neither of them had been looking forward to that scene, for different reasons.

"Oh? Is it something you want to talk about?" Tension threaded through Luke's voice like a tightly wound guitar string.

Jimmy huffed out a laugh. "Oh, it's not what you're thinking, believe me. I told you how we repeat stuff over and over? It's like that, except naked and freezing. It must be like having sex in the penguin enclosure at a zoo as part of a breeding program, except no one's got an erection."

"No one?" There was a hint of relief in Luke's tone.

God, he loved this man, who always did his best to give Jimmy the benefit of the doubt.

"Nope. Not unless it belonged to that sadist of a director. At least he had the decency to close the set, but there were still a number of people there, and it was the least sexy thing I've done in my life."

Luke chuckled. "Is it okay that I'm glad?"

"I'm glad, too. But Aaron warned me the naked shoots often get leaked to the Internet, so you might see some suggestive shots tomorrow."

"I'll live. I hope. I trust you, implicitly, but it still might not be easy seeing you with another guy."

"You know I love you, and it means nothing, right?"

"I know. I love you, too." Funny, Jimmy had never thought about being able to hear a smile in someone's voice, but he heard one in Luke's right now. Probably more obvious because he didn't have any visual cues to work from.

"So… what does he look like naked?"

"About what you'd expect. Remember in that last one we watched before I left, *Model Revenge*? He wore that tiny bathing suit that left nothing to the imagination. Well, there wasn't much more to see. We wear these little socks over our dicks, so there's no dick-to-dick contact."

A relieved sigh gusted out of Luke. "I'm glad. I want to be your only source of dick-to-dick contact."

"Mmm. I wish you were serving up some dick-to-dick contact right now."

The sound Luke made was nothing more than an aroused purr. Jimmy shucked his clothes off one-handed and lay back down on the bed, ready to enjoy some much needed phone sex with the love of his life.

LUKE SLUNK through the grocery store, hunched over his cart like he needed it to prop him up. The muggy heat of the summer outside made his T-shirt cling to him, but the aggressive chill inside made him cold and clammy. Jimmy had been away almost two months now, and Luke missed him more every day. He had no idea what to do with himself. The rest of the day stretched out endlessly. He'd already done everything to the house he could do without Jimmy's input. As much as he appreciated his friends' help—and appreciated that he had friends to help him—the upgrades to the house had gone far more quickly than he'd anticipated. He had nothing, absolutely nothing to distract him. Even work, which always meant longer days in the summer, didn't do enough to distract him. All it made him do was resent how much it interfered with him getting on a plane and going to visit his partner.

God. This was worse than after his divorce. After his divorce, he'd been lonely, but he hadn't realized that loving someone who wasn't around was a much more painful version of loneliness. Crime and forensic dramas weren't nearly interesting enough to distract him from how empty the house felt. He missed Jimmy's presence like the ache of a missing limb. He missed making dinner for him, planning nights out, discussing their day. Even when Jimmy had a bad day, he was always enthusiastic about something, and he never failed to brighten Luke's day. Now, his life had plunged back into shadow, and he was more acutely aware of how miserable he'd been before he met Jimmy. The only bright spots were the frequent texts and the occasional phone calls. The calls were so difficult to squeeze in, and Luke hated it.

Even if he was able to schedule a few days off, enough to make it worthwhile to fly all the way to the West Coast, how much time would he spend in Jimmy's sublet apartment, waiting for him to finish filming for the day?

Without Jimmy, cooking had become dull and pointless again, so it was no surprise Luke found himself in the frozen food aisle, his standard fare since his divorce. The wall of identical cardboard boxes shook him. He didn't want to go back to where he'd been. Shaking off this depressing funk entirely might not be possible until Jimmy got home, but he could at least avoid falling back into his lonely rut. He missed Jimmy about a hundred times more than he missed Kelly after their divorce, but this time he had friends to help him through it, and he ought to take advantage of that.

An alert sounded on his phone. Another listing for James Alexander had popped up. Most times he was eager to click on Internet news about Jimmy. He was so fucking proud of his partner, who seemed poised to take Hollywood by storm. But ever since the smuggled stills of the nude scene had been posted online, as Jimmy had warned him, he was also apprehensive about clicking those links. Jimmy was a good actor, and some of his facial expressions in those shots, while he was all up close and personal with Aaron Young's naked body, were a little too similar to ones Luke had seen at home in their bed. No matter how much he believed Jimmy and knew in his heart they weren't real, it was hard not to feel pain that Aaron was holding the man he missed more than his left arm.

With trepidation, he clicked on the link. And immediately left the site. It was yet another version of the ones he'd already seen. He didn't really need to see them again, nor did he need to risk someone noticing he had two naked men on his phone while standing by the ice cream. Last thing he needed was someone thinking he was some sort of pervert.

He was going to obsess about this all fucking night if he didn't do something. He pulled up his contact list.

"Bennett, you want to catch dinner and a movie?"

"You okay?"

"Just another naked picture."

"Shit. I can't even imagine. Must suck."

Luke sighed. "Yeah. So, are you free tonight?"

"Sure, but I think you need a beer or three, not a movie. Let's go to the pub. I'll call Graham and Hector. We'll make a night of it."

"Okay, sounds good."

He noticed Bennett didn't offer to call Peter. Peter was a great guy, but he almost never went anywhere without Scotty. Who was also a great guy, but Bennett sensed that seeing a happy couple together would only make Luke more lonely for his own partner.

"I'll pick you up in a couple of hours, okay?"

A couple of hours would give Luke plenty of time to get home, shower, and change.

"You don't have to go out of your way. I can drive."

"Oh, Luke, you need more beer than you'll be able to drive home on."

That could be true. "You're probably right. See you soon."

Luke grabbed a few essentials that didn't include frozen dinners before heading home to get ready for a night out with his single friends, a mini Rainbow Blues gathering.

WITH ANY luck, this would be the last day of filming. Two months had been like two consecutive eternities, and Jimmy was still expected to spend another two months in California. He never got used to the different pace, never became comfortable with the changes he had to make for filming to work. But here, on the last day, the end in fucking sight, Jimmy realized something important.

All this time Jimmy had thought he was an attention whore, and now he'd come to realize he was actually an energy vampire. The movie set was dead. No energy from an appreciative audience, no ego boost from the applause, no tears shed or sniffles. No laughter. The challenge of doing scene after scene, repeating lines of dialogue over and over to ensure the cameras could be moved and catch the right cut... that wasn't a challenge that fired his blood. Doing an entire play from memory, with few to no flubs, in front of an audience? That was a challenge he thrived on.

There was nothing on this set that gave him the energy he craved. He'd always thought it was the most glamorous job ever, but each day was a chore, and the restrictive food and exercise only annoyed him more. Even seeing the dailies didn't spur any excitement. Not like the last minute preparations backstage at the playhouse, accompanied by the hum of an eager audience settling into seats.

Like sunshine breaking through the clouds, the shackles of the "lost dream" fell away. He didn't want to be a film actor, and this was the last film he was ever going to do. As soon as he could, he was getting the fuck out of Hollywood and heading back to Luke and the playhouse. Hell, he even preferred the sullen energy of the kids in his classroom to this overprocessed repetition.

"Cut! James, this scene is supposed to be heartwrenching, not joyous. Don't fucking smile while you're saying your lines."

"Sorry."

This time, keeping his focus was a hundred times more difficult, because he had a call to make to Matthew, the entertainment lawyer, and an idea he wanted to float past him.

CLENCHING HIS phone tight in his hand, Jimmy stabbed at the display to call Damian, while double-checking to make sure the bathroom door was locked. Too fucking bad for anyone who needed to take a leak right now.

"Pick up, pick up, pick up." He needed to get this sorted now, because this was fucking ridiculous.

"Well, if it isn't our famous movie star," Damian sang into the phone. "Calling to crawl back to the small stage?"

If Jimmy wasn't so fucking angry, he might have teased Damian back. "In a manner of speaking."

"Wait, what?" Damian's voice got all serious. "What's going on?"

"I need help, Dame. I need to you call Matthew. Urgently. I've tried the one number I have, but I'm just getting his voice mail. You're friends with him, so you must have another number."

"What's wrong? Do you need me to fly out?"

Jimmy closed his eyes and took a deep breath, trying to prevent his tears from spilling over. Damian was his best friend, and one he knew wouldn't be making a play for Luke while Jimmy was out of town.

"No. But I need some advice about this contract. You remember how they want me here to do PR for the film after the shoot wraps?"

"Yeah, it seemed a bit early."

Jimmy shrugged, even though Damian couldn't see him. "They also didn't want me to tell any interviewers that I have a partner, which seemed weird at the time, but I didn't think too much of it."

"Uh-oh. This doesn't sound good."

Damian knew how much he loved Luke, and how much he hated keeping things under wraps.

"Exactly. They want to publicize a romance between me and Aaron."

"I'm sorry, they want you to date Aaron Young? I mean, I like Luke, but Aaron Young." Damian's tone was teasing.

"Damian." Jimmy couldn't keep the edge out of his voice. "It's all fake. Publicity for the movie."

"Okay. So what?"

"So I hate this. I hate acting for film, I hate the strict diets, I hate lying. I miss the live audience, the feel of being on stage. Hell, I even miss those bratty kids at school and teaching. But most of all, I miss being with Luke. This isn't what I want to do with my life. I want to come home."

"You're sure? You do this and you'll be burning bridges you might not be able to rebuild."

"I've never been more sure of anything in my life." Dreams could change, and he'd been blind not to realize his had changed the minute he met Luke.

"You might still have to do PR, but I'd be surprised if there wasn't a way you could wiggle out of a fake romance. Especially if you don't care if you ever have another movie role."

Jimmy snorted. "You can repeat that in as many variations as you want, but I'm not changing my mind."

There was a rumor of another, much bigger role that might be coming his way, but Jimmy didn't care, not one fucking bit. He wasn't doing this again, and he wouldn't miss it for a second. As soon as he got some legal advice, he'd be getting on the first plane back to Luke. He'd fly back to do additional promotion as necessary, but there was no way he'd need to stay in LA for two months solid for regular promotion.

"Do it fast, okay?"

"I'm on it."

"You think I'm an idiot, don't you?"

Damian laughed. "No. I could have told you you'd hate film acting, but I knew you needed to try. Besides, Hollywood's loss is my gain. We're doing *The Mousetrap* next. I'm saving you the detective's role."

Jimmy sagged against the door. "Thanks."

A knock on the door had him whispering into the phone. "Gotta go. Get me that lawyer, quick."

He breathed a moment, trying to compose himself. It was selfish of him to have locked the door to a public bathroom with multiple stalls, but he'd needed some time away from everyone. He had a trailer on set, but he never felt comfortable in it.

"Hey, sorry about that," Jimmy said as he opened the door, not really paying attention to the person on the other side. Until he was pushed back into the bathroom by Aaron, and the door locked again.

"What the hell?" Aaron wasn't trying to get a bathroom blow job, was he? He'd gotten the sense early on that Aaron was attracted to him, and while Aaron was good-looking, he wasn't Luke, and Jimmy would never cheat. As soon as he'd explained to Aaron he was involved with someone, Aaron had never pushed the boundaries, not even once. In fact, Aaron had been the only bright spot about Hollywood, becoming a true friend over the past two months.

"Are you okay?"

"What?"

Aaron gripped his shoulders. "James, I know that proposition surprised the shit out of you. I thought for a minute you were going to deck Missy."

He'd wanted to, but Jimmy wasn't much of a fighter. Even with the weight of righteous anger behind him, he figured a tough as nails

PR person could break him in two, no matter that Missy Wong was a girl half his size.

"You can't really expect me to go along with that nonsense, can you?"

Aaron snorted and let him go to start pacing. "Of course not. I don't intend to go along with it either."

Stupidly, he felt a bit hurt, which Aaron saw and laughed.

"Don't get me wrong. Another time, another place, we might have made something happen. But I can see how much you love your partner. And I came out to find that same kind of love for myself. Not to make a mockery of it with a fake relationship for a publicity push."

"They can't... can't make us, can they?" Jimmy hoped someone would have warned him if his contract had locked him into something this ridiculous.

"I've already got a call into my agent. I can't say anything about the contract you signed, but my guess is that they're going to try and class this as some sort of 'miscellaneous' public relations obligation. Without my cooperation, a decent agent or lawyer should be able to get you out of it, although they are going to try and push that agenda on us and hope we'll just cave."

"I'm not caving. I've called a lawyer, and I'm going home as soon as he says I can." At the moment, he didn't even care if he got paid for this movie or not. He and Luke would muddle through somehow until he went back to teaching after his unpaid leave of absence.

"Going home? You can't let this change your mind about Hollywood! I have it on good authority they want you to play Aquaman."

Jimmy raised his eyebrows. "Aquaman? Surely I'm too old to play a role like that, even if I wanted to."

"You know you look great for your age, and the dieting and exercise is a total pain in the ass, but you're sleek, toned, and getting buff. You'd make a great Aquaman. You could have Luke move out here. Construction jobs are everywhere."

"I appreciate the vote of confidence, but I made up my mind to go home before this even came up. I love acting on stage, and I hate acting for film. If I loved it, yeah, I'd consider asking Luke to move, but I don't, so there's no point in disrupting our lives any more, you know?"

"I wish I could convince you otherwise, but I'm happy you know what you want to do with your life. Today's the last day we're on set, which means we can both drink. Wanna head out for some celebratory drinking and eating of fatty, bad-for-us food?" Aaron grinned like a little kid ready to sneak cookies from the cookie jar.

"I don't know. What about the call I've got into my lawyer?"

Aaron shrugged. "Well, it's already six, and you don't need bail. My guess is that the earliest you'll hear from any lawyer would be tomorrow. Besides, we might get called back to do a few more takes, once they've taken a look at the stuff from today, so you can't leave tonight. C'mon. Come out and celebrate. You just made your first movie! Even if you never do another one, how can you not celebrate this?"

Aaron made some good points. Jimmy had done something most people only dreamed of doing. "Okay, let's do it."

"Then let's get the hell out of here before those PR bull dogs attack again."

The knowledge that he was so close to going home to Luke buoyed up Jimmy's mood so much that he was ready to celebrate. Ready to celebrate that this hell of a production was over. Ready to celebrate returning to his real life. And during his epiphany on set, when the director had verbally smacked him around for looking happy, he'd also realized he had a perfect idea for an "out of the blue" gift for Luke.

"If you don't mind, I need to make a stop somewhere. Pick something up. If we can't do it without you being recognized, I'll go on my own."

"I have a few tricks up my sleeve. Let's go."

"After you." Jimmy held out a hand, and Aaron unlocked the bathroom door. He took a glance outside before stepping out and beckoning Jimmy to follow.

CHAPTER 13

THE ALERT notification went off on Luke's phone, and he pulled it out, almost dreading what he would find. As soon as Jimmy had left, he'd set up the alert to notify him if Jimmy's name was posted on the Internet. There would be interviews or something with Jimmy, and Luke wanted to see them right away. He was so fucking proud of his partner.

The pride didn't go away, but each article he'd been alerted to had chipped away at his heart. Because each article was filled with pictures of Jimmy having a good time without him, if they weren't the ones of him kissing Aaron Young on set. And although Jimmy had said he missed Luke and was miserable with all the restrictions, every picture Luke saw featured Jimmy smiling. Smiling and beautiful. In expensive restaurants and exclusive clubs. Hollywood clearly agreed with Jimmy, and it was getting harder and harder to believe that their short separation was ever going to end. How could Luke possibly compare with all that Hollywood had to offer?

More and more, those stories had prompted him to go drinking with his friends, trying to forget the love of his life was a continent away, hanging out with celebrities and spending most of his days and sometimes his evenings, with the young, sexy Aaron Young. Reluctantly, Luke pulled up the alert and clicked through to the story.

A New Romance for Aaron Young?

Inside sources on the Walking Wounded *set say Aaron Young and his costar, Hollywood newcomer James Alexander, have gotten pretty cozy with each other. These photos, leaked from the closed set, show a lot of chemistry between the two men, and they were even seen drinking and laughing together at Crave.*

With his breath rattling in his chest, Luke scrolled down. The shot of Jimmy and Aaron, mostly naked and standing next to each other, he'd seen before, as he had the one of them kissing. Those were, according to Jimmy, stills from the set that shouldn't have been leaked out. This was the first time he'd seen the bloggers take the romance angle, and just thinking about Jimmy and Aaron together sent stabbing pains through his gut.

He scrolled down further. The cramping in his gut intensified, and he had trouble catching his breath. The next picture showed the two of them coming out of a men's room together. Jimmy had already told him there was very little deviation from the play, and Luke had seen the play enough times to know there was no men's room scene. He'd also been out long enough to know two guys in the bathroom together could very easily mean the budding romance, or at least budding lust, between Jimmy and Aaron might well be true. True to the point they may have already gotten off together in some random men's room at the studio.

Jimmy wouldn't do that to him. Jimmy hated cheating. But that didn't stop the insidious fear from taking root in his heart.

Like a rubbernecker unable to drive past an accident without slowing down, Luke scrolled down. The picture of Jimmy happy and smiling, Aaron's arm slung around his neck, made him feel as if his heart had been ripped from his chest.

He slid down the wall and forced himself to read the words below the image.

Aaron Young shocked the entertainment world by coming out earlier this year. Rumors abound that James Alexander is the front runner to play Aquaman in the upcoming movie, which should catapult him into the stratosphere of A-list actors. Undoubtedly, we'll see more of this superstar couple in the upcoming months.

Aquaman. Jimmy was going to play Aquaman? Luke tried to wrap his mind around it. Jimmy was going to be a movie star. A famous movie star. Not that Luke had any doubts. Jimmy was such a good actor, and Luke was so proud. With a boyfriend like Aaron Young, Jimmy could go far. Luke would only be holding him back.

He'd been a fool to think this movie was a one-off. Jimmy was meant for better things than sharing a house with a middle-aged construction manager.

Tears ran unchecked down his face as the realization tore his soul in two. He was going to have to let Jimmy go. He couldn't selfishly hang on to Jimmy, not when the best thing for Jimmy's dream would be for them to break up. Even if Jimmy still loved him, or thought he did, staying together would only make things more painful when Jimmy realized Luke was nothing more than a useless reminder of his former life.

In agony, he stared at the countertops and cupboards he and Jimmy had picked out together in those frantic, bittersweet moments before he left for Hollywood. His mouth opened in a silent scream and sobs wracked his chest.

He was never going to cook for Jimmy in this house. They were never going to have the barbecues they'd talked about. Christening each room by getting naked and fucking each other's brains out was never going to happen. The only memory of that would be in the master bedroom.

Even if he could afford the house on his own, how could he live here? How could he live in the house that was supposed to be for them both and not be bombarded at every turn by the palpable lack of Jimmy? Trying to paint on walls primed for Jimmy's artistic input would be impossible.

It had been the best eight months of his life, and they were over, all too soon.

There would never again be a reason for an "out of the blue, I was thinking of you" present. That one thought exploded through the last shreds of Luke's control, and he tipped over onto the floor and cried until his nose was swollen and his eyes were painful and dry, every last tear shed.

JIMMY CLAWED his way back to consciousness. Light stabbed at his eyes, and his mouth was as rank and gritty as if he'd been eating sand. The pounding in his head made an unpleasant counterpoint to the roiling in his gut. It had been a long fucking time since he'd been this abysmally hung over. But then, he'd gone two months without a speck of sugar, fat, or alcohol.

Last night. Jimmy groaned. Last night he'd completely overloaded all three by accident. Overloaded. It hadn't seemed too much at the time, but he'd based his consumption on his pre-cardboard eating days and heavier weight. His stomach turned over again, keeping time with the mariachi band in his head.

Fuck. He was too old for this shit. He just hoped he hadn't done anything that would piss off the school board too badly. Because he wanted to go home to Luke, back to his life of being a teacher and part-time stage actor. It was a good fucking life, and he loved it.

First, though, he had some serious love for the ibuprofen in his bathroom. He lifted himself up, slowly, and shuffled to the bathroom as quickly as his head and stomach would allow.

Once there, the sight of the toilet triggered an almost painful need to piss. He took care of business, downed a couple of glasses of water with the pills, and after his stomach decided to accept his offering, took a cool shower to help clear his head.

By the time he got out—and he wasn't entirely sure he hadn't dozed off somewhere in the middle of soaping himself up—his headache had abated to a more manageable throb, and his stomach was now equally angry and hungry. Jimmy judged that a step in the right direction and toweled off carefully, not wanting to disrupt the delicate equilibrium he'd achieved.

Naked, he wandered back into his bedroom. He knew for a fact there wasn't one fucking thing in the apartment he wanted to eat, but he wasn't sure he had the energy to go out and scavenge for something.

As he pulled on a pair of boxer briefs, his phone buzzed, vibrating atop the nightstand. Grabbing it, he saw he'd missed a number of calls—how the hell had he slept through the incessant buzzing, he didn't know. The most important one was the one from his lawyer.

After playing the message, his shoulders slumped in relief. It might take a few days, but Matthew would make sure he didn't have to play out some farce of a tabloid romance. What a fucking relief. Even after the success of *Brokeback Mountain*, Jimmy had been surprised that *Walking Wounded* ended up as a movie, never mind anticipating that they'd want to make up a gay romance as a publicity stunt. It had just never even occurred to him. Matthew's message had said as long as he was willing to do typical publicity events, there was no reason to stay in Hollywood once filming wrapped.

Which it had done yesterday. Jimmy flopped back down on the bed. A short nap, then he was booking a flight home.

WHEN JIMMY woke up again, it was just after noon, and he didn't feel so much like death on a cracker. He scrabbled for his phone in the bedding where he'd dropped it. There were a slew of new texts, a voice mail from Aaron, and a bunch of voice mails from numbers he didn't recognize.

He skimmed through the texts from his family. He must be still drunk, because they didn't make any sense. None seemed urgent, though. No one was dead or hospitalized. They merely seemed upset with him. He scrolled down to the new message from Damian.

You need to call me ASAP! I must know what Aaron Young is like in bed. DETAILS!

That made even less sense, but at least there was a link attached to the text.

A New Romance for Aaron Young?

Inside sources on the Walking Wounded *set say Aaron Young and his costar, Hollywood newcomer James Alexander, have gotten pretty cozy with each other....*

Jimmy scrolled through a set of damning photos, his horror growing with each one. The one of them coming out of the men's room yesterday was like a physical blow to Jimmy's alcohol-irritated stomach. Nausea roiled in his gut, and he closed his eyes, taking a few deep breaths. When the urge to hurl passed, he called Aaron.

"Did you get my message? James, I am so sorry."

"Fuck, no, I didn't listen to the message, but did you see this article? What the fuck is this?"

"Apparently the powers that be thought they could ram through this publicity stunt. I've got my agent on it, but not much we can do about what's out there."

Jimmy's headache was back, hot and angry. "I can't believe this."

"My guess is that reporters and bloggers and shit will be trying to get in touch with you for an interview. If you don't recognize the number, don't answer."

Oh dear God. All those voice mails. At least there wasn't a picture of him buying the gift for Luke. Aaron had come through about ducking everyone, because he couldn't imagine having some stupid blogger assume he was giving that gift to Aaron, not Luke.

"Assholes."

"Yep. No job is perfect."

"I was planning to check the flights back home, leave as soon as possible. I'll just have to lay low until I can get out of here."

"I'm going to miss you, Jimmy. I know we'll see each other for publicity events, but I had a great time working with you. And if you change your mind about acting, you let me know. Good luck with the damage control."

"Damage control?"

"With Luke. Tell him I'm sorry this happened. If I hadn't come out, maybe they wouldn't have bothered trying this."

"Uh, yeah. Talk to you later."

Jimmy ran for the bathroom and puked.

After his stomach stopped spasming, he drank some more water and stumbled back to the bedroom. Surely he didn't have to do any damage control with Luke, did he? Luke had to know it wasn't true.

Although apparently his entire family thought it was true, for God's sake. His messages made a lot more sense in that context. They all thought he was cheating on Luke in front of the media. For fuck's sake, he wouldn't do that to anyone, let alone the man he loved more than anything.

But there wasn't a text or a message from Luke. Jimmy couldn't decide if that was a good thing or a bad thing. Or maybe it was a Luke hadn't seen the article thing.

Fuck. He was getting the first flight out of here.

Amazingly, for a small fortune, he could get on a plane in three hours. With two stops, he wouldn't get home until six in the morning, but he booked it and called for car. With an hour to pack, he should still be able to make it to LAX in plenty of time. He left another message for Matthew, telling him he was leaving town immediately. If anyone needed anything from him, they could go through Matthew. Bastards.

Before he even started, though, he had one more thing to do.

Unfortunately, his call went straight to Luke's voice mail.

"Hey there. Long story to tell you, but filming's done, and I'm going to be home in the morning. Can't wait to see you. Love you."

His finger shook, ever so slightly, as he disconnected the call. Luke was probably just busy. Or forgot to charge his phone. Or maybe was in an area without service. He wasn't screening Jimmy's calls. He couldn't be.

CHAPTER 14

EXHAUSTED, JIMMY tried to get comfortable in the airport chair, ball cap pulled low over his eyes. The cap had been a necessary purchase at LAX when he realized the blog article had been more far reaching than he'd assumed.

Fuck. Jimmy squirmed in his seat. They had people trapped at the gate. The least they could do was make the seats almost conform to the human body.

He rubbed at his eyes before pulling out his phone. It was way early in the morning to call anyone, but he'd tried calling Luke at LAX, right before boarding, and at his last stopover in Denver. He needed to hear Luke's voice, make sure Luke didn't believe some stupid story on the Internet.

The PA system announced boarding for his flight, and Jimmy made another call, however douchey it may be to call at this hour.

"'Lo?"

"Hey, Damian."

"Jimmy? What the fuck time is it?"

Jimmy didn't know. Geography wasn't his strong suit; he wasn't sure whether he was in the same time zone as Damian or not.

"Can you pick me up at the airport?"

"Now?" Damian was incredulous.

Jimmy rubbed at his eyes again. "No. My flight gets in at six fifteen. This morning." Overnight flights sucked big donkey balls.

"Uh, sure. Might as well, since I'm already awake."

"Thanks. I gotta go. We're boarding now."

Jimmy disconnected the call before Damian woke up enough to ask more questions. He wasn't interested in answering any of them in a place as public as the airport.

Maybe on this leg of the flight he could get a bit of sleep.

"I CAN'T believe they did that to you." Damian was still in shock after Jimmy had told him the whole story, which had taken almost the entire drive from the airport to Jimmy's house.

"I know. I just hope Luke hasn't freaked out."

Damian shrugged. "He seemed like a pretty even-tempered, down-to-earth guy."

Jimmy pulled out the house keys he hadn't used in two months, although he'd touched them lovingly more than once when the loneliness had gotten to be too much.

"Where's Luke's car?"

"Maybe he's working? Or didn't you say he sometimes goes out to brunch with his son?"

Jimmy snorted, striving for normal. "You're a gay man. When was the last time you went out for brunch at seven thirty in the morning?"

"Okay, true. But sometimes construction guys work on Sunday, right?"

Luke had worked a few weekend jobs since Jimmy had been away, but that didn't explain why he wasn't responding to any of Jimmy's voice mails or texts.

"Yeah. Maybe." Jimmy got out of the car and helped Damian unload his suitcases from the trunk. He patted his pocket to make sure Luke's present was still there, same as he'd checked about a million times since he'd left LA.

"I'll come in with you, okay?"

There was a funny note in Damian's voice, and Jimmy glanced over. His friend was agitated, although he was trying to hide it. Shit on a shingle. Damian *was* afraid Luke had flipped out, and that Jimmy was walking into a domestic brawl.

"Fuck, Damian. Even after everything I told you, you think I cheated on him, don't you?"

"No! Seriously, Jimmy, I don't. But I don't know what Luke thinks. It looked bad."

If those shithead bloggers fucked up his relationship, Jimmy was going back to Hollywood to beat them about the head with a baseball bat. Or maybe shove their keyboards up their asses.

"Come on. The sooner I find Luke, the sooner I can straighten this out. Luke loves me and knows I love him." Damian couldn't know how important that was, how special, because he'd never been in love before.

Jimmy opened the door, and the faint scent of Luke almost made him stagger. How had he lived for two months without that?

"Luke? Are you here?"

Pointless to call, because he could sense no one was in the house. Damian dragged his suitcase inside.

Jimmy walked into the kitchen and gasped. "It's so beautiful, Damian. He sent me pictures, but I had no idea." He brushed a hand along the cool granite countertops. It almost looked like a magazine spread, except their kitchen was much smaller than those featured in magazines.

"You just going to wait here until he comes home?"

Damian's words brought him back to his current dilemma. "I don't know. Maybe I'll try calling Zach or Bennett a little later."

Jimmy hadn't ever called either of them, but Luke had given him those numbers a while ago.

"Want me to hang around? I'm up now. You can tell me more stories about Hollywood."

Since he wasn't going to be able to sleep until he'd talked to Luke, he might as well have company. "Sure. Let me see if I can figure out how to make us some coffee. Have a seat."

Coffee. Oh fuck. That was an indulgence he hadn't had since starting that damned diet. He was almost salivating. He assessed the cupboards, trying to figure out where he'd put coffee. The first one he opened was the right one, and he wanted to crow with success. He and Luke were still in tune.

There were some papers on the counter and Jimmy picked them up, wondering if they'd give him some clue as to where Luke had gone.

He picked them up and started to read. His breath came fast and hard, blood pounding in his ears, coffee forgotten.

"Jimmy, Jimmy, what's wrong?"

Light-headed and dizzy, Jimmy waved the sheaf of papers at him. "These are papers to sell the house. Luke signed them yesterday." Colored flags had been attached where Jimmy would have to sign to put their house—their home—back on the market.

How could Luke do this without even talking to him? If he'd eaten anything since he'd last puked, he'd be puking right now.

"Damian, was the article really that awful?" Jimmy's voice cracked. This couldn't be happening.

"Come on, you look like you're going to keel over. Sit down." Damian guided him to a chair.

Something crunched under his feet, and they both looked down.

"Uh, Jimmy, is this Luke's phone?"

Frowning, he stared at the mess on the floor, barely able to comprehend what he was seeing. On the floor by the table lay scattered pieces of plastic, and on the wall, a blackish streak and crack in the wall as though someone had thrown the phone with great force against it.

Jimmy's pulse sped up. "What…. You don't think there's been a break-in, do you?" Jimmy lowered his voice, pleading. He almost wished a break-in would explain it, but somehow he knew that article was to blame. Luke had seen it and was furious. The demolished phone certainly explained why Luke hadn't returned any of his calls.

Damian gave him a sympathetic look. "I don't think so, sweetie."

"Why, Damian? Why wouldn't he at least wait to talk to me?" Jimmy knew the article looked bad, but he was hurt that Luke hadn't had more faith in their relationship.

"Sweetie, you haven't seen each other in two months. And how many actual phone calls did you manage?"

"Three, but we talked about that. He understood." Luke had sworn he'd understood that their schedules were at complete odds. Jimmy hadn't liked it any more than Luke.

"Three. Long distance relationships are hard, and everyone knows actors often get their heads turned by costars. I know not all the tabloid stuff is real, but there's no smoke without fire, right? And it's not like we haven't seen it at the playhouse from time to time." Damian's words were reasonable, logical, but they hurt.

"I should never have gone." Jimmy wiped at the tears that wouldn't stop coming.

"Don't say that. You've done something most of us never have a chance to do. But…."

"But…." Jimmy repeated softly. "Luke might never forgive me."

He clutched the small box in his pocket as though it were a talisman that could ward away this pain.

"You won't know anything until you talk to him."

Jimmy pulled out his own phone and scrolled through his missed calls, hoping Luke had called. There were so many of them, but he had missed one.

"Zach called. Just before I landed. Didn't leave a message."

The phone rang in his hand, and Jimmy answered before he even registered who was on the caller ID.

"Luke?"

"No, asshole, it's Zach. Are you screening my calls?"

"Uh, no, I…."

"Whatever. Just thought you should know my dad was in a car accident."

Jimmy's head swam, and if he hadn't already been sitting down, he'd have fallen. "What?"

"Don't know if you care or not, but he's going into surgery."

"Zach, of course I care. What hospital?"

"Why? Gonna get your people to send flowers? Don't bother. I don't know why I even called."

"Zach, please." Jimmy could barely get the words past the lump in his throat.

At least Zach told him which hospital before clicking off. Jimmy looked helplessly at Damian.

"What happened?"

Jimmy swallowed a couple of times before he could say the words. "Car accident. Memorial Hospital."

"Let's go."

Dazed, Jimmy let Damian guide him from the house, taking charge the same way he did at the playhouse. How bad had the accident been? When? Where?

Jimmy wanted answers, but he thought Zach would be more likely to give them to him in person.

"THERE." DAMIAN pointed, and Jimmy saw Zach and Ryan seated together.

Jimmy rushed over. "Zach. Please tell me how he is."

Zach's eyes widened. "How the hell did you get here so fast?"

Ryan reached out a hand. "Sit down. You look like hell."

Then he looked a lot better than he felt. But he couldn't sit yet. "Zach. Jesus. Is he okay? What happened?"

Zach pushed himself out of the seat and got in his face. "What do you care? He's been fucking miserable, and it's all your fault. And you come back now? When he's hurt? If that's what it takes, he doesn't need you."

The attack had Jimmy reeling, both metaphorically and physically. Damian stepped up behind him, propping him up.

Zach was right; Jimmy should have come home long before this. Clearly both he and Luke hadn't been entirely honest with each other, otherwise Luke wouldn't have made such a drastic decision without talking to Jimmy, but that was something Jimmy would have to work on, as long as Luke made it out of this okay.

"I've been traveling almost twelve hours. I was coming home. For good." He wasn't about to get into details of his relationship with

Luke's son, but he didn't think Zach was going to unbend if Jimmy didn't do something to placate him.

"Exactly." Damian's agreement wasn't much, but it was something. "Jimmy's a smart cookie, but he hasn't developed teleportation in the past couple of days."

"Damian!" Sarcasm wasn't going to help.

Zach scrubbed his face, stress making him appear a lot older than he was. "You're right. I'm sorry. I just...."

"You're worried about your dad," Ryan piped up. "We know. But look at Jimmy. Really look at him. He's just as worried as you are."

Jimmy threw Ryan a grateful smile. "I am. I love your dad, with all my heart." He thought maybe Zach and Ryan hadn't seen that stupid article, and he hoped they wouldn't. Not until he had a chance to talk to Luke about it.

Zach did as Ryan instructed, and his reddened eyes started to water. "God. When they called me, I don't think I've ever been so scared."

Jimmy took a deep breath. He wanted to shake Zach, get him to tell him how the fuck Luke was, but he was maybe the substitute parent in this case. He had to be calm for all of them, even though he was quickly discovering that maybe wasn't his forte.

"Did you tell your mom?"

"I did, but my sister's got chicken pox and my step-dad's out of town. She's trying to find someone who'll babysit a sick kid, but at the moment, I'm just updating her by phone."

"Okay, and what was the last update?" Jimmy did his best to keep his tone even. Everyone in the waiting room was tense, and it wasn't fair to subject them to his and Zach's drama.

"For God's sake, Zach, sit the fuck down." Ryan had just lost patience with Zach's dithering. "Jimmy, come with me to the cafeteria. We'll get you a cup of coffee. Looks like you might need it."

Ryan threaded his arm through Jimmy's and led him away while Damian sat next to Zach.

"He's freaking out." Ryan's tone was apologetic. "It's the first time I think he's had to deal with a hospital and his parents. When it wasn't his mom giving birth, that is."

"I can tell he's freaking out, but I'm about thirty seconds away from my own meltdown. Please." Jimmy's voice cracked in his desperation. If someone didn't tell him something, he was going to leap over the desk into the nursing station and start flipping through files.

"As far as we know, he went out to a bar last night and got shitfaced. Then he walked out in front of a car and got hit."

Jimmy blinked. He wasn't going to think about why Luke was getting shitfaced, but he had to revise the gory images he had in his head of mangled metal and the Jaws of Life. But an unprotected human against a couple tons of metal didn't necessarily translate to fewer injuries.

"And?"

"Fortunately, the car wasn't going fast, but he broke a femur. He's in surgery now getting pins put in. I think the prognosis is pretty good, actually."

"This is my fault."

Ryan looked at him disapprovingly. "How could you cheat on LJ? He's one of the best people I know."

Fuck him sideways. Apparently Zach was the only one who hadn't believed Jimmy would cheat. Or at least, Zach was the only one in the world who hadn't seen that fucking article.

Jimmy lashed out with a fist and hit a wall. A nurse glanced up, eyes narrowed.

"Sorry, sorry."

They continued on toward the cafeteria.

"I never cheated. It's a long story, and one Luke deserves to hear first. But that article was complete bullshit."

"Really? I mean, I was shocked when I read it, because you two seemed so in love, but if there wasn't some truth to it, why would LJ get so drunk? He's not much of a drinker."

Ryan's gaze slid sideways, but Jimmy didn't press. Luke had never come out and said, but Jimmy suspected Luke had long ago given up getting buzzed around Ryan to make sure Ryan had a place he felt safe.

"No, he's not. And he didn't talk to me about it. I thought Luke would at least give me the chance to explain." Jimmy's voice wobbled. He was so fucking worried about Luke, but he hadn't expected one miscommunication to result in Luke wanting to dissolve their relationship. That didn't seem like Luke. Not when he'd always been so forthright, even to the point of being too forthright. "I thought this might end up being something we'd laugh over."

"Really? He didn't talk to you about it? That does seem weird. I know how much he missed you. Maybe it was just that messing with his head."

Jimmy hoped so. "Will you help me? With Zach?"

Ryan nodded and bought him a coffee. Was this some sort of weird karmic revenge that his first cup of coffee in two months was at the hospital cafeteria waiting for his partner to get out of surgery?

LUKE BLINKED his eyes open. The light was bright, and his head was swimmy, but he had no trouble recognizing a hospital room. He didn't recall being the one on the bed before.

"Hey, you're awake." Jimmy's voice, dusty and crackling like old parchment, sounded about as normal as Luke's vision.

Jimmy's beloved face moved into his line of sight, eyes bloodshot and deeply shadowed, but still as gorgeous as ever.

"Jimmy," Luke croaked out. If Jimmy's voice was old parchment, Luke's was a dried out old fossil. Jimmy squeezed his hand and smiled down at him, a sad little smile.

Luke hated it when Jimmy was sad, but he didn't have enough spit in his mouth to say so.

"The nurse left some apple juice for you. Want some?"

As his heart swelled with love for the world, he nodded. Apple juice. Sounded like the best thing ever.

Jimmy brought a plastic cup with a bent straw to his lips. He sucked, aware his lips were cracked almost to the point of bleeding, and his throat ached.

All too soon, Jimmy pulled the heavenly straw away, and Luke grunted.

"Not too much. You can't overdo it."

Luke lay there for a moment, hoping the cotton in his brain would disappear. Made it hard to think.

"What happened?"

"Well, love, seems you had a burning desire to tie one on, all by yourself. Got drunk as a skunk, then you wandered out in front of a moving car. Broke your leg, and they had to take you into surgery to fix it."

He loved Jimmy's voice, and his rambling. But his words didn't make sense. Getting drunk wasn't something he did often, especially not by himself.

"Juice?"

Jimmy let him have another sip before squeezing his hand and looking sad again.

"Don't be sad. I hate it when you're sad."

The grip on his hand tightened. "Luke, you could have died. If that car had been going faster…." Jimmy's eyelids fluttered, and he looked toward the ceiling. "I could have lost you. What were you thinking?"

Jimmy brought his hand up to his lips and kissed it, his tears warm against Luke's chilled skin.

The cotton clouding his thinking began to disperse, and he began to remember. Remembered the article that outlined in a series of photos why his whole world was about to explode. Remembered lying on the kitchen floor, tears running down his face to wet the tile. Remembered calling the real estate agent to get the paperwork started for reselling the house. Remembered the agent being kind enough to accept his explanation that they were planning to flip the house, ignoring the fact he must have looked like some sort of demon-spawn alcoholic with chicken pox from all the crying. Remembered signing the documents and throwing his phone away before driving to a local pub and starting a tab.

Beyond that, there was a blank wall. Until now.

"What are you doing here?"

Luke didn't expect Jimmy to lay his head down on his chest and start shaking with silent tears. Somehow, he untangled the IV enough so he could rest his hand on Jimmy's back.

"I'm so sorry, Luke. Nothing happened, I swear. It was all a publicity stunt. You have to believe I would never cheat on you."

There wasn't enough moisture left in his body for Luke to cry his own tears, but his face still heated in preparation for them. A publicity stunt? He was going to need more information on that later, but one thing he could tell Jimmy now.

"I know you didn't cheat on me."

Jimmy lifted his head, expression incredulous. "You know? Then why do you want to sell the house? Did you...?" Jimmy's breath hitched. "Did you meet someone else?"

The pain in his heart battled with the growing pain in his leg, burning off the muzzy aftereffects of whatever drugs he'd been given. He hadn't wanted to do this, but maybe it was better this way.

"There's no one else, Jimmy. I doubt there ever will be. But I saw that article—"

"I told you. I didn't cheat. It was a stupid ploy dreamed up by the producer."

"That's not what I meant. The article was pretty clear—you've got a great future ahead of you. If you're free of me, you can pursue that, maybe even find a guy who's better suited to Hollywood. This is for the best. Best for you." Luke barely got those words out because they meant no more Jimmy in his life, and with his stupidity in getting hit by a car, he wasn't even going to get good-bye sex to remember him by. Not like he'd ever be able to forget Jimmy. For the rest of his life, he'd be comparing all potential boyfriends, and none of them would come close.

A growl from deep within Jimmy's chest escaped, and he stood up, cheeks flushed and furious in a way Luke had never witnessed.

"Best for me? How do you figure?"

"You were so happy in those pictures. You're supposed to be happy, Jimmy. Or maybe it's James, now that you're an up-and-coming star." Luke wasn't sure, exactly, why this wasn't working out as smoothly as when he and Kelly had had a similar discussion. Of course, this time Luke was devastated, and he'd only been relieved when he and Kelly finally ended their marriage, but he'd sort of thought Jimmy would be relieved, as well, that Luke wasn't going to make a fuss.

"I still hate James," Jimmy snapped. "And of course I was happy in those pictures. Because I wasn't *acting*."

"I don't understand."

"Clearly." Jimmy's tone should have drawn blood.

"But you love acting."

Jimmy held out his palm in a "stop" gesture. "No. I'm going to talk, which I'm good at. And you're going to listen, which you are *normally* good at."

"What's going on in here?" Zach burst into the room, probably drawn by Jimmy's increasingly raised voice.

Luke opened his mouth, but Jimmy stopped him again. "No." Then he turned to Zach. "Your father is trying to dump me out of some misguided notion of being a martyr."

Zach didn't know what to do with an angry, snapping Jimmy any more than Luke did. His glance slid from Jimmy back to Luke, before settling on Jimmy again.

"Well, maybe if...."

"Zach, honey," Jimmy drawled, and it wasn't sweet or nice at all. "I'm going to educate your father in a few truths. Because there are a few things best for *him*. You can stay and watch if you like, I don't mind an audience, but it might not be pretty."

Zach's eyes widened. "He's injured. Are you sure this the best time for this?"

"I'm not going to hurt him, for fuck's sake. I love your father, and he'll recover much faster once he realizes he's a big idiot. Now get out."

Unaccustomed to that sort of direct, uncompromising order, Zach fled. Luke was pretty sure he'd hover outside, but if there was anything Luke could be sure of, besides the fact that Jimmy wouldn't cheat, is that Jimmy wouldn't maliciously hurt him. Zach had to know it too, or his stubborn son wouldn't have left them alone.

"Jimmy, don't do this. Don't give up your dream for me."

Those were exactly the wrong words to say, because Jimmy's eyes flashed, his hands clenched, and he looked like he was suppressing a primal scream.

"Quiet. I'm talking. You listen."

Luke pressed his lips together. He'd never seen Jimmy like this, all that vibrant energy changed from bubbles and light to angry red shards.

"First of all," Jimmy said as he stared at Luke, hands moving to punctuate his words. "This is a partnership. And that means I don't get my way all the time, and you don't get to decide what's right for me without my say so. If our paths look like they're diverging, we should talk. There might be compromises. There might be sacrifices we're willing to make. But you were willing to sacrifice our relationship without talking to me. You will never do that again. Understand?"

Luke cleared his throat. "Yes. But, Jimmy—"

"No. You don't think we could have discussed you moving out to LA as an option? Construction is everywhere, and as close as you are to your son, he's a grown man. Hell, you could even start up your own chapter of the Rainbow Blues. We could have discussed having smaller places here and in LA."

"Oh." Luke had sort of leapt to one conclusion, and he could only conclude it had been fear that made him do so. Fear that Jimmy wanted to leave him behind as he moved into a shiny new life.

"Yes, oh."

"I guess… the distance thing was freaking me out. Not talking to you on the phone, not visiting."

"And you should have told me. Because as much as I hated it, I knew it was temporary." Jimmy's voice softened, and his arms lost some of their exaggerated, choppy movements. "But you were worried this was how life was going to be from now on."

"Or worse." Luke had been afraid the lack of calls had only been a way to ease him into a breakup, and he'd struck first to keep himself from further pain.

"Oh, Luke." Jimmy sat down beside him again and threaded their fingers together. "You were so blunt when we started dating. Blunt enough about your desire to commit that you would have scared away most men. You should have said something."

"You're right. I should have." God, he was stupid. "Maybe we should still sell the house. It will be a while before I can look for work in California."

Jimmy huffed out an exasperated laugh. "This is partly my fault. I told you how different it was, acting for a film. What I never told you was how much I hated it. Despised it. Loathed, even. I kept telling myself that this was my dream, and I was only having difficulty adjusting because I'd gotten in a rut or I'd gotten too comfortable in my backup plan. Teaching was only supposed to be temporary. But I got to the end of that film and on the last day… I felt nothing. There was a small sense of accomplishment, because we were done. But there was no joy. No high. No sense that I was challenging myself. I understand for film actors, getting it right for film is a challenge they enjoy. I didn't. I enjoy the challenge of running through an entire play with no flubs. I like the immediate gratification of an audience laughing or crying or applauding. That's what drives my passion. I even missed teaching, and I'm kinda pissed I'm not going to be able to do anything but sub for this coming semester."

"But…." This sounded too good to be true.

"Luke, even if we weren't together, I would still be coming back to this life. But you're what makes me complete, and I don't want to have to live this life or any other without you."

There were still a few tears left in the well, and they coursed down Luke's cheeks. Jimmy wiped his own eyes and kissed Luke's away.

"This isn't because I got hurt, is it?"

Jimmy narrowed his eyes, and Luke had the feeling he'd be paying for his doubt for a long time.

"As a matter of fact, I was already on a plane home while you were getting shitfaced. When your bratty son called to tell me about your surgery, I was already at the house. Which, incidentally, is how I know you contacted someone about selling it."

Luke smiled, the happiness making his physical pain almost bearable. Jimmy was going to forgive him. Jimmy truly wanted the life they'd started to build together, and Luke hadn't fucked it up beyond all recognition.

"I also have a little gift for you, although I have a feeling I'll have to show you the receipt so you know I bought it before that horrible article was posted."

Luke shook his head. "I'll believe you. I promise."

Jimmy smiled, wide and happy, the way he should always look if Luke had his way. He disengaged their hands, pulled a small blue box out of his pocket, and placed it on Luke's chest.

"Is this…?"

Jimmy had always liked little gifts for no reason, and after the first one, Luke had always made sure his random gifts were blue. This was the first blue gift Jimmy had got for him, though.

Jimmy kept smiling, although tears stood out in his eyes and his voice wobbled. "Out of the blue, I fell in love with you. Will you marry me, Luke?"

All the oxygen was sucked out of the room as Luke processed the question. He flipped open the box to find two silver-colored rings inside.

"Oh, yes, Jimmy, yes."

Laughing and crying at the same time, they kissed. A sweet, molten kiss of promise. One which he'd have liked to have followed with a more physical response.

"Put it away, keep it safe until I get out of here." Luke didn't think he'd be allowed to wear it, not yet.

"I will, don't worry."

"Jimmy, you are going to do the Aquaman movie, though, aren't you? It's a fantastic opportunity."

"Were you not listening to me? They can get someone else to be the fish whisperer."

Luke laughed. He'd never heard Aquaman called that before. Suddenly, his eyes drooped, and fatigue slammed over him like a brick to the head.

"Oh, hon, you're all tired out. You go to sleep, and I'll go tell your son I'm making an honest man out of you."

"Don't go," Luke slurred out.

"Not going anywhere. I'll be here when you wake up again, I promise."

If there was nothing else certain in his life, Luke could trust Jimmy's promises. Happy and content, he drifted off.

EPILOGUE

JIMMY PUSHED Luke's wheelchair around Home Depot, stopping at all the places Luke normally skipped over.

They'd spent an inordinate amount of time looking at ceiling fixtures, which was doubly irritating because Luke was so damned far away from them in the chair. But he loved seeing how excited Jimmy got.

"Karen just about shit herself with jealousy when she realized that I was going to have a couple of months to leisurely plan our wedding while she'd be stuck at work." Jimmy gave a gleeful little laugh.

Since he was on sabbatical and the *Walking Wounded* movie had paid more than enough to support him during that sabbatical, he was determined to spend every waking moment working on decorating their home or planning the wedding. In between taking care of Luke, that was. It was a new experience for Luke, being the one taken care of, but Jimmy was great, and they got along so well that even when Luke got discouraged about how restricted his movements were until his leg healed, Jimmy was able to jolly him right out of his bad mood.

Most of their jollies had involved blow jobs and hand jobs, since that was about the most Luke was capable of, but orgasms with Jimmy were always spectacular. He shifted a little in the seat, readjusting himself while Jimmy made notes on prices and sizes, snapping pics of various light fixtures.

Then they stopped by the paint chips, and Jimmy came a hair's breadth from squealing like a girl.

"Ooh, maybe these two would complement this in the kitchen." Then another color palette would catch his eye and he'd flutter over to it, snatching up various different colored cards.

By the time Jimmy was done, Luke was in awe. "The place is going to look like a rainbow. Are you sure that's all going to look good together?"

Jimmy gave him what Luke's mother would have called the "stink-eye."

"Just who is the decorator in this family?"

"You are."

His fiancé huffed. "Exactly. And don't you forget it."

"Anything going to be blue?"

"Of course not. You know we're saving blue for other things."

Yeah, they were. "I might be wearing blue underwear," Luke said hopefully.

Jimmy snorted. "You sure as hell are not. I've done all your laundry, and you haven't got any blue pairs."

"Maybe I ordered on the Internet." He hadn't, but all he could think about now was getting naked with his fiancé, not whether ochre would clash with sandstorm.

In the blink of an eye, Luke saw Jimmy's focus switch from paint to penis as he winked. "Maybe I'll have to investigate. Let's get this stuff and get home."

Luke grinned. Blue might be a melancholy color for some, but for him and Jimmy, it would always be the color of love.

KC Burn has been writing for as long as she can remember and is a sucker for happy endings (of all kinds). After moving from Toronto to Florida for her husband to take a dream job, she discovered a love of gay romance and fulfilled a dream of her own—getting published. After a few years of editing web content by day, and neglecting her supportive, understanding hubby and needy cat at night to write stories about men loving men, she was uprooted yet again and now resides in California. Writing is always fun and rewarding, but writing about her guys is the most fun she's had in a long time, and she hopes you'll enjoy them as much as she does.

Visit KC at her website: http://kcburn.com/, on Twitter: https://twitter.com/authorkcburn, or on Facebook: https://www.facebook.com/kcburn.

Toronto Tales from KC BURN

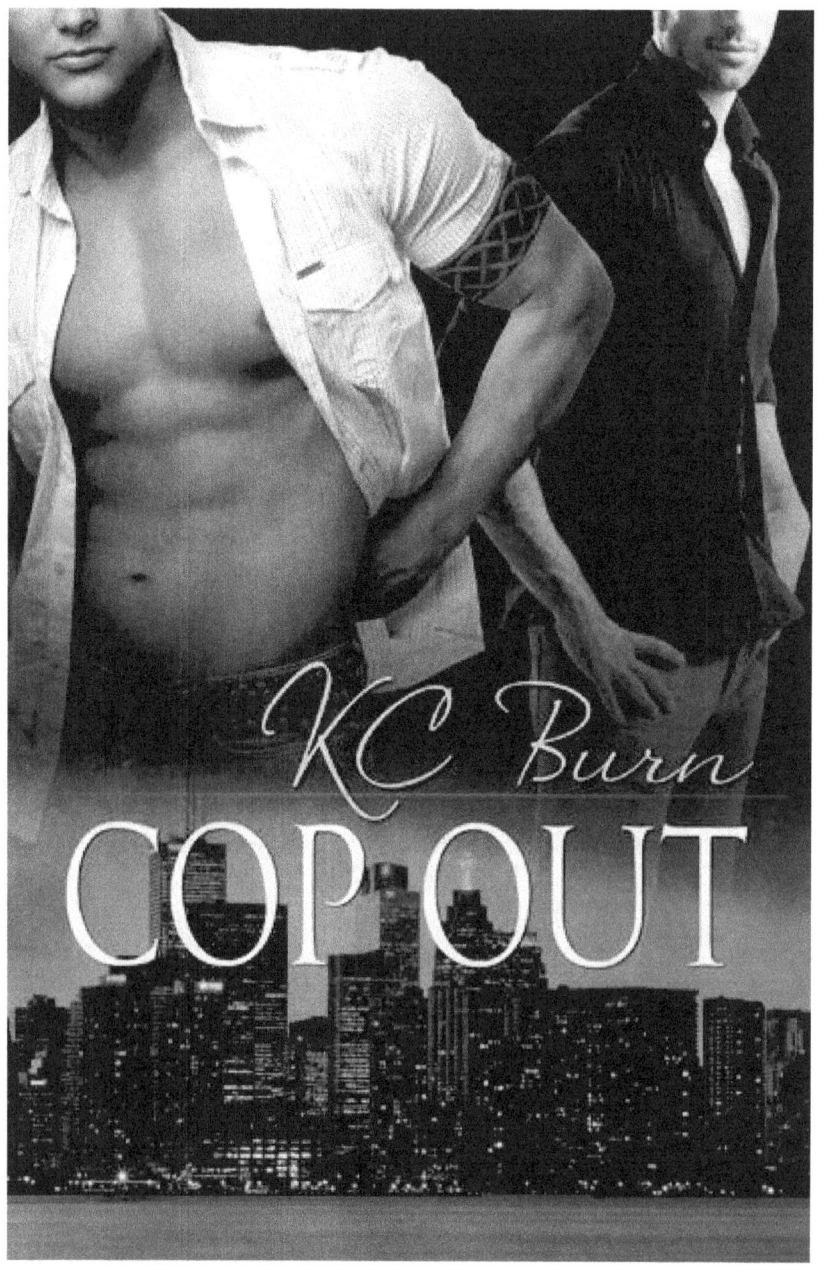

KC Burn

COP OUT

http://www.dreamspinnerpress.com

Toronto Tales from KC BURN

Toronto
Tales

COVER UP

KC Burn

http://www.dreamspinnerpress.com

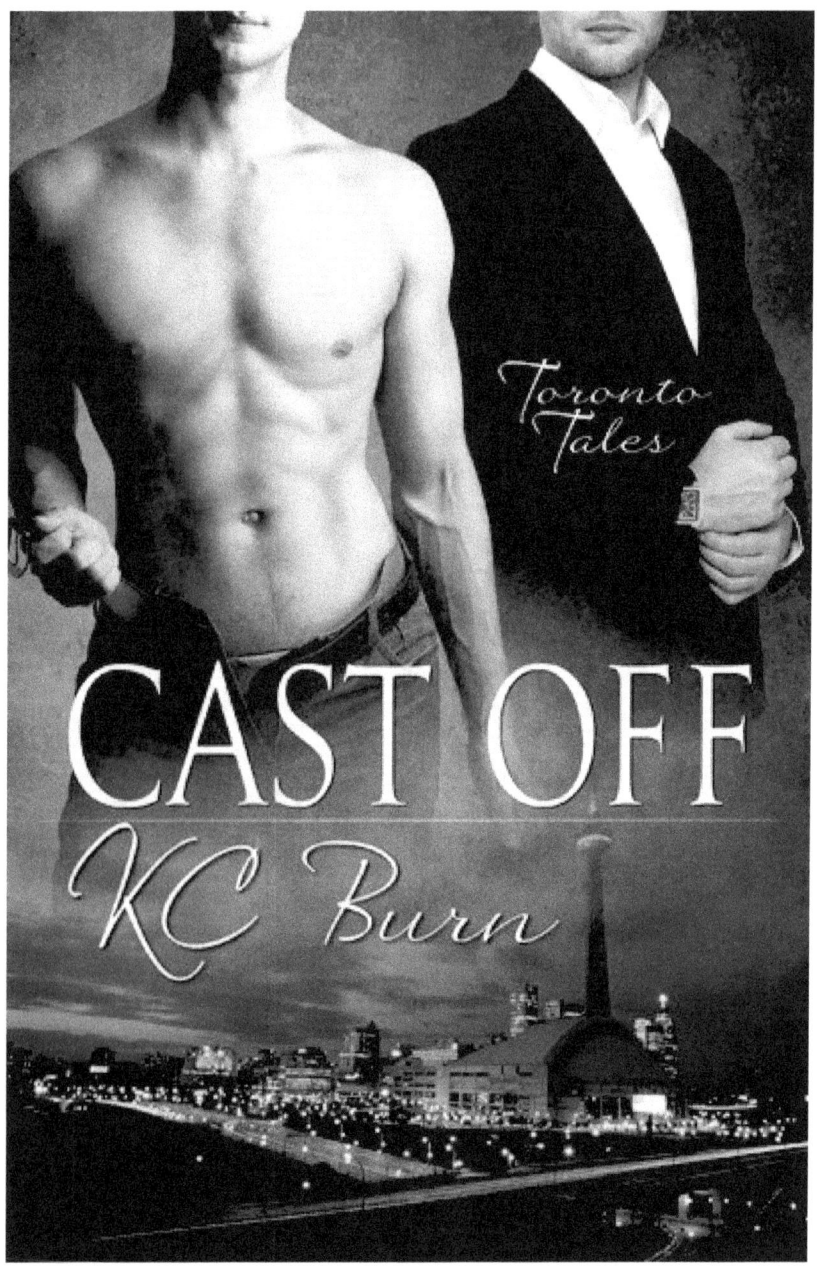

Also from KC BURN

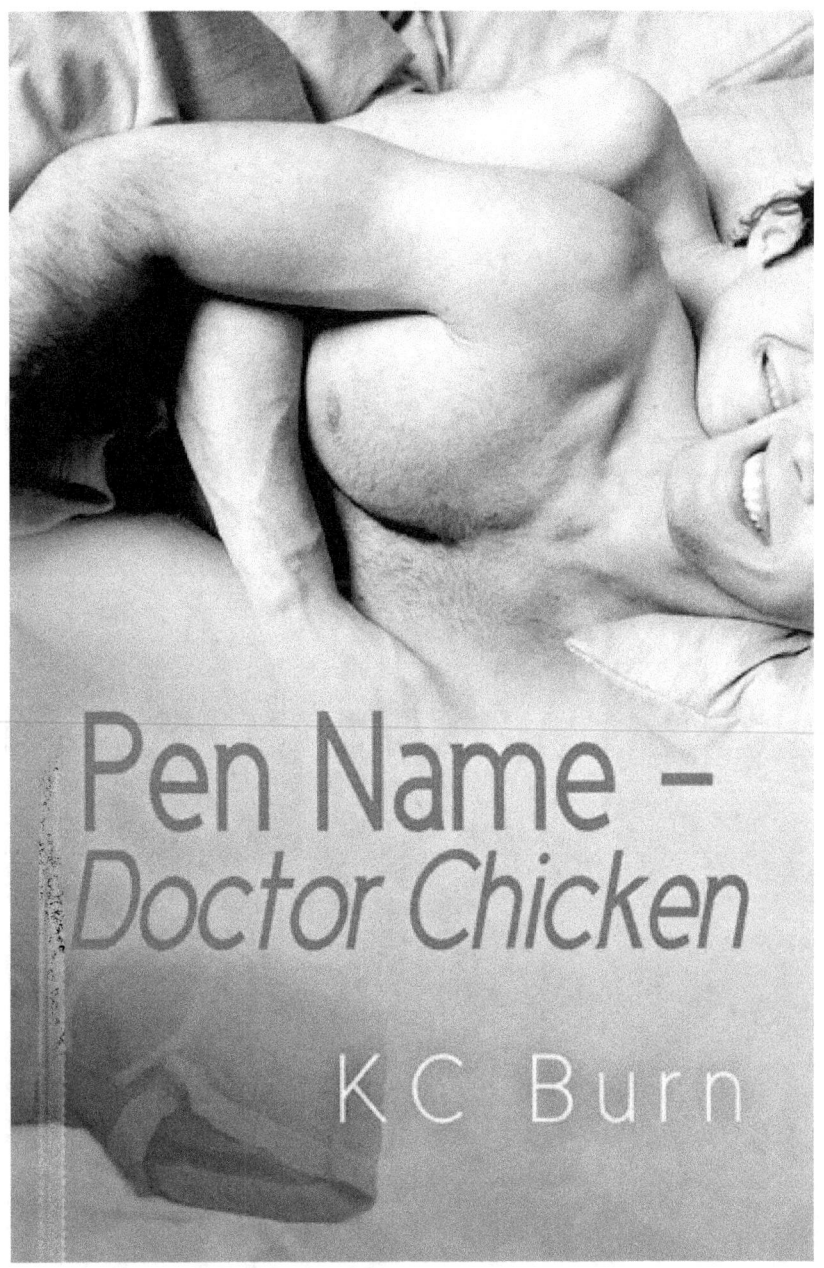

Pen Name –
Doctor Chicken

KC Burn

http://www.dreamspinnerpress.com

www.ingramcontent.com/pod-product-compliance
Lightning Source LLC
Chambersburg PA
CBHW060051260626
47160CB00005B/1654